IT IS WHT IT IS: This is a work of fiction and this statement is included to inform the reader that any celebrity name(s), business name(s), location(s), product(s), and organizations that are stated in the content of this book are real. However, they are used in a way that is purely fictional.

IT IS WHT IT IS

JERZ TOSTON

It Is Wht It Is

By Jerz Toston

Cover Art Created by KREATIVEGRAFIKS.COM

Logo Designs by LeRoy Grayson

Editor: Anelda L. Attaway

Co-editor: Jerz Toston

ACKNOWLEDGMENTS

First and foremost, I to thx Allāh (SWT) wit out Him, none of this would even be possible.

DEDICATION

I dedicate this book to all my loyal fans because I appreciate their continued support and commitment to reading my books.

Ya Fav Author!

TABLE OF CONTENTS

CHAPTER 1 – Jade 01

CHAPTER 2 – Bre 04

CHAPTER 3 – Turk 07

CHAPTER 4 – Philly 09

CHAPTER 5 – Chase Center..14

CHAPTER 6 – Shopping..26

CHAPTER 7 – Give It Up..28

CHAPTER 8 – Heart Broken 32

CHAPTER 9 – Maze 54

CHAPTER 10 – Play My Part 60

CHAPTER 11 – Easy As 1.2.3 72

CHAPTER 12 – Keep'n It Real 76

CHAPTER 13 – Reunited..85

CHAPTER 14 – Doin' Me 96

CHAPTER 15 – Contact..100

CHAPTER 16 – Swerve 105

CHAPTER 17 – Anotha Hit 113

CHAPTER 18 – Lovers 116

CHAPTER 19 – My Young Boy 129

CHAPTER 20 – Catching Up..132

CHAPTER 21 – Heem 142

CHAPTER 22 – Count Down 149

CHAPTER 23 – One Last Time 156

CHAPTER 24 – Free At Last 161

TABLE OF CONTENTS

CHAPTER 25 – Finally 171

CHAPTER 26 – Played 180

CHAPTER 27 – Young Jawn 188

CHAPTER 28 – Knocked Up 196

CHAPTER 29 – R.I.P. 206

CHAPTER 30 – Engaged 207

CHAPTER 31 – Pay Me My Money 216

CHAPTER 32 – Dinner Party 223

CHAPTER 33 – A.J. 230

CHAPTER 34 – Tha Nite Before 245

CHAPTER 35 – Wedding Day 252

CHAPTER 36 – Back 259

CHAPTER 37 – Another Engagement 266

CHAPTER 38 – Grand Opening 270

CHAPTER 39 – Tha Meeting 279

CHAPTER 40 – Pay Ya Debt 289

CHAPTER 41 – Girl Talk 295

CHAPTER 42 – L.A. 297

CHAPTER 43 – It's Over 304

CHAPTER 44 – D.O.A. 309

CHAPTER 45 – Happy Birthday 310

CHAPTER 46 – Prom Night 314

CHAPTER 47 – A New Car 327

CHAPTER 48 – New Year's Eve 331

ABOUT THE AUTHOR 335

INTRODUCTION

Urban Fiction at its best! The life journey of four couples: Jade and Ahmad, Bre and Maze, Turk and Fresh, and Killer and Lexis. Along with four friends, Fresh, Killer, Heem and Tiz, that had tha city in a chokehold because…. "It Is Wht It Is!"

CHAPTER 1

Jade

"Jadeen, Jadeen, Jade get up!"

"What do you want Iciss?"

"I'm hungry."

"You better eat some cereal then."

"I don't want no cereal."

I looked over at tha clock on my nightstand.

"Iciss, do you know what time it is?"

"Morning time, now get up."

"Girl, it's only 8:30; now leave me alone."

"Jade, I'm hungry."

Iciss was my 13-year-old sister who came over to stay wit me whenever my mom had to leave town, which seemed like every other weekend.

"Jade, pleeease."

"A'ight, I'm getting up now."

I could never resist those pretty gray eyes and that smile of hers. Everybody always thinks Iciss is my daughter instead of my baby sister. She was a little version of me. I look just like my mom; she was 45 but didn't look like a day over 30. I was 5'6, with caramel skin, gray eyes, shoulder-length hair, and not to brag, but I had an ass that would make J-Lo jealous. Once I had finished washing up and taking care of my hygiene, I went into tha kitchen.

"Iciss, what do you want to eat?"

"Turkey bacon, eggs and waffles."

"A'ight, after we eat, we'll go get manicures and pedicures."

"Yeah!"

Iciss just loves to be pampered. My mom said I was molding her into a little me. She was right; I made sure she had the best of everything.

"Jade, are you going to call Bre and Turk to go wit us?"

"No, I thought me and you could hang out today."

I went into my closet to find something to wear. Iciss walked into my room holding her pink and cream Christian Dior dress wit her cream Dior sandals. All I could do was smile because she was just like me. I chose to put on my peach Donna Karan dress wit my matching sandals. Once we were dressed, we both knew we were tha shit.

"Oh, I almost forgot," Iciss said, runnin' back into her room.

When she returned, she was rocking her cream Dior frames.

"Sure, ya right," I said, grabbing my frames.

It was tha middle of May but felt like late July.

"Your car can use a little soap and water Sis."

"I know, I'll let Larry hit it while we're in tha nail salon."

I had an S600 black on black wit dub Dueces.

Iciss wasted no time, "Soulja Boy, track five volume 10."

Get My Swag On was her song. We pulled up Larry was just finishing up a car.

"I'm right on time."

"Yup, you want tha works or just a wash."

"Tha works, make sure you really shine my rims, please."

"Gotcha Jade. Who is this pretty friend of yours? Does she have a boyfriend?" Iciss started blushing.

"Larry, you so crazy."

"How are you doing Ms. Iciss?"

"OK, Larry can you put some of that good-smelling stuff in there when you done?"

"Sure thing, Little Lady."

We walked into Miss Lee's to be greeted by Jazz.

"I'm ready for who ever is going first."

"That will be Iciss."

An hour and a half later, we were heading out of tha shop.

"Now that's what I'm talking about Sis."

I paid Larry and tipped him since he did such a good job.

"What do you say we head to Philly to do a little shopping on South Street."

"Now you speaking my language Sis."

CHAPTER 2

Bre

"ATL club see her do her thing might wanta rap, but she'll make you sing. I was on her; she was on him."

"Damn, dis my shit right here. I love this bitch."

"Aunty, you crazy."

"Chasity, didn't I tell you to put that seatbelt on?"

"Aunty."

"Aunty, my ass, put that seatbelt on now!"

We pulled up to Larry's; he was doing another car.

"Hey Larry, do you have time to do my car?"

"About 30 minutes ago."

"I need tha works and make sure you hit my rims good, please."

"Don't I always strap you up?"

"Come on, Chastity, let's go to Ms. Lee's."

"Hey Bre."

"Hey Chas."

"Hey Jazz."

"Jade and Iciss was just here."

"I know, Larry just told us."

"We only got manicures."

So, by tha time we were done, Larry was almost done. He had my 750 looking real clean. I had a 750 Beamer red wit peanut butter guts and a set of 22s.

"All done Bre."

"Larry, just give me 20 dollars back."

"Thanks for tha tip Bre."

Larry was always try'n to get wit either me, Jade or Turk. I couldn't blame him. I was 5'7, with bronze skin and hazel eyes, my hair came to tha back of my neck and my ass was often compared to tha rapper Trina.

"Chas, do you want to go to Philly?"

"Aunty, now why would you ask me a question like that? Of course, I do; you know how much I love to shop."

My brother was always droppin' Chas off on tha weekends. I didn't mind because she was my niece. My mom says I spoil her wit materialistic things. Chas is 14 and likes to wear name-brand and designer things. We normally had breakfast with Jade and Iciss every Saturday morning. But today, I had a few things I needed to take care of.

"Aunty, can we stop at tha house? I need to get my shades?"

"OK, I need to get some more money anyway."

I was only 21, but I was well-off. My bank account was on swole thanks to tha hustlers I had dated. Most of them were from out of town and by tha time they realized they weren't getting any pussy it was too late. Their bank accounts were about 10 to 15 grand lighter. I was no fool; I would put tha money they gave me in tha bank. And enjoy tha shopping trips they would take me on. I had this one guy fly me to Beverly Hills to shop on Rodeo Drive. I'm that bitch you have to pay to play. We always play by my rules no matter what.

"Chas, you ready to go?"

"Yes Aunty."

When we got into tha car, my cell phone started ringing. I knew by tha ringtone it was my friend from DC. I answered just to let him know I had my niece for tha day and I will call him later. He let me know that him and two of his boys will be coming this way later. He wanted to know if I had any friends. I kindly let him know that my two friends were like my sisters. And they didn't deal wit no losers.

"You got me mixed up, Ma. My niggaz get at that dollar."

Just what I needed to hear, but I had to play it off.

"I didn't say nothing bout no money. I was talking about tha looks department. Well, I'll call you when I drop my niece off later."

As soon as I hung up, Chas said, "Turn it up Aunty, that's my song."

I was playing J Holidays Can't Get Enough.

CHAPTER 3

Turk

"Thank you for tha breakfast Turk."

"No problem Mom. Would you like to go to tha nail salon wit me?"

"Sure, I could use a mani and pedicure."

I pulled up to Larry's to drop my car off while I was in tha nail salon.

"Today must be my lucky day."

"And why is that Larry?"

"First Jade, then Bre, now ya fine ass."

"Boy, watch your mouth; you see my mom."

"I'm sorry."

"You just make sure you hook me up, especially my rims."

I had a 645CL charcoal gray on gray wit 22s.

"I'll be back in an hour."

"Hey Turk, Mrs. Taylor."

"Hey Jazz."

"How you doing Jazz?"

"Ok, Jade and Bre were here. But Larry already told you that, didn't he?"

"You know he did."

"Jazz hooked us up, so my mom tipped her."

Larry was just finishing up when we got back there.

"Is this tha same car," my mom asked.

"Keep tha change, Larry."

"Thanks, you know Turk, if you…." I cut him off.

"No, thank you, Larry, my keys."

"Inside tha car."

As soon as we pulled off, "Turquis, can you blame him?"

I was a younger version of my mom, 5'7, dark skin, shoulder length hair, green eyes, yes, you heard me right, green eyes that were real, and an ass fatter than tha singer Beyoncé. A lot of people always mistake me for being Dominican.

"Turk, you can drop me off home. I'm tired."

"I thought you was gonna go to Philly wit me?"

"I was, but I'm tired now."

Once I dropped my mom off, I jumped straight on tha highway. As soon as I did, I wasted no time lighting up my weed. By tha time I got by tha Naamans Road exit, I remembered I had to meet tha cable man at 12 o'clock to fix my Internet service. I got off just to make a U-turn and get right back on. When I got to my house tha cable man was just pulling up.

"Hi, are you, he looked at his clipboard, Ms. Turquis Taylor?"

"Yes I am."

"You're having a problem wit your Internet?"

"Yes."

I explained tha problem to him.

20 minutes later, it was back working.

"Thank you, I really needed that."

"Let me find out you're a YouTube, Facebook junky."

"Pleeease, I need my Internet to shop. Well, once again, thank you, I said, heading toward tha door.

I hopped in my car and headed to Philly to do some shoppin'.

CHAPTER 4

Philly

"Aunty, there go Jade's car."

"Where Chas?"

"Right there," she said, pointing toward tha parking lot.

I pulled in and parked next to Jade's car.

"Let me call that hussy and see where she is."

"Hello."

"Where you at and don't say Philly 'cause I already know that."

"Then why did you ask?"

"Cause I'm standing next to your car."

"Well, walk to Unica for Kids.

"On my way."

Me, Bre, and Jade were like sisters. We had been friends since kindergarten. We made a pact that we would only mess wit Ballers and never fall in love. Anytime one of us caught ourselves falling for a man, we would just cut them off, no questions asked.

"Iciss! Chas!" they both yelled, runnin' towards one another.

"Love tha outfit," Chas said.

"And me yours," Iciss responded wit.

Me and Jade looked at each other and nodded.

"We did this," I said.

"I know, I know."

"Bitch, why didn't you say you was coming up here?"

"You said you had to handle a few things, so I just figured me and Iciss would hang out and shop til we drop."

"I heard that."

"Well, I guess me and Chas will be joining yall now."

"You know what they say, great minds think alike."

We both turned around to find Turk standing in tha doorway. Aunt Turk, Chas and Iciss screamed while runnin' to give her a hug.

"You two bitches didn't have to call me."

"Well, for your information, we didn't come up here together."

"I know, I seen both yall cars in tha parking lot. Jade, I'm going to pick me out some clothes."

"Me too Aunty."

"A'ight, just make sure you let us see before you take them to the counter."

"Not a problem," Iciss said.

"I see we all had tha same plans for today."

"We normally do this together every Saturday anyway."

"There's a party at tha Chase Center tonight."

"Oh shit, I forgot about that."

"Me too, ain't Jamie Foxx supposed to be there?"

"Yeah, you know anybody Doc B invites shows up."

"Bitch you ain't never lied about that."

"Oh, before I forget, yall remember that guy I told you about from DC?"

"What about him?"

"He called me earlier said he would be at tha Chase tonight."

"Are we supposed to get or be excited about that?"

"No smart ass! He brings two of his boys wit him."

"Unh, Uh, I don't think so, tha last time you hooked us up wit one of your friends' friend."

"The last time, shit try every time."

Jade and Turk high-fived each other.

"Well, not this time; he assured me they bout a dollar."

"Well, for your sake, I hope so."

"Excuse me."

"Bitch you heard her! If they don't got no money, then from now on, don't even think about calling me anyway."

"Me either."

"We always put you down wit a profitable thing."

"Turk she all for self."

"Bitch, no I'm not!"

"Don't be mad; we know you're not."

Iciss and Chas came back wit an arm full of clothes.

"Did yall get enough shit?" Turk asked.

"No, but this is all they had that we liked."

Iciss had five outfits that came to $529.00. Chas had seven for a total of $649.00. We paid wit our debit cards and walked out. Of course, South Street was jam-packed as usual. Our next stop was Blondies to grab some shoes.

"I don't know about yall, but I'm going to King of Prussia to buy my outfit for tonight."

"Jade, I'm going wit you," Iciss said.

"OOOOH, can we go to Aunty?"

"We all gon' go; we can take Jade's car."

When we got to tha mall, I parked around by Neman Marcus.

"Girl, I haven't been here in a minute."

"Who you tell'n, I normally go online," Turk said wit a big smile.

"I'm going to tha Gucci store to grab my outfit."

"I think I want to wear some Fendi," Turks said.

"I'm going wit Dior," Bre said.

"Well, let's meet back here in an hour."

As I walked into tha Fendi store, I knew what I was wearing tonight. They had this black and cream Fendi dress that was to die for. And I found these cream open-toe Fendi shoes that went perfectly. Of course, I had to get a new pair of Fendi frames to set it off.

"Wait til they see me tonight."

"Aunty, I think you'll look good in this."

Chas had picked out this red and white Dior dress that I'm sure would show off every curve of my body. I had to give it to Chas on this one.

"Come on, let's see if I can find some shoes to match."

"Aunty, I found tha perfect shoes for you over here."

When I saw tha shoes, she found I was sold. My niece had picked tha perfect outfit and shoes for me.

"You not going to be able to keep 'em off you tonight, Aunty."

They had this sharp-ass Dior watch that I had to have. Chas had found her a nice skirt and shirt also.

"Iciss, what are you doing?"

"Helping you find tha perfect outfit for tonight."

"Well, Imma let you pick my outfit, shoes and sunglasses then."

"Sis I got you."

She sure did get me. Iciss picked me out this brown Gucci dress wit matching shoes and frames.

"Chase Center, watch out, here I come."

She grabbed herself a pair of Gucci shoes and sneaks.

"Come on, let's go."

"We have to stop at tha Prada store before we leave."

Tha Prada store cost me another stack between tha both of us. When we met back up wit Chas, Bre and Chas, everybody had hands full wit bags.

"You'll ready to get out of here?"

"Yup."

"Damn, it's 8 minutes after 7."

"I know by tha time we get home, it'll be time to get dressed."

"I know and I'm starving," Bre said.

"Me too."

"When I drop yall back to yall cars, Imma go get me a cheesesteak."

"That's a good ideal; kill two birds wit one stone."

"Aunty, can I stay wit Iciss?"

"Yall didn't even ask Jade."

"I asked my mom and she said yes."

"Well, if Ms. Sady said yeah, then I guess so."

So, once we had our food, we hit tha highway and headed back to Wilmington. Since Chas was staying with Iciss, she road back wit us. Bre was going to drop her clothes off over at my mom's since it was on tha way to Turks. We were all meeting up at Turk's house. I dropped tha girls off then headed to my house to get dressed.

CHAPTER 5

Chase Center

We pulled up to tha Chase Center; it was only 10 o'clock and tha line was around tha corner.

"Shit, look at that long ass line!"

"Since when did we start waiting in anybody's line?"

"You right about that, Jade. Plus, we doing V.I.P."

"I know that's right."

"Pull up front; let's valet park our car."

Bre pulled up to tha valet. When tha valet came to tha car, he let us know in order to park valet; we had to buy V.I.P. tickets.

"A'ight," we said.

"V.I.P tickets are a buck 50." He said that like we couldn't afford it.

"Give us three, please."

He went back to where tha other guy was standing and came back wit our tickets. When we got out, all eyes were definitely on us. Of course, we gave them something to look at courtesy of Fendi, Christian Dior, and Gucci. Nobody in our town could say shit to us. A lot of people thought we were hustling. In a sense, we were hustling tha hustlers. When we pulled up, we had our anthem bang'n. A Diva is tha Version of a Female Hustler.

There were a lot of nice whips now in valet. I could see tha hate in bitches faces when we went in V.I.P. A few females were coming back out salty.

One of tha bouncers said, "Listen, it's 50 for females and 65 for males."

Somebody yelled, "Damn, who in there, Obama?" I had to laugh at that one.

"Nah, just Jamie Foxx, T-Pain and Lil Wayne."

"Damn, I didn't know that; I thought it was just Jamie Foxx."

"Jade."

I turned around to see who was calling me. It was my cousin, Tasha.

"Do you got any extra $20? A bitch only got 50."

"Here," I said, handing her 100, "enjoy yourself."

"Thanks Cuz, I got you."

I knew she would give it back, but I didn't need it.

"You good, Tasha we family and family looks out for one another."

My cousin Tasha was just as pretty as me. She was just too dependent on her boyfriend and I didn't like that. But it was her life, so I had no say so. We tried to put her down wit us, but she had fallen in love wit Cash. Now three years later, she was still wit his no-good ass.

"I'll see you inside and I love that Prada dress."

We went inside to be greeted by tha sounds of T.I.'s Ain't I. We stopped at tha picture booth to take a couple of pictures.

"You gon' kill 'em tonight, Shorty."

"I know."

"We only need three for now. We'll be back a little later."

"Well, Well, Well, if it isn't my three favorite ladies."

"Hey Larry, you look nice."

"Thank you, I don't need to tell yall that cause I'm sure you already know that."

"So, who you here wit?"

"You know I roll solo."

Larry was good-looking, but none of us looked at him like that.

"Can I at least buy you ladies a drink?"

"We are in V.I.P."

"So am I, you only get to drink tha cheap stuff for free. They do give you a bottle of Moët."

"Wow, we get a bottle of Moët? "He did just say we get tha cheap shit."

"It doesn't matter; I need me a bottle of Bombay."

"You ain't the only one," Turk said.

"Well, I need my Goose."

"Bre, you better get wit tha program."

"That's yalls drink. Imma stick to my Goose."

We made our way to tha bar. When tha bartender came, we ordered two bottles of Bombay and a bottle of Grey Goose.

"Can we have 3 cups wit ice, please?"

While we were sitting at tha table, this guy came up.

"Good evening, ladies. How are you doing Bre?"

"Hey Wes," I stood to give him a hug, "Turk, Jade, this is my friend Wes I was telling yall about."

"So, this is tha infamous Wes from D.C. We've heard a lot about you."

"All good, I hope."

"If it wasn't, you wouldn't be standing here, that's for sure," Bre said, "you here by yourself?"

"Nah, Bankz and Joker came up wit me. Let me find them and I'll be back."

"Hope his friends look as good as he does."

"As long as their money looks good, I don't care what they look like."

"Bitch you crazy."

When West came back, he was accompanied by two sexy niggaz draped in diamonds.

"Turk, Jade, Bre these are my boys Bankz and Joker."

I already knew I wanted Bankz. I loved a man wit braids; not to mention, he looked Dominican and Spanish.

He must have felt tha vibe because she said, "Nice to meet you Angel."

"Angel, my name is Jade."

"I'm sorry, but you look like you were sent from Heaven."

"Wow, I see you got ya game together."

"Baby, that's no game. You fly as shit!"

"Thank you for tha compliment."

"Turk, would you like to dance?" Joker asked.

"Only if you can keep up," she said wit a smile.

"Damn, you looked out for a change; good looking and they smell like money." Bre was all smiles.

"Well."

"Well, what?"

"Don't keep him waiting."

"I've always been tha one to take my time." Turk finally got up.

"Would you like to dance?"

"Do you know how to dance to this kind of music? I know all yall listen to in DC is club and go-go music."

(Ha! Ha! Ha!) "I don't even like this shit; I prefer Plies, Jeezy, or Lil' Wayne."

"Oh, excuse me."

For some reason, his accent made him more appealing. I heard tha females start screaming. When I looked up, I saw Jamie Foxx on stage. He started it off with his club banger Blame it On. When T-Pain came on, they went crazy.

"I'm going to sit back down."

"May I join you?"

"That's up to you."

"In that case, lead tha way."

On our way, I tried to hold my smile in when a group of girls said, "There he is, right there."

"I see somebody has a fan club."

"Nah, they were out front when we pulled up in my Rolls-Royce."

"Damn, this nigga is holding," I thought to myself.

"I know that's not your everyday car?"

"Naw, it's one of my cars; I bring it out on occasions like this."

"Must be nice."

"I deserve to treat myself to nice things."

"Well, if you got it, I always say make good use of it."

"If I may say, Ms. Jade, you look like you do pretty good for yourself also."

"I try."

After they all performed, they sat in V.I.P. All the females were trying to get pictures wit them.

"Yall don't want any pictures wit them."

"You got us messed up; we don't sweat nobody famous or not."

"I most definitely respect that," Bankz said.

"Most females are quick to try and get wit a nigga wit money. Most even go as far as giving a nigga as Steve Harvey calls tha cookie on tha first date, expecting to get into a niggaz pocket."

"See Bankz, that's where they go wrong. Because tha average dude only gon' look at them as a smut and easy ass. If a bitch give you tha pussy on tha first date, how many other niggaz she done gave it to that easy."

"I knew it was a reason I was feeling you, Jade."

"I just don't need no man to buy me shit; I got my own crib, car and cash. I do better than most niggaz."

"And some real; I thought you had a nigga."

"Why? Cause I got on Gucci from head to toe."

"Truth be told, yes and it's tha real deal. And don't mean that in no disrespectful way at all."

"I know, I see a lot of females and males wit knock-off designer shit on."

"If you don't mind me asking, what kind of car you drive?"

"I got a S600."

"Word, I was going to see that."

"What ever."

"Real rap, I was. I had to test tha waters."

"Tha way you talk, I would have never figured you a worker."

(Ha! Ha! Ha!) "I know Wes didn't say we work for him!"

"Wes didn't say anything; I just assumed."

"Never assume, I run DC, I put them on. Everything runs through me."

Bingo, I hit tha jackpot, they all got money, but Bankz is tha one. It took everything in my power not to smile. Tha lights came on and damn, did Bankz look even better wit tha lights on.

"Do yall have plans after this is over?"

Turks said, "I don't know if you noticed, but it's over."

"Would you like to get something to eat?"

"Sounds good to me," Bre said.

"I'm sure you know where to get a good bite to eat from."

"Yeah, we can go to tha Waffle House."

"We out then."

When we got outside tha parking lot was packed. Car stereos were playing all types of music. We handed the valet our ticket; two minutes later, he was pulling up in Bre's Beamer.

"Wow, that's how you doing it," Joker said.

"What, a girl can't drive a nice whip?"

"Where I am from, most of tha females drive Hondas."

"I'm not tha average broad."

"I see."

When he pulled up in his white-on-white Rolls Royce, I watched Bre and Turks' facial expressions. Bankz hit a button and tha top came down.

"Yall make my car look like a hoopty."

"We gon' to follow you."

"A'ight," Bre said, getting in her car.

Bitch do you see that Rolls?"

"Yeah, that's Bankz car."

"How you know?"

"I was feeling him out, so I told him he didn't strike me as a worker. Why did I say that? He thought Wes said that. But I told him he didn't; then he let me know he was tha man in DC. They all got paper, but Bankz is the one."

"You lucky bitch," Bre said.

"You really made up for all tha other mishaps."

"Well, I don't know how long I'm going to be able to put up wit Joker."

"Why?"

"He's too arrogant and cocky. One of those who think because he has money, somebody is supposed to sweat him. He got tha wrong one. I can see me cussing him out before tha night is out. Shit, if I wasn't hungry, I wouldn't even fuck'n go."

"Turk, just chill."

"Fuck that nigga, Turk don't say shit to him if you don't want."

"I got bank, so it doesn't matter and it shouldn't matter to you either, Bre."

"I put yall before any nigga wit money, so, if they all want to go let them, fuck 'em."

"I know that's right, Jade."

We pulled up to tha waffle house; it was a nice crowd already inside and cars were still pulling up. We parked and then made our way inside.

"Six?" tha waitress asked.

"We want a table for two, please." Turk looked at Bre.

"We'll have a table for four, please."

I could tell Turk was relieved. When we sat down, Bankz said, "I hope you don't mind that I got us our own table."

"Not at all, but I do have to say my girl says Joker is too full of himself."

(Ha! Ha! Ha!)

"What's so funny?"

"Everybody says that; females wit class and standards anyway."

"Oh, he's use to chicken heads? The type broads that ain't never had shit, so they deal wit tha bullshit just to get a pair of sneaks and hairdo."

"Exactly, you know the type."

"Wow, well, he got tha wrong one wit Turk."

"You might need to school him tha difference between tha two."

"Been there, done that."

"I let him do him on that note as long as it doesn't interfere wit my doe. I really don't care."

"I feel you on that one."

"What do you do for a living, if you don't mind me ask'n?"

"I work at a bank."

"Do you have kids?"

"No, but I do take care of my little sister. Do you have any kids?"

"Naw, but I take care of a child that I thought was mine. He's 8, I just found out last year that he wasn't."

"If you don't mind me ask'n what made you get a blood test?"

"One day we were at tha mall and my son says dad, there goes my other dad. At first, I just thought that he meant his god dad. Until this guy walked up and asked me who I was. So, I asked him who he was. He told me he was Jaman's father. You should have seen tha look on my face. I tried to remain cool. So, I said yeah, Jaman just said there goes, my god dad. He said, no, you must understood him; I'm his father."

So, his mother had both yall think'n yall was his daddy."

"Yup. Tha next day, I went to get a blood test. Then two weeks later found out that my son I have been taken care of for tha last seven years was not my son."

"So, he turned out to be tha other guys?"

"No, he wasn't his either."

"But you continue to take care of him?"

"Yeah, I couldn't turn my back on him after seven years."

"What about tha other guy?"

"Shit, he kept moving and hasn't looked back."

"Wow, that says a lot about you."

"Yeah, now I am Uncle Bankz instead of daddy."

We talked while we ate when we were done, we exchanged phone numbers.

"Maybe we can get together this weekend if you're not too busy."

"I don't know; you'll have to call me and see. I normally spend tha weekends wit my little sister."

"I'm not trying to get in tha way of that."

"We're normally done shoppin' around 5 or 6." I wanted to see if he would fall for tha bait.

"Why don't you let me take you and your sister shoppin'."

"Your wallet might not be able to handle tha two of us."

He gave me this funny look that said my money is long.

"I spent close to six stacks today."

"You probably don't even wear half tha shit you buy."

"You're probably right."

"Not to be smart, but 6 stacks ain't shit."

"If I sold drugs, it wouldn't be shit to me either."

"Even if I didn't sell drugs, I would still be well-off. I own two salons and a moving company."

"Why don't you get out of tha game then?"

"The money is too good. Just think about it."

"Think about what?"

"Letting me take you and your little sister shoppin'."

"I'll do that," I said, standing to leave, "Turk, Bre are you two ready?"

"I been ready," Turk said, annoyed.

"Joker, what did you do now?" Bankz asked.

"Nuffin', just kept it real like I always do."

"Yeah, you were keeping it real, 'cause you a real asshole!" We all started laugh'n.

"Don't forget to think about my offer Jade."

"Why don't you call me in a few days and I'll let you know."

"OK, sounds like a winner to me."

Joker smiled and said, "I guess another date is out of tha question."

"You can't be serious."

"Actually, I wasn't. You know how many women would love to be wit me."

"Well, I'm not one of them! Too bad you don't have a personality to go wit your good looks. That's why you'll always have chicken heads on your squad. Come on yall, we out. It was nice meeting you Wes and Bankz."

"You too and I apologize for my friend."

"Nigga you don't have to apologize for me!"

"Your right, I don't, but you represent me."

I could tell that Bankz was getting upset.

"Well, make sure you call me," I told Bankz and winked at him.

On tha ride back to Turks, I told them about my talk wit Bankz.

"Damn bitch you was right; he is tha one."

We pulled up to Turks, said our goodbyes, and went our separate ways.

CHAPTER 6

Shopping

It had been four days since I last seen Bankz. He had called to confirm our shoppin' date for Saturday. Iciss let me know that she wasn't going to hold back on her spending. I really didn't expect her to. I happen to have a cousin from DC, so it was nuffin' for me to find out about Bankz. What I did find out, though, was that he was a millionaire thanks to tha drug game and his businesses. I might have to keep him around longer than I planned to.

Saturday finally came and Bankz was up here bright and early. When he seen Iciss, he asked tha question everybody always asked.

"Are you sure that's not your daughter? She looks just like you."

"Well, you should see my mom."

"I could just imagine."

We ended up spending tha whole day shoppin'. Iciss wasn't playing when she said she wasn't going to hold back. Bankz didn't seem to mind. When I told her not to get anything else, Bankz said that she was good. Why did she say that? She really went berserk?

"I see she has good taste."

"My mom says I spoil her."

"You said yall do this every Saturday?"

Yup."

"I know you both have a closet full of clothes wit tags still on them."

"Right again. I'm pretty sure you do too."

"I'll be lying if I said I didn't."

Bankz ended up spending close to 25 grand. Not just on me and Iciss, he bought his son some things as well as himself.

We decided to have dinner before he headed back to DC. I thanked him for tha fun day and told him next week, it was on me. He refused like I knew he would. After dinner, Bankz dropped me off and then headed home.

CHAPTER 7

Give it Up

"Lay ya punk ass down Motha Fucka. You not so tough now, are you Nigga?"

"Fuuck Yoou!"

"No Fuuck Yoou, you stuttering bitch."

"Ya Mooom." (SMACK)

"That may help ya speech out a little bit. Now, where's tha money at and please don't make me ask again."

"It's uuup stttairs."

"Where at upstairs?"

"In mmmy bedroom cllloset."

"Go check it out yall."

When they came downstairs caring tha black duffel bag, I knew we had what we came to get.

"Did yall look inside of it?"

"No."

"Well, what are you waiting on?"

"Shit!"

When I looked, I couldn't believe my eyes. There had to be at least 300 stacks, if not more.

"What are we going to do about him."

In one motion, I pulled out my .45 and squeezed tha trigger. "Problem solved, let's go," I said wit no remorse.   I couldn't be anything less than happy when we counted it up. 625 G's, that's 208 G's a piece. Tha extra stack we'll just put it in our in case of an emergency stash.

A few days later, we were on another job.

"Now remember, he's probably going to play hard, so only pop him in his legs or arms til we get what we came for." We all pulled our masks down.

"I know you didn't forget to pull tha wires for tha alarm."

"Unh, Unh, It always flashes even when it's not on."

"OK, yall ready?"

"Ready as we'll ever be."

"One of yall go around to tha back just in case he's a runner."

I looked through tha front window only to see our Vic sittin' on tha couch playing Xbox. Without hesitation, we hit tha door hard.

"Don't even think about it," I said, pointing my P90 at his head.

"A'ight, just don't shoot."

"Tie him up."

"Do you know who I am?"

"Yeah a motha fucka who's about to tell us where tha money is."

"You Niggaz might as well kill me because I'm not telling you shit!"

"Oh, you gon' talk."

I walked to the kitchen and turned the stove on high. Somebody bring me a hanger. I put the hanger in the fire so that it could get hot.

"Listen, you can make this easy on yourself."

"I'm not telling you shit."

"Fine, have it your way." I raised my gun and pulled tha trigger.

"OOW SHIIIT!" I walked over to him and ripped his jeans where tha bullet hole was at.

"Tape his mouth; things are about to get messy."

"Do you want me to search tha house?"

"Yeah." I grabbed tha hanger, which was now red due to tha heat from tha fire.

"Would you like to tell me where tha money is?"

His voice was muffled, but I could tell he said, "Fuck you."

"Fine, have it your way then."

I took tha hanger and placed it inside tha bullet hole. When I thought he had enough, I took it out and placed it back on tha stove. He was still screaming when I came back.

"Shut ya bitch ass up."

I heard a loud thump causing me to jump. When I looked in tha direction it came from, all I could do was smile. Then there was another one coming down tha steps. Two seconds later, another one was following it; tha look on his face said it all. I looked in all three bags, which were filled wit money. Never did I think that he would have money here. We must of caught him in tha midst of copping.

"Hey we got company."

I ran to tha window to see a Spanish guy getting out of his car. He walked around to tha trunk and came out wit two duffel bags.

"I was right; that's his Connect, I bet."

When he knocked on tha door, we let him in. As soon as he walked in, he was met wit a .44 magnum across his head. He went to reach for his heat but was met by two bullets to tha face. We looked in the bags.

"WOW," I said, "I guess today was our lucky day." I quickly snatched tha tape off his mouth.

"Yooou neever get awwway wit this."

"Who's gonna stop us?" I took my mask off.

"Whhat thhe fuuuck are you doing!"

"You should always watch who you talk to."

I could see the look of hurt in his face. I gave tha nod and my peoples walked up from behind and put two bullets in tha back of his head.

"Come on, let's get out of here."

We decided to go out tha back just in case anybody else wanted to pull up. In total, we came away wit 500 grand, 50 bricks of cocaine and 20 pounds of some exotic weed. We put everything in tha stash spot on tha van and headed home.

CHAPTER 8

Heart Broken

When my phone started ringing, I already knew who it was from the ringtone.

"Hello."

"Hey Bre."

"Hey, Wes what you doing?"

"Nuffin' on my way to Delaware."

"Why is something wrong?"

"I just need to get away for a while." I could tell that something was really bothering him.

"Are you home?"

"Yeah."

"Is it cool if I come by?"

"Sure, Turk and Jade are here, though."

"That's cool, I'll be there in tha next 30 minutes."

30 minutes later, Wes was knocking at tha door. Turk got up to let him in.

"What's up yall?"

"Chillin'," Turk said.

"I can't call it; tell ya boy, he doesn't have to screen my calls. I've been calling him for a week now. I know he said he was going out of town, but he would have called me by now."

Wes blurted out, "He's dead!"

Tha whole room got quiet.

"He's what!" Jade screamed.

"Dead."

"As in D-E-A-D," she said, spelling it out.

"Yeah."

Jade went to stand, but her knees gave way and she fell.

"How did he die?" Turk question.

"Somebody murdered him in his house."

"How did they do that wit tha alarm system he has?"

"They cut tha wires; not only did they kill him, they killed tha plug too."

"Yall don't have no ideal who did this?"

"Not a clue when I find out there's as good as dead!"

Watching Jade cry only confirmed what I told Turk that she was breaking tha pack by falling in love wit Bankz. So, I guess him getting aced was a good thing for us. I could tell that Wes was really hurting behind Bankz being murdered.

"Who would want to hurt him, Wes?"

"I don't know, Jade he didn't have any enemies. What I really think is that someone was trying to rob tha plug. So they followed him and got two birds wit one stone."

"I know they couldn't have been try'n to rob Bankz. Because they didn't get shit, Bankz is worth millions and they didn't get shit from him."

"Are you sure?" Jade questioned.

"At tha most, they got 500 grand in tha re-up. I checked the stash houses and everything is still in them."

"Damn, so now Wes will be runnin' the show," I thought to myself.

Just to make sure, I asked him would Joker know how to run tha businesses.

"Hell Nah, he's just tha gun. I'll be runnin' all of tha businesses. I do know that over tha last 8 months, he falling in love wit you Jade. He was actually going to ask you to marry him," he said, passing Jade a box.

When she opened it, all of our mouths dropped.

"I can't accept this, Wes."

"Sure you can."

"I won't feel right putting this on Wes."

"You don't have to; just keep it."

"Shit, I probably can get a nice piece of money for this," I thought to myself.

"Well, Bre, Turk and Wes, I need to get home. It's gettin' late; not to mention, I have to work in tha morning."

"A'ight, you gon be OK."

"Yeah I'm straight."

"Call when you get home."

An hour later, I was sitting alone on tha bench in 8th Street park on tha west side. I kind of felt bad about Bankz. I went against tha rules by letting myself catch feelings for him. I sat there staring at tha ring; wondering had he proposed, would I have said yes. This is why we say never let your feelings get involved. After another hour, I got up and drove home.

By tha time I finally dozed off, my alarm was going off.

"Shit!" I yelled, hearing my alarm.

I didn't want to get up but I wasn't about to stay home either. When I walked into tha bank, my cell phone started to ring.

"Hello."

"Damn, you had a bitch worried. You didn't call last night or answer your phone. Are you a'ight?"

"Yeah, I'm cool."

"Bre it is wht it is."

"I got work to do. I'll call you when I get off."

"I have a better ideal. Why don't we meet at T.G.I. Fridays for lunch?"

"Sounds good call Turk."

"Already did."

"Well, see you there."

When I walked into T.G.I. Fridays, Turk and Bre already had a table.

"We were starting to think you weren't coming."

"It's been a hectic morning at work."

"I see you don't have your ring on."

"I'm not going to wear that. Actually, that's what took me so long to get here. I stopped to have it appraised."

"How much is it worth?"

"Let's just say I'm going to put it in my safety deposit box. I'll have that to fall back on if I ever go broke."

"Damn, I knew it was worth a lot as big as that rock was. I guess it's true what they say."

"And that's what, Turk?"

"Some must die for others to eat!"

"I don't mean to sound ignorant, but I'm glad he's dead."

"Damn Turk, you a cold-hearted Bitch!"

"Nah, Jade was spending so much time wit him, I knew she was catching feelings."

"Yeah, I was slippin', but what's done is done."

"Did yall hear Wes when he said that they only got chump change?"

"Of course, we heard him." We both looked at Bre.

"Yall already know Imma get all that."

"You might even have to give him some cookie." She gave us a look that said, been there, done that.

"OOOH, Bitch I know you didn't."

"Shit, yes, I did last night. My mind was two steps ahead of yall."

"Well, I hope you put it down."

"When I left, he was still in tha bed."

Ha! Ha! Ha! "You must have really put it on him."

"I did things he didn't think could be done." We all high-fived one another.

When I got back to work, I had three messages tha first two were from my mom and Iciss.

Damn, I forgot all about Maze. He was from CBW over east side. He was like a brother to me; I was suppose to plug him in wit Bankz. Let me call him back and put him down. After three rings, he finally picked up.

"Hey Sis, you a'ight I been try'n to call you for tha past two days."

"Yeah, I'm cool."

"Well, did you holla at that nigga for me?"

"Yeah, but I just found out he got murdered last week."

"Fuck! I was looking forward to doing business wit him. You don't know anybody else you can turn me on to?"

"Bre deals wit his boy, so let me holla at him and see what he can do."

"Do that for me, Sis. I went by tha house to visit mom and Iciss tha other day. Iciss is really growing up fast."

"Who you telling Maze."

"I told mom tha boys gon' be beating tha door down to get to her."

"She says they already are."

"Sis, I see now Imma Fuck a Mafucka up."

I couldn't help but laugh to myself, thinking back on how Maze always tried to run all my friends away. Most of them he did and the ones he didn't, he made sure they knew any chances of them gettin' any pussy was out. Maze is older than me by three years. He's really my Godbrother, but ever since his mom was killed in a car accident, my mom raised him.

"Jade, Jade."

"Huh?"

"Did you hear what I said?"

"No, I was thinking about how you use to run all my boyfriends off."

We both had to laugh at that.

"What did you say?"

"I said, tell Turk and Bre I said hi."

"Boy you a mess. Well, I got to handle a few things."

"Do you want to get a few drinks later?"

"Sure, me and tha girls were going to tha Union Tavern later anyway."

"Sounds like a winner; I'll hit ya phone around 9 o'clock." As soon as

I hung up, I called Bre.

"What's up Jade?"

"Did Wes leave yet?"

"He's about to why? What's up?"

"Let me holla at him about Maze real quick."

"About who?"

"Bitch you heard me, my brother."

"Oh, him, hold on."

Bre still has feelings for Maze even though she tries to deny it.

"Yo, what tha bizz is Jade?"

"I need to get at you about my brother."

"Oh, da boy Mase."

"Maze."

"My bag, Bankz was say'n something about that."

I told him what they were suppose to be doing. Of course, I lied about tha price. Since he let me know he was getting 'em for 10.5 a piece, I told him on tha strength of me, Bankz was given them to Maze for 12.5.

"Jade, I'm going to still honor Bankz word, but it won't be until this time next week."

"Wes I appreciate it."

When Bre got back on tha phone, she let me know that I was always scheming.

"I'm just try'n to put my brother in a better position than he's already in."

"I feel you on that."

"I'll call you later." I couldn't wait, so I called Maze back.

"What up Sis?"

"How much are you paying a brick?"

"24 Flat, but Sis, I'm only grabbing 4 for 96,000."

"Well, you'll be spending 12.5 a piece now."

"Shit! Are you serious?"

"Yeah, I just got off tha phone wit his peeps. Only thing, he won't be ready to this time next week, though."

"Shit, at that number, I would wait a month. That is a reason to celebrate; leave ya wallet home; tonight it's on me, Lil' Sis."

"You don't have to tell me twice."

Later that evening, I decided that since we were only going to Union Tavern, I would dress down. White Ralph Lauren sundress wit a pair of black Cole Haan sandals. Once I was dressed, I called Turk and Bre. They pulled up tha same time Maze did.

"Damn, Maze I like that truck."

"Thanks Turk."

"Damn Big Brother, tha new Caddy truck on 28's you showin' off. We gon' ride wit you," Bre said.

I tapped Turk and we both jumped in tha back.

"Yall so petty and whack."

"Just like old times, huh, Bre?"

"What ever Maze. Put on some of that Meek Millz."

When Meek came on, his shit was knock'n something serious.

"I hope I can find a spot to park."

"Don't worry; my peeps saved me a spot in front of tha club."

Sure enough, there was a spot waiting for us in front of tha club.

"Damn this dumb bitch here!"

"Who Maze?"

"Tha broad Tammy I was telling you about."

"Oh, tha one that followed you home?"

"Yeah."

"I told you about slingin' ya shit all around."

"Sis, I told you I didn't even fuck that psycho ass bitch." Bre started laugh'n.

"What's so funny, Abreale?"

"Wow, Mazell we on a first-name basis now?"

"Jade, if I didn't know any better, I would think they were still in love wit one another."

"I think you're right, Turk."

"Pleeease don't even go there."

"What we had is in tha past, so let it stay in tha past."

My mouth says that, but my heart says something totally different, though. Maze looked over at Bre and smiled.

"Damn, she still as beautiful as ever. I'd do anything to have her back," he thought to himself.

"What you smiling at?"

"You, 'cause you still tha same ol' Bre."

"What's that suppose to mean?"

"Always try'n to hide your feelings behind that tough girl shit."

"What ever Nigga!"

Bre, you might fool Jade and Turk, but I see right through you."

"Unh Umm, are we going sit here all night or are we going in?" Turk asked.

As soon as we hopped out, tha bouncer was calling Maze's name.

"What the deal is Ted?"

"Awe, you know, tha same ol' shit."

"Just four of yall tonight?"

"Yeah."

"Come on thru."

I could hear a few people saying shit, but I didn't care one bit.

"Hey Maze," another broad said.

"Damn, he look good; hook a sister up."

I looked at my brother, who was dressed in a pair of pink Ralph Lauren capris wit a white and pink shirt to match and white S. Carter's wit pink stitching. He topped it off wit his Ralph Lauren frames and C.B.W. chain.

"Girl, one of them is probably his girl."

When we got inside, we were met by tha sounds of Yung LA, Yung Dro and It's Ain't I remix. Maze went straight to tha bar to order.

"Let me get a bottle of Bombay. What yall want to drink?"

"I see you still drinking my drink. Me and Turk will split a bottle."

"Bre, you still sippin' tha Goose?"

"Yes, but I'll buy my own bottle."

"Girl, if you don't fall back. Let me get another bottle of Bombay and Grey goose."

"A buck eighty, please."

Maze peeled off two $100 bills.

"Keep tha change."

"Thanks Maze."

"It's nuffin'' Ma." We found an empty table and sit down.

"Don't look, but here comes psycho broad."

"Why haven't you returned any of my calls?"

"For tha hundredth time, I'm not interested in you."

"Yes, you are; that's why you keep riding by my house."

"Ha! Ha! Ha! You need serious help. I'm ride by your house because my mom lives down tha block."

"What ever Maze."

"Check this out; I already have a girl, so I would really appreciate it if you would stop umm…What's tha word I'm looking for?"

"Stalking," Jade said.

"Who are you?"

"His sister and you are?"

"Tracy, his future wife."

Maze had that look that said help me.

"Baby let's dance," Bre said, grabbing his hand.

"Excuse you," Tracy said.

"No excuse you; please make this your last time bothering my man."

What Bre did next took us all by surprise, including Maze. She took his mouth and massaged his tongue wit hers. I could tell Maze enjoyed it because he grabbed a handful of ass. I tapped Turk under the table.

"Umm, Umm," she said, clearing her throat. They finally came up for air.

"When she breaks your heart, don't come runnin' to me."

"Believe me, I won't."

Tracy rolled her eyes and walked off.

"Thanks, Bre, I owe you big time."

"Shit, if I didn't know any better, I would have thought yall enjoyed that."

"I know I did," Maze said, smiling from ear to ear.

"Boy, please, that's tha last time I do you a favor."

"Bitch please, you liked it too; that's why you didn't say anything when he grabbed a handful of your ass."

Ha! Ha! Ha! Me and Turk busted out laugh'n. Even though they were right, I would never let them know that.

"So, I guess you don't want to dance now?"

"Boy, I'm still the shit on tha dance floor; it ain't been that long."

"Girl, it doesn't take rocket science to see they still have feelings for each other."

"Hey all I can say is if it's meant to be, it will be."

"I couldn't agree wit you more." I was feeling good by tha time we have finished our bottle.

"Hey Sis, yall want another bottle?"

"Sure, why not."

"When I come back, we can flick it up."

"How about you Bre?"

"Nah, I'm still on tha first one. Besides, I'm grooving like a Mafucka."

"A'ight, I'll be right back."

As soon as he left, Turks said, "Don't let tha liquor be ya excuse."

"Excuse for what bitch?"

"You know what she talkin' bout, don't play dumb."

"Bitches pleeeeease!"

After 10 minutes, Maze came back wit two more bottles.

"Come on, let's take some flicks."

There were a few people in front of us.

"Damn, yall some bad ass broads."

"I'm sending some flicks to my mans in tha Bing; can yall get in?"

"Unh Unh, we don't do that boop-boop."

"I didn't mean no disrespect Ma."

"None taken."

"Oh, what da bizz is Maze?"

"Same Shit M-O-N-E-Y!"

"You ready for me yet?"

"Yeah, my bag I meant to call you back. Imma hit ya phone in tha AM."

"That's wht it is."

What's up wit my baby Swerv?"

"He good, that's who these flicks for."

"Is she talk'n about Swerv from 8th?"

"Yeah that's who I'm talk'n bout."

"Let me get in."

"I was wondering what happened to him."

"He's been down for a year now."

"When he touch?"

"He only got four left."

"Do you think I can get his information so I can holla at him?"

"No disrespect Ma but who you?"

"Jade."

"Oh shit, word he told me to give you his info if I ever ran across you."

"Well, let me put it in my phone."

Now he was the only one from Wilmington that was going to get some of this bomb-ass twat. We took a lot of flicks. I even took two by myself for him to have.

After we was done his peeps who name was Killer, said, "I see why he been try'n to find you. Imma make sure I tell him I finally seen you."

"Nah, don't tell him just send him those flicks."

"I'll send him these wit my number so we can call me."

"A'ight, just make sure you send them off."

"Don't worry about that!"

"Maze, she ain't ya girl, is she?"

"Nah, that's my little sister. If she was my girl yall definitely would not have been having that conversation."

"I heard dat, well I'm a hit you in tha morning."

"Yo yall we out, this shit about to be over."

We got outside it was packed. "Aye Maze, you going to tha guards."

"You know it; I gotta drop my sis and her girls off, then I'll be over there."

"I'm not ready to go in yet."

"Me either, I normally don't even do tha guards, but I'll make an exception tonight," Bre said.

"If you want, we can drive just in case you get a date."

"Nah, yall good; I don't do Delaware."

"Since when?" Turk said.

"If yall stay in town long enough, you would know."

We pulled up at tha Thunder Guards people were everywhere. We got to tha line Maze peeps were close to tha front, so we walked up there. Nobody said nothing because even though Maze was a pretty boy wit money. Tha whole city knew he was a gun. Rumor also had it that he had a few bodies under his belt. As we walked in, I could feel the heat.

"This is why I don't come here."

"Damn, it's hot in this joint. We can sit over there," he pointed to a table by a fan.

I couldn't front tha DJ was playing all tha right shit. It wasn't until he played Plies "Bust it Baby" that I got up to party.

"That song is still my shit."

Some dude came up try'n to dance. I didn't mind til he tried to grab my ass.

"Excuse you."

"Damn, Baby I know I'm not Plies, but please excuse my hands."

"That's a cute little line that might work on tha average chick."

But since I'm far from tha average chick, I wasn't trying to hear it. The nigga had tha audacity to pull me up to him and grab my ass. I pushed him back and then cussed his sweaty ass out. He acted like he wanted to hit me until he seen Maze walk over.

"Yo Nigga you got a problem wit my sister?"

"My bag Maze; I didn't know this was ya sister."

"Even if it wasn't, no woman should be subject to this bullshit because she don't want a nigga all up on her ass."

"You right, my bag Dog."

I couldn't believe tha words that just came out of Maze's mouth. He had my panties moist; he really has matured a lot in a year.

"I don't know if it's tha Goose or what, but I want me some sex tonight."

I tried to call Wes, but he was in DC and wouldn't be back up for a few days. Looks like I will be using my new toys tonight. I went to tha bar to get me another drink. Some girl was over all over Maze; I don't know why but I was jealous. I went to pay for my drink, but Maze grabbed my hand.

"Put it back in your purse. I got you Bre."

"I got it, Maze you've been more than generous tonight.

"It ain't about nuffin''."

"I remember when you wouldn't buy me shit."

"That was when I was broke fronting like I had paper. I didn't want you to know that I was fucked up."

"Why not?"

"Because I knew you would stop dealing wit me."

"Actually, I wouldn't have."

"I only left you alone because I knew that you deserve more and at tha time, I couldn't give it to you."

"So that's why."

"Yeah, it wasn't because I was in love wit somebody else."

That made me feel a lot better knowing that. All this time, I thought that I wasn't good enough for him.

"Hey this my shit right here." I made my way to tha dance floor.

"We were so tha same I just couldn't see you just like me all up in tha club pop'n bottles of that bub she just like me."

I felt somebody grab my waist and when I turned to see who it was all I could do was smile.

"You didn't think I was going to let you party by yourself, did you?"

Turk tapped me on my arm, bringing me out of my daydream.

"Look at those two. I say we end our pact."

"Not tha pact of never falling in love."

"Yes, that pact. I mean, look at those two they still love each other."

"I know, a blind man can see that."

"Well, no more pact."

After another hour, we were already to bounce.

"Damn the parties out here."

"I don't do the parking lot Pimpin' thing."

Boc, Boc, Boc, Boom, Boom, Boom. No soon as he said that, shots rang out.

"Get in tha truck now!" Boc, Boc, Boc, Boom, Boom, Boom!

"Dumb Mafucka's ain't hittin' shit."

"Do you know 'em?"

"One of 'em is from my set, tha other nigga from tha hill."

Once I heard tha police sirens, I knew it was cool to pull off.

"Imma tell that dumb ass little nigga tomorrow about hisself. Real killers move in silence; they definitely don't shoot out in front of all those people. If somebody would have gotten shot, he would've definitely been going to jail."

"I know cause, like you said, somebody would tell."

Maze pulled up to my house. I couldn't wait to get into my bed.

"Jade, I'm staying here tonight. I don't feel like driving," Turk said.

"Can one of yall pick me up in the morning I don't think I can drive?"

"Why don't you just stay here then?"

"I'm not sleeping on tha couch Maze is going to give me a ride."

"Unh huh, yeah, right."

"Bitch you think you slick, you try'n ta get some dick."

"Sure, I'll give you a ride," Maze said.

"Well, don't look like you'll be needing us to come get you."

"Yes, I will; stop try'n to play me."

"Well, just call if you need a ride."

On tha way to my house, tha ride was quiet except for the sounds of Keyshia Cole's You Complete Me playing. I wonder if he's try'n to tell me something? Nah, it's tha Goose talk'n to me.

"Volume 4."

"Why you turn that down?"

"I was about to use my phone if that's a'ight wit you."

"Do you."

"Bre, can I ask you something and you be completely honest wit me?"

"Yes."

"I know that you're not fucking these dudes that you deal wit."

"How do you know that?"

"For starters, you don't get down like that."

"You're right. I don't; I just use these niggaz for their doe."

"You don't ever think about settling down?"

"No, you fucked that up for everybody. We being honest, right?"

I pulled up in front of her house and turned my truck off.

"When you walked out on me, I was truly heartbroken. I made a pact with Jade and Turk that we wouldn't fall in love."

"Bre, it hurt me to let you go, but I could not do tha things for you that you wanted done."

"Maze, all I wanted you to do was to love me, that's all."

"It just seemed like you weren't happy."

Wit out saying another word, she took my face in her hands and kissed me. When we came up for air Bre told me to come in.

"Listen, before we do this, I just want you to know there's no turning back."

"I know, what ever happens happens."

I hadn't been in Brie's house for over 19 months.

"Love tha new look Bre."

"Thanks."

She had Gucci everything from her couch to her dining room set.

"Do you want another drink?"

"Only if you got Bombay."

"Why wouldn't I, tha way Jade and Turk drink when they over here."

After a few more rounds of Bombay, I was more than drunk. Not to mention my E-Pill had me horny. As if she was reading my mind, Bre told me to follow her. As we went upstairs, I kept my eyes glued to her fat ass. Bre walked over to her stereo, hit power and Chris Brown Say Goodbye came out. I stood there as she took off her clothes. Damn her body was toned up something serious.

"Are you just gon' stand there?"

"Huh, oh, you had me mesmerized."

"Boy ain't nuffin'' you ain't seen before."

I didn't even take my clothes off before I laid her down on tha bed. As soon as my tongue touched her nipple, a soft moan escaped her mouth.

"OOOOOH YEEEES Daddy, that feels SOOOO SOOOOO GOOOOOD."

I slowly worked my way down her body until my tongue landed between her love nest.

"OOOH Shit Maze."

Bre started gyrating her hips as if my tongue was my penis. I had stepped my sex game up two notches since we last encountered one another in tha bedroom. I stood up and slowly pulled my clothes off. Before I could finish, Bre had put tha head of my penis in her mouth. Tha next thing I knew, she was deep-throating all 10 ½ inches of me.

"Damn, Baby what you try'n to do to me?"

When I couldn't take it anymore, I pushed her back on tha bed. Then I took tha tip of my penis and rubbed it against her lips, teasing her.

"Ummm, put it in Daddy."

I slid tha tip in slowly, causing her to moan a little louder. I decided to make her wait by only giving her another inch per stroke until she had it all.

"Oh My God! Oh My God!"

"You want me to stop?"

"No, No, No, it feels like it gotton bigger." That caused me to smile.

"I can't believe how much it's grown; it went from 8 to at least 11."

This nigga is putting it down something serious.

"Oh, Shiiit," I said as my body started to shake.

"MAZE, I'M CUMMING. OOOH, DADDY, OH MY GOD!"

No soon as I exploded all over him, another one was coming.

"Damn, I'm cumming again, Baby!"

He was hittin' my spot; it was like I couldn't stop my body from having orgasms back to back. I lost count at 9. If I wasn't sure, now I was Wes was my last job. I wanted Maze back. I just hope he feels tha same way I do.

After three hours of hot steamy sex and about an hour of lovemaking, we were both exhausted. Soon as I closed my eyes, I was sleep.

Tha next morning I was awaken by tha smell of turkey bacon, eggs, fried potatoes, and waffles. After I had washed up, I went downstairs. To my surprise, Maze was puttin' a plate wit a glass of orange juice on a tray.

When he seen me standing there, he said, "So much for breakfast in bed."

"Awe, you actually made me breakfast."

"Yeah, after the way you put it down, this was tha least I could do for you. I was going to buy you a car, but that would have been overdoing it," he said wit a smile.

"Boy, please. I guess I better get back in bed," I said, then headed back upstairs.

Damn she fat to death. I watched her ass bounce in those booty shorts as she went back up tha steps slowly. I know she was teasing me and it was definitely working. I gotta get some more of that before I leave.

"I feel really special; no one has ever given me breakfast in bed before."

"Well, you should. I've never done this before."

"Yeah, I bet you haven't."

"I haven't." As soon as I tasted tha food, I was blown away.

"Damn, Maze you stepped ya game up all tha way round tha board.

"Hmm I aim to please." When I finished eating, I was ready for some more sex.

"Is there any chance that I can make sure it wasn't tha Goose making me think tha shot was more than it was?"

"Ha! Ha! Ha! You're real funny Bre!"

"I'm dead serious, though."

"You ain't said nuffin'' but a few words."

"So what you waiting on then?" I asked, putting tha tray on my dresser and talking shit at the same time.

When we were both standin' in our birthday suits, I made tha first move and once again, it was on. This time I gave her just enough to come back for more. By tha time we were finished, if I counted correctly, Bre had another six orgasms.

"Is it a'ight if I jump in ya shower?"

"Do you."

I looked at tha clock on tha wall, which read 10 o'clock. I know Turk and Jade will be calling or coming by soon. When Maze came out tha bathroom, he was fully dressed wit tha same clothes from last night.

"Here's my number; after you finish wit Wes call me," he said and left.

Damn, so he was on the same page as me.

CHAPTER 9

Maze

A week had went by and just like he said, Wes had called me.

"What da bizz is Jade?"

"I can't call it; was wait'n on you to call."

"I'm up here, but I never asked you what ya brother was try'n to cop. I only bought 6. I hope that's not too much."

"Let me call him and I'll hit you right back."

Maze picked up on tha first ring.

"Damn, you must be waiting on a phone call."

"Nah, I was about to call somebody."

"Well, Wes is here; he said that he didn't know what you wanted, so he only bought six. Is that too much?"

"Hell Naw, I was hoping he brought at least 8."

"Well, I'm going to have him meet us at Concord Mall by Strawbridge's."

"Where are you at Sis? I'll come scoop you."

"I'm at home."

"Be there in twenty."

I called Wes to give him tha rundown. I didn't even know that was Maze when he pulled up in this Brady Bunch station wagon.

"Are you coming or not Sis?"

"Oh Shit, I didn't know that was you."

This is my hoopty ain't try'n to draw no attention to us."

"I feel you on that."

"I just hope tha product is good."

"Four are sold already at 28,000 apiece."

"Damn, you really killing tha game."

"I just hope ya peeps is consistent."

We pulled up to find Wes already there. He motioned for us to get out and come to his truck. I let Maze get in tha front while I climbed in tha back.

"Wes, this is my brother Maze. And Maze this is Wes."

"What tha bizz is Homie?" West asked.

"You know, try'n to make it do what it do. Jade told you I only bought six, right?"

"Yeah," he passed me a bag, "check 'em out. This is tha best coke that you'll ever put ya hands on."

"Do you think you can bring me back 20?"

"I can bring you as many as you want. When you need 'em next week?"

"Today!"

"Hold on."

He got on his phone and told his peeps he needed them to bring him 20 more.

"Damn, Bankz was really holding."

"My peeps will be up here in a few hours."

"Cool, but let's not meet here; it's too open."

"Are you familiar wit Hanes Park?"

"Yeah, Bre took me there a few times."

"Well, that's our meet spot."

He hit me wit his number as a passed him tha cash.

"I'll call ya phone as soon as he gets here."

Once me and Jade got back in my car, I put tha bricks into my secret compartment and pulled off.

"I seen how you looked at him when he said Bre's name."

"What you talking bout Sis?"

"Nigga it's me you talkin' to. I know last week you and Bre hooked up after yall dropped us off."

"Who told you that, Bre?"

"She didn't have to; it was and has been written all over her face. So what is tha deal wit yall?"

"You know I neva kiss and tell Sis."

"Boy, this me you talk'n to."

"You know I told her tha real reason I left her alone."

"Oh, you did?" I tried to sound surprised even though Bre had already told me.

"Bre already told you, didn't she?"

"Truth."

"Yeah truth."

"Yes, but don't tell her I told you. She was just happy that it wasn't that you didn't love her anymore."

"Well, did she also tell you that I let her know when she finishes wit Wes and whoever else to call me?"

"Yup, but I don't want him to get upset and cut you off."

"Well, I need to find out who his plug is because I know if he's letting them go to me for 12.5, he getting a lot for dirt cheap."

"Let me handle that part."

"Here Sis," I said, handing her an envelope.

"What's this Brother?"

"Just to show my appreciation for tha hook up."

"Boy, I wouldn't dare to get ya money," she said, handing me the envelope back.

"Thanks, but no thanks."

"Maze, anything I do is outta love not for money."

"I know Jade and that's why I'll do anything for you and I mean anything."

"I'll be sure to keep that in mind."

After I dropped Jade off, I'll called Juice, Zeeky and Tranz to let them know that everything was a go and it to meet me at tha stash house on 38th St. First; I had to meet my peoples from Sussex and Maryland to hit them wit tha 4 bricks they had ordered. Once that was done, I made my way to meet wit my boys.

"What's da deal big Homie?"

"Money Nigga Money!"

"You ain't neva lied about that."

"Look, I got two birds left for yall to break down and hit ya folks."

"Damn, that's it?"

"Naw, I'm waiting on tha call as we speak. I had six, but tha other four were gone before I even got them. Just hit me wit 19.2 apiece."

"This some good shit; I don't know he said it's the best I'll ever had."

"We bout to find out right now."

Juice went to tha kitchen and pulled out everything he needed. He put 4 ½ in tha pot wit 40 grams of bake. He took a spoon, mashed and mixed tha bake and powder into tha rocks were all out. Next, he took a little water and sprinkled just enough to wet tha Coke. As soon as he put it on tha stove, he started to stir it. He was doing what I had taught him. I call it dry cooking tha Coke. Wit then a couple of minutes, it looked like a cookie.

"Run cold water in tha pot," I told him.

Once he did, it rocked up instantly. Juice took a butter knife and went around tha edge of tha pot. Then he flipped it over onto tha paper towels. When he put it on tha scale, it jumped from 4 ½ to 6 easily. Now to get Aunty to try it out.

"Aunty, come down here for a second."

"Yes Baby."

"Can you try this out for me?"

"Sure will."

After about 20 minutes, Aunty came back wit a piece of paper and handed it to me. When I looked at it, all I could do was smile.

"Yo, we struck gold. Aunty said she hasn't had Coke this good since tha 70s. Also, that she couldn't talk that why she wrote a note."

I was upping tha price to 30 grand a pop. My phone started going off.

"Yo."

"I'm ready for you. Meet me where we discussed. I'm only 10 minutes away."

After we met him, I called all my folks to let them know about tha new product in tha price. Over the next few days, shit was rolling and to my surprise, there was only a few left. I called Wes to place my order and this time, I doubled up. He told me he would call me in a few hours. I knew he was with Bre because he said that he was already up this way. As much as I wanted to be wit Bre I wasn't and couldn't let her come between my business. At least not till I find out about his plug.

CHAPTER 10

Play My Part

It had been a week since I had written Swerve and sent those pictures. I even sent him a money order for 300. Even though I know, he didn't need it. Now here I am, staring at a letter he had written me back, scared to open it.

Dearest Jade,

First, all praise due to Allāh. I pray this reaches you in tha best of health and spirits. Sorry, it took so long to respond back. I must admit I was surprised to receive a letter as well as pictures and a money order from you. Thank you, I have been thinkin' about you this past year. I told my peeps if he ever ran across you to get your info if you allowed him to. Upon reading ya letter, I couldn't believe you were actually feeling me that way. To be honest, I thought it was all about a dollar since I have plenty of it. I now know that was not tha case. As you may know, I was set up by a rat and sentenced to five years. Nine outta 10, I'll only do four and I got one in. But tha show must go on, right? I said that to say, tell Maze that tha boy Wes is copping off me. So why deal wit tha middleman? But anyway, I hope that you will find tha time to set up a visit for next week.

Until tha next time we talk.

Love ya friend

Swerve

Wow, that made me more attracted to him. Not to mention, I had gotton Wes Connect. I picked up my phone to make a visit. After trying for 45 minutes, I finally got through and got a visit for next Saturday at 2:30.

"Hello."

"What's da deal Lil' Sis?"

"Got some good news for you."

"What dat is?"

You'll neva eva guess who Wes like is copping from."

"No, I won't so tell me."

"Swerve."

"Who?"

"You heard me."

"How did you find that out?"

"Swerve wrote me back and he said to tell you why deal wit tha middleman when you can go straight to tha source."

"That's what I'm talk'n bout fuck that nigga after this flip."

"Well, I made a visit to see him next week. I put you on there so you could talk to him face-to-face."

"That's wht it is. When is tha visit?"

"Next Saturday at 2:30."

We checked in wit tha CO (Correction Officer) and then had a seat in tha lobby.

"Time to go up for tha visit everyone," tha CO said.

They made me take my hat off and leave it downstairs. When we got in tha visiting room, we had to wait until tha other visitors came out. I knew one of the broads that came out. She spoke, so I spoke back. Swerve was sitting in the first booth. I could see tha other inmates that were in tha hallway staring. I picked up tha phone after wipin' it down. Damn even wit his white uniform on he still look good as shit.

"Hey how are you doing?"

"A'ight now that I've seen you."

"Don't try to fill me up."

"Ma, I'm dead serious; all I've been doing is staring at ya pictures."

"Whatever."

"I didn't think you was going to make a visit."

"Why wouldn't I."

"Maybe you got a man; I don't know."

"If I did have a man, I would have neva wrote you in tha first place."

"Let me know you talk to my brother so I can have tha rest of the time."

"Swerve As Salamu Alaikum Walaikum Salam."

"What tha Bizz is?"

"Try'n to get at a dollar."

"I heard you been dealing wit my folk."

"Yeah, my sis put me down wit him."

"Oh, did she?"

"Yeah, one of her girls been dealing wit dude."

"Oh a'ight. So, if you don't mind me being in your bizz-ness. How much he charging you?"

"12.5."

"That ain't bad; I'm charging him wit 10 flat."

"Say no more; when I dump these last five, it's me and you."

"So how many you copping?"

"I just grabbed 20 5 days ago."

"Damn, and you only got five left?"

"Yeah, I let them birds fly."

"I heard that."

"If you gonna charge me 10 apiece, then I'll take 25 off ya hands when you ready."

"Imma have my nephew Tiz holla at you."

"That's my peeps; he got my number."

"If he don't get at you then Killer will. Do he got ya number?"

"Yeah."

"Well, one of 'em will call you later."

"That's what's up here my Sis."

"I should've made the visit for him."

"I'm sorry."

"It's cool; I'm just play'n wit you."

"I hope this is not going to be ya only visit."

"I'm sure you got all types of broads kick'n da door down to see you."

"Nah, I wasn't dealing wit a lot of broads and the ones I was left when tha judge said five years."

"You know why, don't you?"

"Why?"

"Cause you not out there to spending no money on 'em."

"I wasn't doing that when I was..."

"Boy stop lying."

"I'm serious."

"Well, you said you got four left."

"Nah, like 3 ½."

"That ain't shit; if you want, I'll keep you company."

"Well, I don't want you to do nuffin'' you don't want to do."

"Believe you me, if I didn't want to, I wouldn't."

"Well, do you then."

Tha CEO started flickin' tha light.

"Well, I'll make a visit Monday for next week. You got my number so call me; I accept collect calls."

Numbers don't change till next month. But I'll get my sis to call you on three-way."

"Call me later." I just sat there and watched her leave.

"Damn, Swerve that wifey?"

"No, not yet, but hopefully, she will be."

"She fat as a mothafucka Dog. "

When we got outside, it was hotter than when we went in.

"So, you straight now, Brother?"

"Yeah, that was a good look too."

I didn't do nuffin'' but relay tha message. Not to be nosy, but are you gonna finish this bid with him?"

"More than likely."

"If you not, then don't get it started. I seen a lot of broads do that to niggaz."

"Brother, I'm tha average broad; you should know that."

"I do. A'ight hit me up later Sis. I need to knock off this last bit of work."

"Be safe and I love you."

"I love you too."

When I got in my car, both my phones were going off like crazy. By tha time I returned all tha calls I had missed, those five chickens were dead. I couldn't believe my luck; within two weeks, I went from paying 24 to 12.5 to 10 stacks a bird.

I'm still going to charge Juice, Zeeky, and Tranz eight an ounce.

I couldn't get my mind off Swerve especially seeing how good he looked at that visit. I was brought out of my daydream by tha sounds of my phone. I damn near fell try'n to answer it.

"Hello."

"Hey, Bitch you still going out tonight?"

"Damn."

"Damn what?"

"I was waiting on a call."

"It must be a call from Barack Obama."

"Fuck you Bre."

"Oh, my bag; my brother got that covered already."

"Yup, he sure do. Yeah, I'm still going out." My other line clicked.

"Hold on a minute Bre. Hello."

"You busy?"

"Who's this?"

"You got that many Niggaz callin' you?"

"No, that's why I asked who's this smart ass."

"It's Swerve."

"Damn, my fault but you sound different."

"Probably 'cause I had food in my mouth."

"Didn't ya mom tell you neva talk wit food in ya mouth?"

"She told me a lot of things not to do." We talked until tha phone said one minute.

"When you gon' call me again," I asked.

"I was gon' hit you right back."

"Well, I'm a forward my calls to her phone 'cause I'm bout to get dressed." Tha phone hung up on his end.

"I'm bout to forward my calls to ya phone."

"OK." As soon as she did, my phone rang.

This is HRYCI wit a collect call from its Swerve. If you accept this call, do not use three-way or call waiting or you will be disconnected. To accept this call, dial five now.

"You gon' blow ya sister's phone bill up."

"Nah, I pay tha bill every month."

"So, if it's cool wit you, I'll just get her to forward tha calls to ya cell until tha new numbers go in next month."

"I'm a'ight wit it; I just don't want to inconvenience anybody. Listen, Jade, I know you independent and I'm not try'n to even change that."

"Boy."

"Nah, let me finish. I respect you for wanting to keep in touch wit me. I'm not expecting anything from or outta you but your friendship. Even though if I neva caught this bid, you probably would have broken ya pact by now!"

"Boy P-L-E-E-A-S don't flatter ya self."

We talked until his last call at 10:30.

Shit, let me jump in tha shower before Turk and Bre come. When I was in tha shower, I couldn't get Swerve off my mind. Tha next thing I knew, I had my index, ring and middle finger inside my pussy, pleasuring myself. It had been a while since I had anything in there. So, I was past due, to say tha least. When I was done, I washed up and then got out.

"Jade, Jade."

"What!" I yelled down tha steps.

"You not ready yet?"

"No, I just got out tha shower."

"Well, hurry up; you know how Doc B parties be."

I didn't even buy anything to wear shit. I walked into my closet and picked out a cream and chocolate Monique Hueller dress that still has the tags on it. I had bought this dress over six months ago. I grabbed my Christian Louboutin shoes that I got to go wit it. Once I was dressed, I had to ask myself why I never wore tha outfit. Damn it fit every curve. I threw on my Ray Ban shades and my diamond Ms. Jade necklace wit tha bracelet to match. Sprayed myself wit J-Lo's To Die For, then headed downstairs.

"Bout time Bitch!"

"I know it's damn near 12."

"You was about to get ya slow ass left."

"I know my way to tha Doubletree."

"Shut up and let's go before we don't get in."

"Us not gettin' in, imagine that. Who is driving cause I'm not?" 1 quickly said.

"Bre is driving"

"Oh, I am?"

"Yup."

We pulled up to valet like always. We went straight in, no waiting in line.

"Now, who ain't gettin' in?"

"Excuse me, Shorty you got a man?"

We all turned around to see Wes and Joker standing there all smiles. Turk frowned her face at tha sight of Joker.

"What's up Turk?"

"Hey."

"Damn, I know you ain't still trippin' about last time? I'm sorry I was out of character. What up Jade?"

"I can't call it, just staying outta tha way."

"I feel you."

"Hey Brother," I said, talking to Maze.

"What up Sis?"

"Damn, you looking good."

"You too Turk."

"Thanks, you real fly wit ya Emporio Armani on."

"I see you know ya designers."

"But of course I do. What up Bre you look'n sexy as usual." She started blushing.

"Thanks, Maze I'm feeling that."

"Thanks."

"I know this Nigga ain't flirting wit my man's peeps," Joker thought to himself.

"What up Maze," Wes said.

"Same ol' shit."

"Hit me when you ready for some more work."

"Damn, did that nigga just try to play me?"

"Oh, Nah, I'm good now; my peeps hollered at me."

"Hey ya folks ain't gon' want nuffin' but what you was just hittin' 'em wit."

"Yo, Wes you ain't got to go into all that; fuck him his loss, not ours."

"Who tha fuck asked you anything Nigga you just a bad carrier."

(Ha! Ha! Ha!) Turk busted out laugh'n.

"Bitch, what you laugh'n at? Aye, Wes, you need to put ya man in check."

I seen where this was headed, so I stepped in.

"Why don't both yall chill out!"

"If you love ya brother, you better get him!"

"Nigga did you just threaten me?"

"Come on, we all just came to have a good time."

"My man enjoy ya night; you neva know it may be ya last," Maze said wit a smile, "Bre, maybe we can have a dance."

Maze walked off, he called somebody on his phone. For some reason I had a bad feeling about that call.

"Hey ladies, why don't we take a few pictures."

"A'ight."

"I'll see you later," Wes said.

"I don't know, but I don't think that Joker knows who Maze is."

"I know. Did you see tha look on his face when Maze told him it might be his last night?"

"I hope he does kill tha arrogant son of a bitch."

"Next."

"That's us, come on."

We took a few pictures; I made sure to take enough to send Swerve. Just when we were done, Maze came out.

"Am I too late?"

"Nope, come on."

"I got these Shorty."

"You know ya money good Maze."

"I know it is, all tha money you get from me."

"While yall here, when tha party's over, don't go out wit dem niggaz."

He didn't have to tell us twice. Bre and Turk looked at me; I just shrugged my shoulders.

"Bre, can me and you take a picture by ourselves?"

"Sure, we can."

While they were taking their flicks, Wes and Joker came out.

"Who tha Fuck this Nigga think he is. I got his Bitch Ass after this."

"Jade, did you hear him?"

"I heard him."

"Can I take a picture wit you Bre."

"Yeah when we finish."

"Check this out, Maze you being real disrespectful. If I didn't know any better, I would think you want her."

"I do, but Imma let her finish up wit you."

Damn, I can't believe he told him that.

"Wes is history after tonight."

We went back inside to tha bar. After another hour, I was ready to leave.

"Yall ready?"

"Yeah, let's go."

When we got to tha door, I seen two people across tha street by Wes car wit hoodies on. When tha valet brought our car back, we got straight in.

"Look at that dumb mafucka all drunk," Turks said.

Boc, Boc, Boc, Boom, Boom, Boom.

"Oh, shit yall look."

We turned around just in time to see Wes and Joker falling to tha ground. Just to make sure they were dead, tha two gunmen stood over top of them and fired close range in their heads. You see tha brain matter splatter. The gunmen took off in opposite directions. Maze walked past our car and winked at me. I no longer had to wonder if what they said about my brother was true. The wink confirmed it all.

CHAPTER 11

Easy As 1.2.3

"Are you sure there's at least 300 grand in here?"

"I'm positive. Have I ever been wrong?"

We parked a block over so not to alarm anyone. We knew there would only be two people in tha house. Tha sweet thing was we had a key to tha back door, thanks to his girl. We had to bust her down 50 grand. Once we got to tha door, I looked through tha window to make sure they were upstairs like she said they would be. We pulled down our masks and then entered tha house.

"Yall look in tha basement behind tha shelf. Press tha wall and it should pop out."

I crept up tha stairs; once I got to tha top, I could hear tha sounds of soft moons coming from tha end of tha hall. I checked tha other bedrooms along tha way to be sure no one else was in tha house. When I got to where tha sounds were coming from, I peeped through tha half-open door. Only to find this nigga hitting her doggy style.

"Umm Unh," I said, clearing my throat. They both jumped.

"What tha fuck!" I pointed my .45 at his head, silencing him.

"I have a few questions, but I'm only going to ask them one time. Where is tha money at?"

"I don't know what." SPTT SPTT.

"Oh shit, you mothafucka!" I made sure both shots hit him in his legs.

"Now, let's try this again. Bitch you better shut tha fuck up! Now where tha fuck is the money?"

"Baby just tell them where it is."

By now, I was joined by my squad.

"Listen, I don't keep that much cash here. I'll have to take you to it."

"Do you think we that dumb nigga? Just give us tha address. They'll get it while I stay here. If it's there, you get to live. If it's not well, you already know what the deal is."

"Damn, I thought they would fall for that."

"Tied them up; now what is tha address and remember whether you two live or die is solely up to you."

I wanted to go since I knew B-More like tha back of my hand. But I had to make sure this nigga didn't try no bullshit. They left and I let them know that if I didn't hear from them in a half an hour, then I would assume tha worst.

"You know I'll find out who you guys are."

"Is that a threat?"

"It is wht it is"

(Chirp) What tha deal is?

(Chirp) We got it.

(Chirp) How much is it?

(Chirp) Three duffel bags of money and one wit heroin.

(Chirp) A'ight you know where to go.

(Chirp) See you when you get there.

(Chirp) Don't forget tha bag in tha kitchen.

(Chirp) Gotcha.

"Well, it was nice doing business wit yall."

I was about to leave when I heard him say we were all dead.

"Now, I was going to let you live, but you just fucked it up."

I took my mask off so he could see my face.

"What tha fuck!"

"I know I'm tha last person you expected to see." He looked over to his girl.

"Bitch you set this up."

SPT, SPT, SPT, SPT. Four shots to his face shut him up instantly.

"I'm going to have to shoot you to make it look good."

"OK."

"I'll call tha police on my way out."

I put tha tape over her mouth. SPT, SPT two shots to tha stomach. I pulled my phone out.

"I would like to report gunshots at 331 Shire St."

I walked down tha steps and grabbed tha bag on my way out. I had to smile to myself, knowing that by tha time somebody discovered them, they both will be dead. I never called tha police. I couldn't take tha chance on her trying to blackmail us after she got her money. My motto witnesses to crime.

By the time we had counted tha money, we were all tired. We were happy, to say tha least wit our take.

"Damn, I told yall that nigga Dreadz was holding."

"This makes that score we got from Bankz look like pennies."

"I know and we still haven't gotton rid of tha drugs."

"I know, but I know somebody in Jersey that will take this heroin off our hands. No questions asked."

"I can't believe the Nigga had over $2 mill in his crib."

"That Nigga runs tha whole B-more, plus it's not like he can just waltz into a bank it say hi I'd like to deposit $2.8 million."

"I know, but I would have been putting a little at a time in there."

"You know those Jamaicans aren't tha brightest of tha bunch."

"I was thinking about opening up some type of business. I have some stock that's been doing extremely well these past few months."

"Come on, let's get outta here and head home."

CHAPTER 12

Keep'n It Real

Tha last year flew by; I've been to see Swerve every week for tha past year. We're still just friends; neither one of us has taken initiative to see if tha other is willing to take tha next step. Bre and Maze finally started seeing each other again. As for Turk, she still doing her. She is also on tha verge of opening up a woman's and children's clothing boutique on Market Street Mall. As soon as I got into my Caddy truck, my phone went off.

"I'M LOCKED UP AND THEY WON'T LET ME OUT THEY WON'T LET ME OUT I'M LOCKED UP."

All I could do was smile. After pressing five, I was greeted by hey Sexy.

"Hey."

"Was you busy?"

"No, on my way to pick Iciss up."

"Now, where are my two favorite girls going?"

"Chas birthday is next week, so we going up top to grab her a outfit. You know Iciss wants to come see you."

"I don't want her to see me in here."

"I told her that, but she said she still wants to see you."

Just as I was pullin' up in front of my mom's tha phone said one minute remaining.

"Are you going to call me right back?"

"Yeah." I hit tha horn to let Iciss know I was outside.

"Hey Sis."

"Hey to you."

When my phone rang, Iciss started smiling.

"Let me talk, let me talk."

"Hold up damn."

"Why did you use ya your prepaid account?"

"We been over this a thousand times. I know I told you that you can call as much as you want. I pay tha bills. Jade, I got over a stack on this. I need to use it cause Insha Allāh (if it pleases Allāh) if this mod goes through, I'm outta here."

"I hope so, I was going to call Malik to see how it was looking, but I wanted to check wit you first."

"Hold on for a second, here Girl."

"Hey Brother, how are you holding up in there?"

"I'm good; how are you doing?"

"Fine."

"You ain't got no boyfriend, do you?"

"No, I don't got no boyfriend."

"She better not have no boyfriend."

"Did Jade tell you I want to come visit you?"

"Yes, she told me."

"So, I'll be there."

"Look, I have a contact visit coming up in two weeks."

"I was going to ask Jade to come."

"So why don't you come if she says yes."

"You know she's going to say yes."

"What are yall talking about? Say yes to what?"

"Swerve has a contact visit in two weeks. Do you want to go wit me?"

"Wit you girl, give me my phone. "I'll see you in two weeks Brother."

Over tha past year, they have gotton really close.

"Who said I was going," I said, snatching my phone from her.

"Hello."

"Oh, so you not coming?"

"Yeah right, stop wit tha bullshit."

"What? You said it not me. I need Iciss name."

"You know it already."

"Are you allowed to have food?"

"Yeah."

"Is there anything particular you want?"

"Can you cook?"

"Now, what kind of question is that?"

"Excuse me; I was just asking not all woman can cook."

"Well, I can burn my ass off."

"Well, I want some fried fish, fried potatoes, corn, cornbread and beef pepperoni pizza from tha gas station on 30th St. Oh and some shrimp."

"Is that all."

"Yeah, if it's too much, I'll have my sister cook it and you can pick it up."

"Don't disrespect me!"

"I wasn't, I know that's a lot to cook."

"Boy P-L-E-E-E-A-S-E."

(One minute remaining)

"I'll call you back later so yall can get your shop on."

"I can do two things at once. I happen to be multi-talented."

"It's about to be count time. I'll hit you after dinner."

"OK."

"Bye Brother!" Iciss yelled.

When I hung up Iciss said, "I can't wait till he comes home."

I lucked up getting a spot in front of Unica.

"A DIVA IS A VERSION OF A FEMALE HUSTLER, A FEMALE HUSTLER."

I looked at my caller ID there was no name. I wasn't going to answer, but whoever it was hung up and called right back.

"Hello."

"Hey Sexy."

"Who is this?"

"Damn, you don't know my voice?"

"Evidently not if I asked who you are!"

"No need to be upset it's Spit."

"Spit from 8th?"

"Yeah."

"How do you get my number?"

"Ya peeps gave it to me."

"Well, why are you calling me?"

"Damn, it's like that?"

"How many times did you try to holla and I told you I wasn't interested? That's what I thought. Please don't call my number no more."

"Bitch you really think you are tha shit, don't you?"

"I must be you keep try'n to get at me wit your broke ass, and ya moms a bitch!"

"Who tha fuck you..." Before he could say anything else, I hung up.

"You OK Jade? Who was that?"

"Some clown ass nigga that's been try'n to holla for tha past few months.

"He from tha same block as Swerve?"

"Yes."

"Why don't you tell him about it then?"

"Because he's not my man, that's why!"

"What are yall waiting for? It's obvious yall like each other."

"Listen to my 14-year-old sister giving me advice about relationships."

"Jade, if nobody don't know you I do. I seen you play a lot of dudes. So, for you to stop for a guy that's in jail and not on his way out, it's only four letters to describe it."

"What's that?"

"L-O-V-E! You been to prison every week for tha past 12 months faithfully. Yall can play, but I see through it."

Damn, I was in love but in denial. We spent tha remainder of tha afternoon shoppin'. My phone started ringing.

"What up Hoe?"

"Shit up top."

"You didn't have to call a bitch."

"Me and Iciss came up to get Chas something for her birthday."

"Fuck I forgot all about her damn birthday next week. Tell Iciss Hi"

"Turks says hey."

"Hey aunty Turk."

"When you coming back this way?"

"In the next 45 minutes. We bout to go to Ishkabibbles to grab something to eat, then we on 95."

"Call me when you get back; I'm try'n to go to McKenzies to have a drink."

"Sounds good to me."

When I pulled up to my mom's Maze truck was parked in tha driveway.

"Iciss you better grab ya bags."

She ran back to get her bags and then ran into tha house.

Hey Mom, hey Maze."

"Sup Sis."

"Don't need to ask where yall been my," mom said pointing to tha bags that Iciss had.

"Yeah, we went to get Chas an outfit for her birthday."

"Bre did say Chasity was having a party next week."

"So, what brings you by?" Iciss asked.

"I can't come check on you and mom. Plus, I came to drop some money off for yall."

"That's music to my ears."

"Who is this Eric dude that called here?"

"Gosh, he's my friend from school."

"He sounded like a grown ass man."

"He's only 16 and we're just friends."

"I know one thing for certain and two things for sure you better not be fuckin!"

"Maze watch your mouth."

"Sorry Mom but I'm dead serious."

I didn't say anything I just looked at Iciss.

"Ain't nobody even having sex."

"You better not be," my mom quickly said.

"See that's where parents go wrong."

"What's that supposed to mean Jade?"

"Listen, Mom when you told me not to have sex that only made me curious. Curious because I wanted to know why you didn't want me to do it. Mom you should've sat me down and talked to me about birth control and condoms."

"I've already had this talk wit Iciss, so she knows to let one of us know when she decides to have sex. Ain't that right Iciss?"

"Yes it is Big Sis."

"I'm cool wit that but I still want to meet this Eric guy."

"Mom."

"Don't Mom me."

"Yeah 'cause I had to go through the same thing wit him."

"Did she mom?"

"Yeah, she sure did so I don't know what to tell you. If you think you gon' be able to sneak around. Huh, just remember I know a lot of people in a lot of places. At tha end of tha day Little Sis I love you and nobody will ever take advantage of you!"

It was the day before my contact visit and I couldn't wait. Shit I'm running late for my visit. I only had 15 minutes and I still had to stop and get a money order. When I got to tha visit they were about to go up.

"You almost didn't make it Jade," tha CO who is always there let me know.

"I know, I had to stop to get this," I said giving her tha money order.

She printed out my receipt and we went upstairs. Swerve was already sitting in tha first booth when I walked in.

"Hey you," I said wit a smile.

"Hey Ma, how you?"

"I'm a'ight considering you haven't called me since Wednesday."

"I thought you might need a break from me calling."

"How much did you say you get paid to think?"

"Ha! Ha! Ha! You got jokes huh .I wanted to see how much he was actually feeling me if he was at all.

"I'm not going to be able to come to your contact Visit tomorrow." As soon as I said that I could see tha disappointment in his face.

"Is everything all right? S-I-I-I-K-E," I yelled sticking out my tongue.

"Jade you better stop play'n wit me like that. Shit I've been looking forward to this since you said you would come."

"Do you still want tha same food?"

"You know it."

"Since we have to be here by 5:30 I'm going to start cooking at 2:30; that way it will still be hot."

"Even if it's not, we got a microwave."

"Almost like home huh."

"Not even close."

"Tell Maze I got that money and flicks he sent me tha other day."

"That reminds me I brought you a money order. I know you said not to bring you any money but I did so be a'ight wit it. I only bought you a deuce.

You're only allowed to have a nickel on tha books."

"Wit tha money you just dropped off put me in a stack. They just sent me a letter from tha business office saying I had to send 300 out. What I normally do is once it gets down to a buck I tell Killer or Tiz to send me another four."

"So how did you end up wit another eight?"

"Because I had three then your brother sent me a nickel."

"Well, you can send it to me if you want."

"I'm not going to send it out fuck 'em."

"Well, if you change ya mind tha offer still stands."

"That's what's up."

The CO flick tha lights which meant it was time to go.

"I'm not going to call I'll see and Iciss tomorrow."

CHAPTER 13

Reunited

Meanwhile across town Bre was sitting in front of the Dominican café waiting for Maze.

"You ain't gotta worry Harlem world cause I got you in tha studio spittin' nuffin'' but tha hot shit."

Look at him pulling up wit that smile on his face.

"I don't know what you smiling for I've been sitting here for 15 minutes."

"My fault, I had to handle something at tha last minute."

"You could have at least called me to let me know."

"I'm sorry I'll make sure to do that the next time if it happens. Come on let's order something to eat, I'm starving."

As we were walking in two broads were coming out.

"Hey Maze."

"Sup Tamika."

Nuffin'' my brother is looking for you."

"Is he?"

"Yup."

"Do me a favor call him and give him my number." She dialed his number then handed me tha phone.

"Hello."

"What up Little Homie you looking for me?"

"Who dis?"

"Maze."

"Damn you a hard nigga to catch up wit."

"I'll be on tha move plus I changed my number."

"I know and so did I."

"So, what's good?"

"Same 'ol same 'ol."

"Take my number and call me in two hours cause I'm about to bust a grub wit my peeps."

"A'ight I got you."

After I hit him wit my number I handed Tamika her phone back.

"Thanks."

"Don't mention it," she said wit a seductive smile.

I looked over at Bre to see if she had seen her. Luckily she didn't or I would have never heard tha end of it.

"Hey Marisol, let me get steak wit red beans and rice and a side of fried bananas."

"Should I put extra steak and sauce."

"Please."

"Do you want your usual?" she asked Bre.

"Yes and give me a side of tha fried potatoes too."

"Is this for here or ta go?"

"For here," I said not giving Maze a chance to answer.

We sat down while Marisol got our food together.

"I seen that chick give you that I want you smile."

"Damn she don't miss shit," I thought to myself.

"I know you did." I lied but it sounds good.

Me and Bre have been seeing each other for the past 7 months. I thought it would be hard for me to stop messing with all tha other females that I was a custom to dealing wit. Truth be told, it was tha total opposite. It was as if everything we felt for one another came right back.

"Thank you Marisol."

"You're welcome, I have to make sure you two are OK all tha money yall spend in here."

"I know that's right."

"Hmm, Hmm, Hmm, this shit is banging like a mufucka!"

"Maze, are you going out tonight?"

"I don't know why?"

"I was hoping we could spend some time together."

"Well, why don't we go to Plush."

"If that's really what you want to do."

We got up I pay tha tab and tipped Marisol.

"Hey Sexy, I'll pick you up by 10 o'clock. Oh, not that you don't already know girl, you sexy as shit."

"Boy, now you got me blush'n all crazy."

He kissed me then we got in his car.

Damn, it's almost 10 o'clock and I'm not even dressed yet. I better get a move on it or I'll never hear tha end of it. No soon as I finished getting dressed, I heard Maze pulling up. Damn, I was right on time. Maze blew tha horn for me to come out. I put on a little Kimora Lee Simmons (KLS), then headed downstairs and out tha door.

"Wow nice car."

"Thank you."

Maze was driving his 72 Lasabre white on white, sitting on 28's.

"Bre you gon' be tha baddest chick in tha club tonight."

I was looking good in my Dior Homme dress and matching stilettos.

"What you smoking, it smells good."

"Just a little Sour Diesle that I got from 8th and Indy up Philly. Do you want to hit it?"

"Yeah, let me try it out. Shit I never smoked any kind of weed except purple haze."

This weed was good as hell. I only took about eight pulls and I was high as shit. Between tha Sour D and tha Goose by tha time we pulled up to Plush I was grooving. We let tha valet park tha car as we headed to tha door. Tha line was a little too long for me. Maze must have felt tha same way because he grabbed my hand and led me to tha front of tha line. He hit tha bouncer wit a hundred and we were let in.

"Blame it on tha Goose, gotcha feelin' loose, Blame it on tha Tron, got you in a zone. Blame it on tha a-a-a-a-alcohol."

"Yo this cut be having 'em go crazy in tha club."

"I know, look at 'em."

"Come on let's hit the bar."

We walked to tha bar to get a few shots of what Jamie was just singing about. Well, I did anyway. Maze was hooked on tha Bombay Sapphire just like Turk and Jade. Once tha barmaid brought our drinks back we headed over to tha dance floor.

"Let me buy you a drink, Imma take you home wit me I got money in tha bank."

Bree was doing her thing. Don't get it twisted I was no slouch when it came to dancing. Especially wit my e-pill in me you couldn't tell me shit.

"I need another drink."

"Me too."

"Come on then."

"Imma run to tha ladies room, be right back," she said kissing me on tha forehead.

Damn how can a club not serve bottles?

"Excuse me is there any way I could talk to tha owner?" She picked up tha phone after a few yes and no's she hung up.

"I have some bad news and good news."

"Hold on let me guess. Tha good news you have bottles but tha bad news is it's gonna cost me."

"Wow, cute and smart man."

"A'ight, Let me get two bottles and 2 cups wit ice."

She came back punched a few keys on tha cash register and said, "275 dollars."

"I would hate to see how much a bottle of Ace would cost."

I peeled off $300 bills.

"Keep tha change."

When I turned around I saw some dude posted up in Bre's face. When I walked up dude was asking her if she knew who he was.

"No, I don't and it really doesn't matter to me who you are!"

Since she had it covered I walked over to one of tha tables and sat down. Bre started to walk over followed by tha same dude who is just spittin' game to her.

"Sorry it took so long but it was beyond my control."

When she sat down dude act like I wasn't even sitting there. I didn't give a fuck who he was I wasn't going to be disrespected.

"Aye My Man." He looked at me like I was crazy.

"Yo she good," I said what a smile.

"This is ya girl?"

I didn't know how to answer that, so I said, "Nah we friends."

"Well then it's fair game, right?"

"Nah, it ain't fair game, I'm here wit him."

"Take my number, call me when you get bored wit him."

(Ha! Ha! Ha!) "You a funny dude." I said.

"What's that suppose to mean?" he asked.

"Listen My Man, I know you not use to females turning you down, especially since you have so much money. But it does happen."

"Damn this could be a good look for Turk," Bre thought to herself.

"Listen, why don't I give ya number to my sister she could use a friend."

"Nah, now you try'n to make me look desperate. Plus, I don't do tha blind date thing."

"Hey suit yourself."

I went through my phone until I found what I was looking for.

"See I," said handing my phone to him.

(WHEEEW) "Damn she bad as a Mafucka are those…"

Before he could finish, I said, "Yes, they are real eyes."

"Well, tell her to holla at me."

"What did you say ya name was again?"

"Cream."

"Aye My Man I wasn't try'n to disrespect you. If you would've said she was ya girl I would've stepped off."

It ain't bout nuffin' Homey."

When he left, Bre said, "We going to see how much money he really has. We'll see if he lives up to his name."

"I don't blame him for wanting you, Bre you're beautiful."

"I am?"

"Why you say it like that?"

"Because what are we doing Maze, huh?"

"I thought we were taking it slow."

"Can I be honest wit you Maze?"

"Of course, you can."

"We were together for three years; I would like to think we know each other. So, I say that to say we either going to be a couple or not. If I was your girl ave had to go thru that bullshit wit Cream."

"Nah, if you was my wifey Cream might be on a T-shirt."

We stopped at tha Wawa before we jumped on tha highway.

"So, are you staying wit me tonight?"

"Well, I thought that you would stay wit me tonight."

"Oh, so you are allowed to have company? I was beginning to think you had a girl."

"You should know better than that Bre."

"I want to hear my song. You do know what song that is, don't you?"

"It's track 10 volume 15."

"Don't wanna make a scene, but I really don't care when people stare at us sometimes I think I'm dreaming so I pinch myself just to see if I'm awake and I gotta be tha one you want I got ta be tha one you need."

Bre always could sing that's one of tha things I loved about her. I pulled up to my crib then hit tha button so tha garage could open up.

"I see you finally took my advice and moved out of tha city."

"Yeah, I just bought this house a few months ago. But I was just finished doing everything that I wanted done to it."

I punched in tha security code then went inside. Once in, I went into tha kitchen opened up tha cabinet and punched in some more numbers.

"What was that about?"

"Well, I have it set up to where after you get it you have three minutes to punch in tha second code or tha police are immediately notified."

"Don't have to worry about anybody breaking in here."

I couldn't believe how nice his house was.

"I'm really impressed wit what you've done wit tha place."

"Thank you, I tried to do tha damn thing."

"Oh, you did tha damn thing without question."

Tha whole downstairs was Gucci. While upstairs was a mixture of Prada, Ralph Lauren, Fendi and Louis Vuitton. He gave me a tour of his 5 bedroom, 2 ½ bedrooms, den, basement, 2 cars garage as well as his big backyard.

"Maze this is a big house for one person."

"Hopefully I won't have to be in here alone too much longer."

"What's that suppose to mean?"

"Just what I said. Brie I was thinking about what you said earlier."

"I said a lot earlier."

"When you said that we already know each other. So, if you're willing to be a couple so am I?"

"Well, it's about time."

"Excuse me."

"You heard me, I said about time. I thought you would never make it official."

"Bre you could have done that."

"I wanted to wait til you were ready."

"That's funny, so was I." We both fell asleep in each other arms.

When I woke up in tha morning I was still laying in Mazes arms.

"Why are you staring at me like that?"

"A guy could get use to this."

"So could a girl."

My phone started to ring. "What's up Sis?"

"Hey, can I speak to Bre?"

"How do you know she's wit me?"

"Boy her phone ain't on so where else she gon' be."

"Hold on."

"What's up Jade?"

"I need a favor."

"I'm listening."

"Can you pick up my clothes from DunRite's before six?"

"Why can't you pick them up?"

"Me and Iciss are going to see Swerve."

"That's right, his contact visit is today. A'ight I'll pick ya clothes up for you."

"You and my brother are spending a lot of quality time together. Let me find out you're caught up."

"Look who's talking Ms. I'm caught up wit Swerve."

Ha! Ha! Ha! We both laughed at that.

"Who would have ever thought."

"I know right."

"Hey, it is wht it is. Hold on ya brother wants you."

"What Boy?"

"Tell my Nigga I said what tha biz is."

"Will do and please don't hurt my best friend again!"

"You don't have to worry about that I'm not going nowhere this time."

"A'ight, I'll call you when I get back from my visit."

"What does she say?"

"Nuffin' just that if I hurt you again I have to deal wit her."

"Maze I don't want to be hurt again."

"Brie I promise you won't be and I never make a promise I can't keep. Besides I got money out tha ass now."

"I'm not wit you for your money and I never was. I got my own money anyway!"

"I'm sure you do. Bre can I ask you something wit out offending you or you getting upset."

I looked at tha seriousness in his face and said, "Yes."

"I know what you, Jade, and Turk do to get your money. I never had a problem wit that as long as yall were safe. But how many of them did you actually sleep wit?"

"One." I watched as a smile came across his face.

"Yup, just one and that's tha truth. My game is strong and tha only reason Wes got some was because I felt sorry for him after Bankz got killed."

At that moment I took her in my arms and made soft, sweet passionate love to her.

CHAPTER 14

Doin' Me

I'm tha only one wit out a man in my life. Jade has Swerve and Bre has Maze. I'm just freelancing. I pulled up at Thriftway; it was a lot of cars in tha parking lot. I had to wait for somebody to pull out before I finally got a spot. I grabbed a cart and went into tha store. I pulled out my list and started to shop. By tha time I got everything on my list tha lines had went down some.

"Excuse me, are you paying for that stuff wit cash?"

"Why?"

"Because if you are, I got some stamps for sale."

"That was music to my ears."

"How much you try'n to sale?"

"I'll pay for your stuff and you just give me half."

When tha lady finished ringing me up my stuff came to 340 dollars. I gave homegirl 175 and asked her was there any way I could get in contact wit her every month to buy stamps. We had exchanged cell numbers wit tha agreement to call each other next month. I paid some kids to help me carry my bags to my car. Shit, while I'm right here, let me check to see if they got a charger for my car. When I walked into tha store, there were only a few people in there.

"May I help you?" tha dude behind tha counter asked.

"Do you have a car charger for tha iPhones?"

"Hold on, Pete do we have any more car charges for tha iPhones?"

"We only got one more in tha back. Hold up Ma let me get it for you."

He came right back.

"It's $24.99."

"No problem."

I handed him a $50 bill. He gave me my change but held onto my hand.

"Excuse you," I said, snatching my hand away.

"Damn my bag; I was just so mesmerized by your beauty."

"That's different."

"Huh."

"That pickup line, that's different."

"Nah, sorry Ma that wasn't no pickup line it was tha truth."

"Well, I'm flattered."

"Why didn't you just get ya man to pick that up for you?" he asked, pointing to tha charger.

"You real funny, you know that. I would rather you just come at me straight forward instead of that bullshit game you try'n to spit."

"Nah Ma, actually I wasn't try'n to spit no game at you. I know niggaz be on ya heels all day every day but not me." He walked away to tend to another customer.

"Wow," I thought to myself; he just set me straight.

Fuck I should have just came at her like she said. But how could I after she pulled my card tha way she did. Oh well, I'll run into her again.

I pulled off slowly, thinking that he might run outside to ask for my number. When I turned on 4th & Madison, I seen a bunch of people standing around as if something had just happened. I got to tha corner and some guy waved to me. I didn't know him, but I waved back anyway. Why did I do that?

"Yo Sexy, pull over let a nigga holla at you for a sec."

I figured I would pull over just to see or should I say hear, what game he would come at me wit. I had heard everything from ya mom should have named you beauty because you're beautiful. Two is your name Angel because you look like you came from Heaven. When he walked to tha car, I rolled down my window so he could say whatever he was going to say. What he said surprised and caught me off guard.

"Hey Pretty, I didn't even think you was going to stop, let alone pull over. I don't got no lame ass game to spit at you. Besides, you probably done heard every line known to man." I couldn't stop myself from smiling.

"All I can say is what you already know you bad as shit. By the way, my name is Fresh and if possible, I would love to treat you to dinner whenever you're available."

"Now, normally I would decline, but since you kept it real and was so original, I'm going to give you my number."

"Nah Ma, you take my number and call me when you're ready for that dinner or lunch or even breakfast."

"A'ight," I said, taking out my iPhone.

Once I had his number stored, I put my phone away.

"Hey, does that store sell purple haze wraps?"

"Yeah."

I got out just so he could watch me as I walked to tha store. When I got back to my car, he told me to make sure I use his number.

"One thing about me Fresh, is I don't play games."

"Then we have something in common already. If you don't mind me asking, what's your name?"

"Turk."

"What you smoking on?"

"Sour D."

"Two things in common, that's all I blow."

I had to admit Fresh was a cutie. 6'-0, Brown eyes and long braids, oh yeah, did I mention he was dark like me? I was definitely calling him. I know he had a couple ones because of tha iced out "F" that hung from his chain.

"Turk, you make sure you get at a nigga."

"Oh, I will."

I turned the volume up and let Rick Ross's here I am come banging out. Shit, I hope my ice cream didn't melt. Fuck, speaking of melting, I forgot to put that damn ice back in tha freezer. My next-door neighbors' sons were outside, so I paid them to carry my groceries inside for me. I had a few messages on my answering machine. Tha first one was from my mom.

"Hey Turk, it's Mom just checking on you, call me."

Tha next one was from my grandma.

"Hey Baby, it's grandma thanks for tha package. When you and tha girls gone come visit? I hope soon, love ya."

That was all that was on there. Visiting Nana sounded like a winner; the last time we went to Miami, we had a ball. Jade and Bre are so caught up they probably don't want to go. It's about time for me to settle down. I had to laugh at that me settle down. Ha! Ha! Ha! Damn, it's only 3 o'clock. I might as well take a nap and get rested for tonight.

CHAPTER 15

Contact

"Iciss, Iciss."

"Huh."

"Get up and get ya self together."

"What time is it?"

"It's 3 o'clock."

"What time do we have to be there?"

"Swerve said no later then 5:30."

"Shit!"

"I know you better watch ya mouth."

"My bag."

"I don't know what to wear."

"Me either, I think I'm gon' just throw on my black Yves Saint Laurent (YSL) jeans wit my silver YSL shirt and silver Givenchy sandals."

An hour later, we were both dressed. Iciss decided to wear her white Ideen sundress wit her black Cole Haan sandals. We were looking good as usual. I had my stylist press my hair so I could wear it down. Only because Swerve says, he loves when I wear it like that. And, of course, Iciss had to wear hers tha same way. Her hair was longer than mine. By tha time I smoked my blunt, it was 4:30.

"Jade, come on, so we won't be late."

"Here I come."

"Are we taking tha Benz or tha Denali?"

"Tha Denali."

When I pulled into tha visitors' parking lot, a couple of other people were pulling up also. We got tha food and headed to tha front entrance. We had to check in and then let them check our food. I guess they want to make sure you don't try to smuggle anything illegal in. After about 40 minutes, they called us so we could go in. Tha guard told somebody on tha walkie-talkie to hold movement on tha first floor of tha gym. We walked down tha hall through two sliders until we got to tha gym.

"Jade, can we grab our food now?"

"Yeah, everybody else is."

We found a table and set up everything. 15 minutes later, they start coming in.

"I don't even know what he look like."

"EEEL, I hope none of them ain't him," she said, pointing to tha three dudes that just came in. "Hell no! There he go."

Iciss jumped up and ran over to him.

"Hey Brother," she said, hugging him.

When they got to tha table, I stood up and gave him a hug. Damn, it's so good to be in his arms.

When we sat down, Iciss said, "Yall so fake."

"What you talkin' bout now?" I asked.

"You know you want to kiss him."

"Lil Sis, we just friends, Jade not my wifey."

"What, you mean to tell me that you're not a couple after all this time."

"Damn Jade, Iciss look like ya daughter, not ya sister."

"I know; I hear that all tha time."

"Now you know she don't look as good as me."

"Iciss please," I said.

"Are you going to eat ya food?"

"You didn't put no voodoo on it, did you?"

"Boy pleeease, like I need to do that."

"What exactly is that suppose to mean?"

"If you don't know then neither do I."

"I think what she is say'n is she already has you."

"Mind ya business Iciss."

"Is that what you say'n Jade?"

"How could I be say'n that and we just friends?"

"Umm, Umm, Umm, what soul food joint did you buy this from 'cause it's jumpin'?"

"Don't disrespect me; I cooked this myself."

"Unh, Unh," Iciss said clear'n her throat.

"My fault, wit tha help of my baby sis."

"Now I'm really impressed, beautiful and you can burn in tha kitchen."

"She's a keeper, wouldn't you say Big Brother?"

"Fo' sho, Fo' sho."

We talked and I realized that I was actually falling in love wit Swerve. I could tell by tha look in his eyes he was feeling tha same way about me. Since we were both headstrong, neither of us would admit it to one another.

"Everybody take a minute to say bye to your love ones," tha guard announced.

Iciss gave Swerve a hug.

"I'll be to see you once a month."

"That's what's up Little Sis."

I stood up and gave him a hug. "If yall don't kiss."

"Mind your bus..."

Before I could finish, he had his tongue in my mouth. Before I knew it, my arms were wrapped around his neck.

"Damn," I said as he grabbed my ass.

It's been so long since I've been touched by a man. I've been so caught up; I've been acting like Swerve is my man instead of my friend.

"OK, that's enough Mr. Jones," tha guard yelled, "all inmates stay seated visitors over here."

"Make sure you call me tonight."

"I wasn't; I was just going to reflect off this visit."

"Boy, you better call me; I'm not play'n!"

"So, are you guys together or still friends?"

We both looked at each other and simultaneously said, "Together."

"Bout time; it's only been a year."

"Mr. Jones, if you want another visit, I suggest you have a seat."

"She just mad because I won't give her the time a day, but I'll call you in an hour."

"Ok."

"That visit seemed like it was over fast."

"I know, I was thinking tha same thing."

When we were leaving tha gym tha guard had tha nerve to roll her eyes.

"It's not my fault."

"Excuse me," she said. I just smiled, blew Swerve a kiss and kept it moving.

As soon as I got into my truck, I lit my blunt up.

"Gosh, you couldn't wait to get in here and light that up."

"You want some?" I asked, testing her.

"EEEEL, no, I don't smoke that stuff!"

"You better not; if you would have said yeah, I was going to beat you down."

Tha whole ride home, all I could think about was my new man Swerve."

"Hey Jade, now when somebody tries to holla at you and you say you have a man, you won't be lying."

"Iciss, shut up smarty-pants."

"I get it from tha best of them."

"True that."

CHAPTER 16

Swerve

"This tha only thing I don't like about these visits."

"Who you telling? Was that wifey and her daughter?"

"Yeah, that was my shorty, but that was her little sister."

"She looks like she could be her daughter."

"I know I told 'em tha same shit."

"Yo, did you peep tha way Ms. Smith was ice grillin' you and ya shorty?"

"Tank, I didn't even pay her no mind. I was focused on my visit."

"I know that's right. You better than me 'cause I would've been knocked her off. Or at least got some of that head of hers."

"Fuck her; like I told her, she ain't on my level! I wouldn't even look her way on tha streets, so I'm not gon' do it just cause I'm in here. She in here around a bunch of thirsty niggaz who be coming at her. Huh, so she thinks she tha shit when she not."

When I got back to the pod, I decided to call Jade tomorrow. My whole uniform smelled like Jade. Damn, after a whole year, we finally made it official. When I call her tomorrow, I'll let her know that I'm not going to be on no bullshit. I was laying in my bunk thinking about Jade when somebody tapped on my door.

"Damn Nigga that visit got you fucked up."

I didn't even bother to look up. I already knew Pooh wanted to crack jokes, but I didn't feel like it today.

"They said you had tha baddest chick in tha visit."

"That shouldn't surprise you, should it?"

"Nah, ya girl Ms. Smith came up here hatin' like a mafucka. I was standing by tha microwave while she was talking to Ms. Wynn."

"Man Fuck Ms. Smith that bitch getting on my damn nerves."

"Damn, I hope Carpenter Grant this mod."

"Insha Allāh (if it pleases Allāh)

"He will. I figure He might wait another six months until I hit my three-year mark."

"Damn, that shit flew by."

"Shit, not for me it didn't. I shouldn't be here anyway. That shit they found wasn't mine. I don't even know how a jury found me guilty of that shit."

"I know that's why your mod is going to get granted."

"Insha Allāh."

"I'll get wit you tomorrow it's almost count time."

"Asalamu Alalkum."

"Walaikum Salam Rahman to Allāh."

When my celly came in, I could tell that he was upset about something. I never got into his business; I always waited for him to ask me, as he often did.

"Did you have a good visit Swerve?"

"Good, Heem it was tha best visit I had in 30 months."

"Damn that good?"

"Yeah," I said as I went to tha sink to make Wudo for Salat.

Heem followed suit. when he was done; we offered Isha. I pulled out my photo album so I could see my baby. How did I let myself fall in love wit a woman I've never touched physically? I even respected tha fact that she told me what she did to get her money besides working at tha bank. I decided to write her a letter to let her know exactly how I feel about her and our situation.

"You must of had one hell of a visit."

"Why do you say that?"

"Because you flying her a kite."

"How do you know I'm writing her?"

"Nigga you've been my celly for tha last year and I only seen you write one letter. You had a visit and then you were lookin' in ya photo album now you at tha desk. I'm not a rocket scientist, but it's not hard to figure out."

Ha! Ha! Ha! "You a funny young boy Heem."

"Man, my girl be trippin' on some bullshit Cuz. She thinks I'm going to come home and be on my dumb shit. Swerve this two years has matured me. I even cut all my other broads off for her. She's been holding me down, so I'm going to commit myself to her and only her."

"That's what's up if you're serious."

I finished up my letter and put it in tha door so that tha CO could grab it when he came around to do count.

When I woke up tha next morning, there was only one thing on my mind. J-A-D-E! I got myself together and headed out for work. They had me working in supply which was OK. All we did was hand out supplies to tha pods and bookings. While we were on tha first floor, CO Sutton stopped me so that I could sign for my legal mail. I had finally got a response for my mod that my lawyer had put in. I decided to wait to get back to my cell before I read it. For tha remainder of tha day, I just kept hoping that Carpenter granted me tha last two years level IV. When I got back to my pod, I made the Zhur Prayer that I missed while I was at work. I sat on my bunk to read my legal mail.

"WHEEEEEW!" I yelled at tha top of my lungs, causing tha CO to come to my door.

"Is everything a'ight Swerve?"

"Yeah, everything is great."

"This is tha best news yet; I can't wait to call Jade to tell her tha good news."

Later that night, when I called Jade, she was mad that I didn't call her last night.

"So why didn't you call me last night like I told you."

"I just came back, looked at my photo album and wrote you a nice five-page letter."

"Five pages wow, you must of had a lot to say."

"I just needed to express myself. I was going to wait until our visit Saturday, but I figured I would give you a heads-up."

"Well, I won't respond, but we can talk about it at tha visit."

"My mod came back today."

"Well, did he agree to what you wanted?"

"No."

"It's OK; you only got 2 ½ left and I'm not going nowhere, I promise."

"Hold on, he denied what I wanted, but he didn't make my three mandatory and suspended tha other two for year level 3 probation."

"So that means you only have 6 months left then."

"No, I have 5 months left. I max out October 15th, so start stocking up on your lingerie."

"I already have enough of that stuff still with tags on it."

"Let me find out..."

"Find out what?"

"That you stocked up on sexy lingerie."

"Just cause I haven't had a man in tha last 13 months doesn't mean I never had one."

I called another two times before count. I really wanted to tell her how I felt, but I decided to let her read tha letter.

"2:30 visits!" tha CO yelled out.

Me, Tank and Heem all walked to tha door. When we got by secondary, there were already people waiting for their visit. The CO read off tha names of tha people who would be down and up.

"My peeps Slice told me he maxes out in 4 days Insha Allāh."

"A'ight, let's go no talkin' in tha hallway, gentlemen."

Ms. Cooper already had tha door open when we got there. "All visits up," I heard them say over the walkie-talkie.

"Well looks like a lot of yall not going to have a visit." I think they get a kick outta people getting a ghost for their visit. She let tha other visits out then told us to go in. I went to tha first booth as I always did. When Jade walked in she look beautiful as always.

"Damn look at them, they act like they never seen a female before." I turned around to see everybody lookin' in.

"It's not that they haven't seen a female just not one that looks this good."

"Now you got me blushin'."

"So, what they talk'n bout?"

"Who"

"Jus a jail phrase."

"Oh, Ok. Well, I got ya mail and it's funny because I feel tha same way. At first, I tried to brush it off. But I had to be honest wit myself first."

"Listen, Jade I know you real because for tha past 13 months, you've been here every week when you did not have to be. Then when you thought they denied my mod, you were willing to stay for tha remainder of my sentence. That says it means a lot to me."

"Well, I know that you had bitches busting ya windows out to come see you."

"Yeah, they were, but once you came and let me know that you would be here every week, I kicked them to tha curb. I always knew you were something special, that's why when we were kickin' it for those few months before I got locked up, I never tried to have sex wit you. Even though I knew how you and ya girls got down I seen past all that. I just neva got tha chance to really get to know you. Now that I have my assumptions were right."

"What were ya assumptions?"

"That you were a thurl bread and that you just needed someone to love you."

"So, I guess you're that somebody, huh?"

"I'm hoping I can be that special guy. Jade, I have to be honest I've had my heart broken and I said I would never fall in love again. But as we know, we can't control our feelings. So, I am willing to take another chance at love with you."

"Since we're being honest, me and my girls have made a pact that we would never fall in love. After I started to come see you we decided to end tha pact. That's why they say never say never. I'm not one of those insecure women and I don't need to keep tabs on no man. You've never did anything or said anything for me to have a reason not to trust you. But let me make this real clear to you if you ever cheat and I find out it's over, no second chances. I look at it like this; there ain't nuffin' that you can't get from me that they do. If I'm not doing something you want, just let me know, simple as that. My shit is that good that you shouldn't have to go nowhere!"

"I feel tha same way you do."

We had covered a lot of ground, so much that we didn't realize that tha CO was flicking tha lights.

"Well, I love you and I'll call you tonight."

"A'ight I love you too."

"Damn nigga you act like you didn't want the visit to be over."

"Shit I didn't, can you blame me."

"Ay Swerve her pictures don't do her no justice. She's way more beautiful in person. I seen wifey gettin in ya shit."

"Yeah she mad because she asked me what I was gon' do when I get home."

"Let me guess you told her hustle."

"Sure did."

"Swerve I don't have no drug charges. I got two years for shooting a nigga. That's my problem guns. As long as I stay away from the .45's, .38's, and 9's I'll be straight. It's all about M-O-N-E-Y!" he said spelling out money.

"I didn't tell you but I'll be out 30 days after you."

"Oh, shit ya mod got granted."

"Yeah but instead of level IV he gave me 1 year level 3."

"You came off better wit that then level IV."

"I know, I'm not complaining."

"I know you not."

"So, what do you plan on doing out there?"

"It ain't no secret Imma get at a dollar."

"Maybe we can link up? By tha time you come home I should be at least coppin' a half chicken."

"That's what's up."

I never let him know that I control 90% of Wilmington. He will find out once I got out. If he was really going to be up a half brick in 30 days, then I know he has potential. For tha past year, I've picked his brain about every and anything. One of tha things I found out is that he can be trusted. He's proven that time and time again.

CHAPTER 17

Anotha Hit

It's been a few months since Bre turned me on to Cream. He was definitely a sucka for a pretty face. He had money; I know that because he is a showoff. He took me to his stash house and even had me help him count money. Today he supposed to take me shoppin'.

"I need to stop and put this money up, OK."

"Yeah."

He pulled up in front of his stash house.

"Come in for a minute."

I really didn't feel like it, but he was treating, so who am I to complain?

While he was at tha table counting tha door came crashing open. Cream went to reach for his piece.

"SPT, SPT"

"Don't even think about it or tha next two won't miss. Tie his ass up and tha bitch too." As soon as he grabbed me, I screamed.

(Smack) "OOOW, What tha Fuck!" I yelled.

"What do you want? She doesn't have anything to do wit this."

"She does now and I think you already know wht it is we came for."

"This is all I have."

(Ha! Ha! Ha!) "You must think we're stupid, don't you? Nigga We been watching you for a few months now. So, we already know this is only chump change. So, either you tell us where tha rest of th money is or we'll kill you both and find tha money ourselves. Tha choice is yours; we are going to give you a few minutes to think about it. Times up so much for a few minutes."

Damn, I neva thought that anybody would have tha balls to try this. I was prepared just in case though.

"Downstairs behind tha bookcase is a safe. Tha combination is 34–31–16."

"I'll check; you stay here wit them; if they try anything, kill 'em." I went down in tha basement and found tha bookcase. When I punched in tha numbers tha safe came open. All I could do was smile. I took tha money and put it in tha bag I had wit me. When I got upstairs, my partner asked if I got it.

"Yeah, I got it."

"Let's get outta here then."

"Ok."

"WHEEW they fell for it."

"Before we go, Cream is going to tell us where tha real doe is." Tha look on his face said it all.

"Now, don't get me wrong, that was cute and tha average person would have went for it. But since I'm not tha average person, I'm not going for tha decoy. In fact, I'll let you keep tha money that was in there so you can get back."

I cocked my pistol, "Now, where did you say tha money was again?"

"What you got is all I have."

"Right, shoot him."

"Wait, Wait, a'ight upstairs in tha back room. Move tha bed and tha floor will slide. Then punch in 44–4–44."

I told my partner to handle it this time.

"Let me know if it's another decoy. If it is you're dead along wit your bitch."

10 minutes later, my partner was coming down wit two duffel bags.

"Let's get out of here!"

"Thanks Cream, we'll be back when you get ya money back up."

We made out wit close to a half mill and didn't even have to kill nobody.

CHAPTER 18

Lovers

I was either staying wit Maze or he was staying wit me. I couldn't front; I was so in love. It was like we picked up where we left off at. Maze wanted me to move in wit him, but I didn't think we should yet. I had cut all ties wit my friends that I was using for money. My cell started ringing.

"Hello Aunty."

"What's up Chas?"

"Nuffin' I just called to check on you. I have not spoken to you in a few weeks."

"I know I've been busy."

"Wit who Uncle Maze?"

"Girl, you too grown."

"I am 16 now. Can we hang out this weekend?"

"Sure, we can do some shoppin'."

We talked for a while longer before hanging up.

"Hey Sexy."

"Boy you startled me."

"Why, what was you doing that you shouldn't have."

"Boy please, I was on the phone with Chas."

"How's she doing?"

"Okay, she wants to hang out this weekend."

"I was thinking about going to Union Tavern tonight to have a few drinks; you wanna go?"

"Nah, why don't you call Turk or Jade to go wit you."

"I already did."

"Oh, so I was the last resort, huh?"

"No Baby, I just knew you were gonna say no."

"Well, I'll be here when you get back."

I pulled up and it was a lot of people for it to be a Wednesday night. I stood in line for about 5 minutes before I got in. I wonder why it's so packed in here tonight? I found a spot at tha bar and ordered a drink. "Don't I know you from somewhere?" I turned to see who was talking.

"No, I'm sorry you must have me confused wit somebody else."

"I'm pretty sure it's you. Isn't ya name Sheena?" he said wit his words slurred from being drunk.

"No, that's not my name." He pulled tha bar stool closer to sit next to me.

"Bartender, can I get another one?" I said, pointing to my drink.

"So, do you have a man?"

"Yes I do."

"He let you come out by yourself?"

"I'm grown." He kept try'n to holla at me as if he didn't know I had a man.

"You stuck up Bitch," he said, half spitting on me.

"Listen, will you please leave me alone," I said, standing up. He grabbed my arm, causing me to fall back on my stool. I threw my drink in his face.

"Don't you ever fuckin' touch me motha fucka!"

"Bitch I should fuck you up!"

He had his fist balled up like he wanted to hit me. I pulled my phone out and called Maze.

"What up Baby?"

"This faggot ass nigga just put his hands on me."

"Who?"

"Bitch you can call who you want. I ain't going no fuckin where."

"I'm on my way." Before I could say anything else, tha phone hung up.

"Who ever you called better come strapped!"

"You must don't know who I am. Imma fuck who ever you called up just because."

10 minutes later, I saw Maze walk through tha door. I knew it was gon' to be some shit by tha look on his face.

"Where he at?"

"I pointed to the picture booth."

"I know you not talk'n bout bitch ass Smiley."

"If that's the one in the middle, then yeah."

"Does he know you called me?" "No, he said he was going to fuck up who ever I called."

"He got a couple ones, but he ain't even built like that."

"A'ight, don't let him know you called me."

Maze made a phone call, said a few yeah's, huh's and nah's, then hung up. The last time he made a phone call, Wes and Joker ended up dead. Smiley walked over to us.

"Maze, what's the deal My Nigga?"

I didn't answer I just looked at him. I didn't care too much for him anyway.

"So, where ya peeps at?"

He had two of his boys wit him, but I wasn't tha least bit concerned about that.

Then I said, "This tha nigga you talkin' bout Babe? Smiley, I don't appreciate you disrespecting my girl."

"Who tha fuck you talkin' to nigga!"

"Smiley, If you like ya life, I suggest you do two things. Apologize to her and pipe tha fuck down Nigga!"

"Fuck you and that."

Before he could finish his sentence, Maze punched him in his face, knocking him down. I grabbed a bottle off tha bar and smashed his boy in tha face. Tha other dude didn't want no parts of it. By tha time either of them had gotton their selves together, security was already there.

Imma kill you motha fucka, Imma kill you!"

"Be careful what you say."

The bouncer that was closer to us let us know we had to leave. Smiley and his boys couldn't get outside fast enough. Boom, Boom, Boom, Bong, Bong, Bong, Tat, Tat, Tat and screens were all you heard.

"That's for putting ya hands on my aunt Nigga."

I could tell that one of them was still alive. But by tha time tha ambulance gets here, he'll probably be dead.

"Come on Baby let's go."

"I'm parked over there, same place as me."

I kind of felt like it was my fault that they got killed. But when I looked at my arm, I quickly dismissed that. Tha next day, my arm was sore and bruised. I walked to tha corner store to get a newspaper. Tha front page read, "Three men shot to death outside local bar." I didn't want to wait to get home to read tha paper, I read it as I walked home. No suspects is all I needed to see. I found myself smiling when I read the part that said, "the killings were about these men putting their hands on someone's aunt." Maze was pulling up when I got to tha house.

"Hey you up early."

"I'm always up early."

"Anything interesting in tha newspaper?"

I turned tha paper toward him so he could see tha headline. "Interesting, what they talking bout?"

"Nothing, no clues, suspects or anything else. They did say it was over a domestic dispute wit an aunt."

"I knew they would; that's why I told them to be sure they say that."

He grabbed me in his arms and said, "Baby, I'm sorry you had to witness that."

"Nothing I ain't seen before." He gave me a puzzled look but let it go.

"I just won't tolerate anybody and I mean anybody disrespecting you!"

Then he kissed me on my forehead and asked if I wanted to get some breakfast. We ended up going to Hometown Buffet.

"Maze, just in case you don't know or you just need to hear it, I love you!"

"And I you Abreale."

Just tha sound of him saying my whole name had my panties moist.

"Uh Oh."

"What?"

"You got that look in your eyes."

"Wow, is it that noticeable?"

"You act like I don't know when my girl is in tha mood for a little sex."

"So, let's get outta here so you can take care of mama."

We got up and then headed to my truck.

"Hey lets, never mind."

"What was you going to say?"

"Don't worry about it."

"Babe, you know I hate that."

"Nothing, I was just going to say let's do it right here."

"In my truck?"

"Yeah, nobody will see us wit tha dark tent."

"You feel a little wild too, huh?"

Long story short, we got it in right there in my truck in tha middle of the Hometown parking lot. For some reason, it was damn near tha best sex we had. I think it was tha fear of being caught. When we were finished, this old couple was staring inside tha truck. Maze started tha truck, scaring tha shit out of them. On tha way home, he let me know that he never wanted to be wit out me in his life again. I felt tha same way. If a bitch thought she was going to get my man, she had another thing coming. I let them have him for 18 months. Now he's mine again and I'm not letting go this time.

"Do you have plans for later?" I asked.

"It depends."

"Depends on what?"

"On if you have plans for us."

"I was thinking about a romantic dinner for two at my house."

"Well, in that case, I have plans."

"See you at 9 o'clock," I said, getting now.

"Hey."

"Yes."

"You forgot something," he said wit his lips poked out. I gladly put my lips against his.

"Maze, let me know if I'm too clingy."

"I will and you do tha same, love ya."

"Love you too."

Later that night, while I was preparing dinner, Jade had stopped by.

"Hey Girl, you got it smelling good up in here."

"Yeah, me and Maze are having a romantic dinner tonight."

"Lucky you."

"I know. How much longer does Swerv have before he comes home, two years?"

"Hell no! Didn't I tell you?"

"Tell me what?"

"His mod got granted; he has 90 days left."

"Bitch you lying!"

"No, I'm not."

"I know you can't wait so he can knock tha cobwebs off tha Twat."

"Ain't no damn cobwebs on this Twat."

"Bitch please, you ain't had no dick in 18 months."

"Damn, I didn't realize it's been that long. I'm happy to see you and my brother are so happy together."

"So am I."

"Well, let me go so that yall can enjoy your dinner."

"Maze ain't even here yet." No soon as I said that, tha front door came open.

"WHEEW, you got it smelling tasty up in here, Babe. What up sis?"

"Little bit of me and a whole lot of you."

"Word in tha streets is Swerve gave his time back and he will be home any day now."

"90, to be exact."

"I know you can't wait. Tha bitches is going to be mad when they see tha second baddest chick in tha city on his hip."

"Excuse you."

"Yeah, you know I got tha first."

"I heard that; let them be mad. I was tha one holding him down for tha past 18 months. If he wanted them, he would have neva cut them off."

"I know that's right," I said, high-fiving her.

"Well, yall enjoy dinner."

"Sis, you going out tonight?"

"I was thinking about it."

"I'm going to Pinnacle to see Jeezy and Jim Jones."

"Oh, you are?"

"Yes we are."

"Count me in; what time you leaving?"

"After I eat and get a shot, Imma get dressed."

"Boy," I said, punching him in tha arm.

"Just hit my phone when you ready."

After Jade left, I prepared our plates.

"Bre, you cooked my favorite."

I knew he would enjoy tha steak, baked potatoes, shrimp and steamed broccoli wit cheese. Maze didn't leave a trace of food on his plate.

"Babe, that was blazing; you put ya foot in it."

"Thank you," I said, blushing. I looked at my watch to see what time it was.

"Do I have enough time to get myself something?"

"It's not even 10 o'clock yet; you have plenty of time, especially since you know what spots to hit," I said, winking at him.

We hit tha bed and wasted no time at all. 30 minutes and 4 orgasms later, we were both in tha shower.

"Bre, I hope you didn't mind tha quicky."

"Not at all; I'll take a four orgasm quicky any day of tha week."

Once we were out tha shower, I looked at my closet to find me tha perfect outfit for tonight. "Bre, why don't you wear that Dior Homme dress you bought?"

He only wanted me to wear that because it showed off my body.

"You must have been reading my mind; I was putting that on anyway."

He went wit his black Gucci capris and shirt wit his black low-top Gucci sneaks and no socks.

"Damn, we look good together."

I stood next to him and looked at us in my full-length mirror. He was right and even though him and Jade were not blood sister and brother you wouldn't be able to tell they look just alike. When we got tha stairs I could hear Jade pulling up.

"She's right on time; come on Bre let's go." It was humid outside.

"What's up Maze and Bre?"

"Hey Turk."

"What tha biz is Turk?"

"Just try'n to have a good time tonight."

"I feel you on that Girl. Turk, what's tha deal wit that nigga from Philly?"

"Ever since that situation, I dealt ain't wit him. I don't got time to be caught up in somebody else bullshit."

"Give me tha, okay and he'll be a mural."

"No, it's cool. I don't wish him dead."

Turk was always a forgiving one out of the bunch.

"Jade, you driving?"

"I didn't want to."

"I'll drive Baby."

Maze handed me his keys. When I hit tha highway it was on, I pushed 100 tha whole way up.

"You drive just like him," Jade said.

"I must be rubbing off on her."

"Damn, look at that line."

"I know, it's long as shit we ain't waiting in no line, you know Cousin B my peoples."

Maze pulled out his phone; within seconds, he was talking.

"Yeah, I'm parking me and three, OK."

"We good he'll be at the door."

Sure enough, he was at tha door waiting on us.

"Damn, Maze you didn't say you had three bad females wit you."

"Two," he said, pulling me close to him."

"I definitely respect that, Baby Boy. Which one of you is available?" he asked.

She is," Jade said, pointing to Turk.

"I do have a mouth," Turk said, talking to Jade.

"Are we going to stay out here all night or go get a party on?" I asked.

"Oh, my fault, come on."

"Kev, give me four V.I.P. bands."

"I'll see yall a little later. What did you say ya name was?"

"I didn't!"

"No need to be feisty."

"I wasn't and it's Turk."

"Well, Ms. Turk, would you like to accompany me tonight?"

"Are you sure your fan club wouldn't mind?" I asked, pointing to tha females that were staring at us.

"Nah, I don't have a girl and tha groupie thing is a turn-off."

"I hear you; it's probably all game, though."

"Ma, I don't play games unless it's Madden NBA Live or Fight Night."

"Wow, a man who likes video games."

"You go meet and greet. I'll be in V.I.P. you got that Ma?"

"Bitch, you always playing hard to get."

"You have to, if you don't they would think it's easy as 1-2-3."

My phone started to ring.

"Hello."

"Hey Sexy, long time no hear."

"You're tha one who never returned my call."

"It's loud; where you at tha club?"

"Yeah."

"Go to tha ladies' room and call me back."

"A'ight, I'll be right back yall."

"Must be somebody important for you to go call back."

"OOOH, Bitch let me find out."

"Ain't nuffin' to find out; now excuse me."

"Hello."

"Now I can hear you."

"So why didn't you return my call?"

"I had no ideal you called."

"Whatever Fresh."

"For real, if you did, it never came through."

"Maybe that's because tha person that was on it said he would give you tha message. But you knew that since you had him answer my call."

"I told you, Turk I don't play games. I thought that because I told you that I was 19, you didn't want to Fuck wit me."

"Damn, you said that like I'm some old lady."

"I didn't mean it like that."

"Oh, 'cause I was about to say I'm only five years older then you."

"Well, now that we got that straight, call me as soon as you leave tha club."

"You might be sleep."

"I doubt it; I'll be on tha block or at tha Thunder Guards. Just make sure you hit my phone."

"Damn Bitch that must of been an important phone call as long as you was in there."

"That was my young boy."

"The one from 5th you was telling us about?"

"Yup."

"What is his name Turk? I might be able to give you some insight on him."

"Fresh."

"That's my young boy; he's on my team. I can't say nuffin' bad about him. He get at a dollar. You might be a little too high maintenance for him, though."

"Who said I was hollering at him for his doe."

"That's a first," Jade said wit a big smile on her face.

"I know there's a first time for everything."

Jeezy and Jim Jones turned it out; after they performed, we decided to roll out. On tha way home, I called Fresh; he said he was at tha Guards and wanted me to come thru.

CHAPTER 19

My Young Boy

After Jade dropped me off to my house, I was thinking about just going to bed. That thought was quickly erased when my phone rang.

"Hello."

"What you do go home?"

"Yeah."

Oh a'ight, I guess I'll get wit you some other time then."

"I had to get my car; I was riding wit my girls."

"I know it's late, so if you want to go in that's cool."

"I'm bout to go to Wawa. I'm starving like a hostage."

"Well, why don't we go to Denny's."

"I don't eat pork and no, I'm not Muslim."

"I don't eat pork either."

"We can go to tha Waffle House. Where do you want me to meet you at?"

"You can meet me at tha park."

"Tha park on 6th and Madison?"

"Yeah, is that outta ya way?"

"Nope, I'll be there in 15 minutes."

When I pulled up, it was packed for it to be 3:30 in tha morning. I parked on tha corner and then called Fresh's phone.

"Hey Ma, I'm walking to ya car now."

Some dude came to my car, but before he could say anything, Fresh let him know to fall back. "My bag Fresh, I didn't know she was ya peoples."

I could tell Fresh was well respected around here.

"Hold up, Turk let me tell my young boy I'm bout to be out; I'll be right back."

"Hurry up, I'm hungry as shit." He was back within seconds.

"You driving or am I?"

"Since I'm already in tha car, I'll drive."

"Is it cool for me to smoke in ya car?"

"Smoke what?"

"Weed, what else you think I'm talkin' bout."

"You could've been talkin' about those nasty ass cigarettes."

"Nah, I don't even like tha smell of those things."

"Me either but ain't it funny how we will blow some weed, though."

"My aunt says tha same thing when I tell her she can't smoke in my car."

"I'm glad it's not crowded tonight."

"Oh, so you come here often?"

I studied his face to see if he was going to lie to me.

"Yeah, I come here about three times a week."

When we walked in tha waitress was all smiles until she saw me.

"Table for two tonight, huh?"

"Yes please." She walked us to a secluded table in tha back.

"Can I bring you something to drink while you look over tha menu?"

"My usual please."

"I'll have spring water in tha bottle please."

"I'll be right back."

"She doesn't seem too happy that I'm wit you tonight."

"She's been try'n to holla at me for tha past few months."

"Why didn't you get at her she's not bad looking."

"I know; I just wasn't interested, that's all."

She brought our drinks back, then our orders. We had good conversation like we did when we had dinner. By tha time we finished eating, it was a little after five.

"Turk thank you."

"For what Fresh?"

"Having breakfast wit me."

"I should be thanking you."

"Why is that?"

"For tha good conversation."

I can't front, I thought Fresh was just some young boy who wanted to just hit. Now, I'm realizing how wrong I was. I guess that's why they say never judge a book by its cover. I dropped Fresh off wit tha promise to call him later. When I got in tha house as soon as I hit my bed, I was out.

CHAPTER 20

Catching Up

I had 60 days before my man came home. And I couldn't wait. It's hard to believe that it's been almost two years since I started going to see him. Even if his mod didn't get granted, I would still wait for him. I never thought I would say this and mean it, but I'm head over heels in love wit him. There is a fear that he might come home and break my heart. When I said something to him about it, he assured me that he wasn't and that he would never intentionally hurt me. After my visit, me and my girls decided to have some us time. We went to TGI Fridays to get our drink on and catch up on what has been going on wit one another.

"So, what's the deal wit you and Swerve Jade?"

"Well, as yall know, he'll be home in less than 60 days."

"We barely see you now, so I know we won't see you then."

"Yes you will. I talked to Killer and Tiz because I was thinking about throwing him a welcome home party at tha Chase Center."

"That sounds like a good ideal," Turk said, "enough about me; I see you and my brother are happy."

"What makes you say that?"

"Hmm, let's see, maybe it's all the time yall spent together."

"Forget you Turk."

"Don't be mad; it's a good thing."

"I'm not mad; truth be told, I couldn't be happier."

"It shows all over your face. So enough about us was up wit you and Fresh?"

"Nuffin' we just friends."

"Unh Huh yeah right."

"I know Maze told me how you and Fresh have been spending all this time together."

"What ever!"

"You don't have to be afraid to tell us that you're feeling that young boy."

"I know, I don't he's just my friend. But trust me, if something does come of it, you two will be the first to know."

I don't know why I didn't just tell them that I'm really feeling Fresh.

"So, how much money you hit him for so far."

"Truthfully, a couple pair of Chanel shoes wit matching handbags." Jade put her hand on my forehead.

"Have you really lost your mind?"

"She's lying to us Jade."

"About what?" I asked, already knowing tha answer.

"Bitch you is feeling Fresh. Ain't no way you gon' not wear his pockets out." Tha sound of my phone saved me.

"Hello."

"Oh, hey you."

Jade and Bre were staring dead in my face.

"Sure, we can go see Obsessed later."

"Hold on for a second," I said, clicking over.

"Hello."

He let me know that he's gotton a new number and would call me later.

"Had to be Fresh tha way you were smiling all hard."

"Shut up Bre!"

"Turk, we're all sisters ain't too much we don't know about each other."

"Or when one of us is lying," Jade added.

"Are you say'n I'm lying?"

"Yes we are."

"Damn, you bitches get on my nerves," I said wit a big smile on my face.

"OOOOOH, I knew it," Bre said wit a smile of her own.

"You felt like you couldn't tell us?" Jade said wit hurt in her voice.

"I didn't want yall to clown me."

"Clown, you Turk, we better than that, besides you can't help who you like. I knew you liked him anyway. You have been spending too much time wit him."

"Is it that obvious?"

"Duh yes it is. So have you given him tha panties yet?"

"No! It's not that sweet and I'm not that easy!"

We talked for another two hours then we paid tha tab.

"We have to stay in touch."

"We will; let's make a pact to call each other at least once a week." We all joined pinkies and twisted them. We all started laughing.

"What yall laugh'n at?" Turk asked.

"The last time we made a pact, it was never to catch feelings or fall in love."

"I know and look at us now; me and Jade are in love and Turk got feelings. Shit we all caught up. Who would have thought?"

"Not me that's for sure."

"Me either."

We got in our cars and went to separate ways.

When I got home, I checked my caller ID to see if anyone had called. Swerve called 3 times. Why didn't he call my cell phone? I pulled it out of my bag. Shit, he did call. I forgot to turn it back off vibrate when I left tha doctor's office. Just as I was about to put it down, it rang.

"I'm locked up they won't let me out they won't let me out. I'm locked up." I picked up and let the computer talk and then I pushed five.

"Hey you."

"Hey Baby, I'm sorry I didn't get ya calls earlier. But I forgot to take it off vibrate when I left tha doctors."

"Oh, you had me a little worried when you didn't answer either phones."

"I had lunch wit Turk and Bre; we were catching up."

"How are they doing?"

"They a'ight all caught up, though."

"Is that a good thing or a bad thing?"

"It's a good thing."

"Then what's the problem?"

"Ain't no problem, it's just that."

"Just that what, Babe?"

"We made a pact that we would never fall in love wit any man."

"So much for that, huh?"

"That pact ended when Bre fell in love wit Maze again and I fell in love wit you!"

"Wow I feel really special knowing that."

When tha phone said one minute remaining, he said he was calling right back. He called back a few times. We talked all tha way until it was time for him to lock in for 3 o'clock count. He let me know he loved me and would call after dinner.

I pulled up to my house to find Maze already there.

"Honey, I'm home," I said, walking in tha house.

"I'm in tha bedroom."

I dropped my purse on tha table and headed upstairs.

"I'm surprised you're in tha house."

"I was going to take a nap. I figured if I came here, then I could turn my phones off."

"Your home early. I took a half a day so that me, Turk and Jade could have lunch and catch up wit each other."

"I'm pretty sure yall had a lot to catch up on."

"Not really, just a bunch of girls' stuff."

"You might as well take a nap wit me."

"I was doing that anyway."

Before I made it home, Fresh called to ask if I could swing by tha park. On my way to tha park, I decided that tomorrow I was going to buy me a truck. It was time for a new whip, not that there was anything wrong wit my 645.

As soon as I pulled up to tha park, Fresh walked up to my car.

"Pull up tha block because…"

Boom, Boom, Boom! Pop, Pop, Pop, Pop! Before he could finish, shots rang out. All I could do was scream when one of tha shots hit my car. Fresh came around to tha passenger side and got in.

"Pull off." He didn't have to tell me I was already doing that.

"Who was that and were they shootings at you?"

"Nah, that was these two young boys beefing over a block."

When I got a few blocks away, I pulled over so I could see tha damage that was done to my car. When I got out and seen tha hole in my car, I snapped all tha way out.

"Baby, calm down; I'll get it fixed, it ain't about nothing. Just take it and put it in tha shop and I'll pay for it."

"Do you know who them boys are?"

"Yeah, so don't worry about it; they gon' pay for it, believe me. I called ya phone to tell you not to come to tha park."

I looked at my phone which showed two missed calls. I had my music up, so I didn't hear it.

"So how was lunch?"

"Good, me and my girls got to catch up."

"That's what's up."

"I know we haven't been spending that much time together as of late."

"I hope I'm not tha cause of that."

"Partly."

"Well, I'll fall back. I don't want to come between you and ya friends."

"You're not, they have men in their lives, so that's why we haven't been together."

"I know Bre mess wit Maze, but if I may ask, who does Jade mess wit?"

"She deals wit Swerve from 8th Street."

"I know who you talking about, that's my cousin."

"Stop lying."

"I'm serious; my mom and his mom are sisters."

"Well, why do you deal wit Maze and not him?"

"Because Maze gave me my start, so I kept it real."

"I can respect it."

I took a mental note that he was loyal; nowadays, it's hard to find that in a man. We ended up at Canby Park.

"Turk, can I ask you something?"

"Ask away."

"We've been talking for a few months and I was wondering where we're headed, if we're headed anywhere at all?"

"*It's about time*," I thought to myself.

"To tell you tha truth, Fresh I didn't want to get in tha way wit ya other broads, so that's why I kept it casual."

"I may be a bit younger, but I ain't no player. I'm definitely feeling you and I hope that we can take it to tha next level. A lot of my boys, even me, said that you are out of my league."

"Well, you just let them know that tha person they said was outta ya league is now ya girl."

He grabbed my face and kissed me.

"So, you make sure you put all ya little friends in check. I don't want no drama and I don't fight over no man. But don't let this pretty face fool you; I can go." He started smiling.

"What do you smiling at?"

"You."

"I'm funny now?"

"No, not at all. I just like being around you."

"That's good to know."

"Turk, do you have anything planned for tomorrow?"

"Yeah, why?"

"I was going to say let's spend tha day up New York shopping."

"Maybe we can go after I finish doing what I have to do."

"I guess, depending on what time you get done."

"Well, I'm only going to buy me a truck."

"I told you I would get ya shit fixed; you don't have to buy a new car."

"I was doing this before this even happened."

"Damn, you holdin' paper like that?"

"Do you mind if I tag along?"

"No, that's up to you."

"Well then, it's a date."

I know she probably thinks that I think, since she my girl, I can hit. I'm gon' wait til she ready; I'm in no rush. We ended up talking for a few hours before we realized what time it was.

When we pulled back up at tha Park, Fresh said, "There that Motha Fucka go."

"Who Baby?" I asked.

"Hold on, Ayo Baby Boy, let me borrow your ear for a second. That was some dumb shit you did earlier!"

"I know, but I was just defending myself."

"Neither one of yall gave a damn about all tha kids that were out here. Both yall gone split tha cost of my girls car," he said, pointing to tha quarter size hole on tha side of my car.

"A'ight Fresh, it ain't about nothing; I didn't mean to hit her shit if I was tha one who hit it.

Imma send that nigga to tha boneyard Fresh."

"Baby Boy, you need to let that beef die down first."

"I didn't fuck wit Jay, but since he spent a nice piece of money every week, I let him breathe."

"Well, tell that Nigga I'm willing to dead tha beef."

"Now you using ya head."

"Imma set up a sit-down wit you two in tha next few days."

"Cool, I need 9 anyway."

"I'll hit ya phone in about 30 minutes."

I made tha call to Jay and told him about tha hole they put in Turk's car and tha sit down. He was cool wit both as I knew he would be. When I got back to tha car, I could tell Turk was a little upset.

"My fault Babe for taking so long. I had to make sure them Niggaz knew I didn't appreciate that shit that went down."

"Fresh, I don't want you to get in no bullshit behind this."

"You don't have to worry about that; they respect me around here!"

"I know that I'm just saying, though."

"You have to trust me Turk."

"If I didn't trust you, I wouldn't be wit you. One thing about me is you have to earn my trust and these past few months, you've done more then that."

"So, you been testing me?"

"Yes and no."

"Well, nice to know I passed."

"Yeah, you sure did wit flying colors too." I grabbed his face and planted a kiss on his cheek.

"I hope that this works out because if it doesn't then I'm done wit love. It's hard to believe I've never had a man before. A real man anyway, I don't count the niggaz I played who thought they were my man."

"I'm about to go to my mom's house for a little while."

"Give me a call later; maybe we can slide by tha Cas-bar and have some drinks."

"A'ight, I'll hit ya phone when I leave my mom's."

When Fresh got outta my car I could still smell his Furdose. Something about that Furdose that makes me horny.

As soon as I got home, I went to my bedroom. Then open my drawer to tha right and pulled up my close friend. We had gotton close in tha past few months. So close, in fact, I didn't take long before my whole body was shaking. I jumped in tha shower and headed to my mom's house.

CHAPTER 21

Heem

"Hello."

"What tha bis is."

"Same shit, different day."

"I need you."

"Same thing?"

"Nah, I need a half chicken this go round."

"You know that's 12 flat, right?"

"Yeah I got it."

"Meet me at tha same spot in 45 minutes."

I took a ride over to my aunt's house to get tha rest of tha money. I was only going to get 9 but decided to get a half. Swerve had 60 days left and tha way things were going, I would be up to a whole pie by then, if not more. My aunt let me keep my money in her house as long as I didn't bring any drugs into her house. I got to tha meet spot and Killer wasn't there yet. After about 10 minutes, my phone rang.

"Yo I'm here."

"I know; see tha woman in tha black Escort?" I looked to my left and there was an old lady sitting in tha black Escort.

"I see her."

"Give her tha money and she'll give you tha work."

When I got in tha car, she told me to put tha money under tha seat and grab tha bag. This lady was old enough to be my grandmother. But I had to be honest; it was smart tha police would never expect her to be riding wit a half a brick and whatever else she might have in there.

I made my way out Claymont, where I had purchased an apartment that my little cousin was staying in. I paid tha rent while she paid tha utilities. I told her that she was not under any circumstances to have any company. I didn't want or need anybody to know about this spot. If she had a date, she was to go to a hotel or his spot. I didn't see Alexis's car when I pulled up. I went in and went straight to work. Wherever Killer was getting this work from, it was definitely tha best in town. It was no problem turning 9 into 12 and still be oils. I turned on tha stereo and let Jeezy tell me how to cook and distribute the work. Jeezy always motivated me even though this album The Recession, is old everybody is still bumpin' to it. My phone rang, it was my peeps from Milford.

"What it be like Heem?"

"You know in tha kitchen wit it."

"I need a half this time, but I only got 25,000 I'll hit you wit tha other duece next go round."

"How long is it going to take you to get up here?"

"I'm 45 minutes away."

"I'll be waiting on you." Alexis walked in just as I was sitting my phone down.

"Perfect timing Cousin."

"What? I just came home to get my debit card."

"I need you to make a run." She started smiling, knowing she was about to make an easy nickel for driving.

"You know that's music to my ears Heem. How long are you talkin' bout?"

"As soon as I'm done doing this up."

"A'ight, oh yeah do you know Misty been asking about you."

"Fuck her; she couldn't even make a visit or send a nigga a card tha whole 3 I was down."

"I told her that, but you know she was wit that crazy Motha Fucka Ben."

"She didn't care when I was hittin' before I fell."

"True."

"I know that's ya girl, so you gon' to stick up for her."

"Yeah, but you my blood and blood is thicker than water."

"Only in certain cases, you need water to live; you learn that in the basics better cherish ya aces bullets in tha faces of jokers we fire Nigga we laugh at smokers." I hit her wit a verse from tha Lox's Can I Live.

"Boy, you crazy? Are you ready yet?"

"Yup, let me put this stuff away."

When I was done, I put tha bag in her car.

"Now, just remember drive regular. I'll be a few cars behind you."

I called my peeps to see how far away they were. He let me know he was 15 minutes away. I watched as Alexis pulled into tha Pizza Hut parking lot. I always parked in Wendy's just to make sure nothing crazy was going down. Once tha transaction was completed, I called my peeps to make sure they were straight. Then I called Killer back to see if I could get a whole chicken. He told me to meet him at tha Dollar Tree on Miller Road in 30 minutes. Tha way this is going, I'll be at two pies when Swerve come home.

2 hours later, I had cooked up one pie and hit my young boys wit some

work. One of my young boys was having a problem wit this nigga on the 22nd. I was a gun, so niggaz on every side of town respected my handle. I still played tha block cause ain't nothing like that block money. I believed in keeping a low profile; that's why I drove an 89 Honda Accord LX with no rims, just a system.

Beezer walked up to my car and gave me dap.

"Asalamu-Alaikum"

"Wailakum-Salam so what's going on out here?"

"Nothin' I can't handle," he said, lifting his shirt up, exposing his .45 automatic.

"Listen Beezer, you not going to be able to get money and beef is just not going to work."

"Trust me, I know." I seen his ice grill so I turned around.

"Heem what up Cousin?"

"Mac what up?"

"Do you know this kid?"

"Yeah, he on my team."

"Lil Nigga why didn't you say that when I asked you tha first time?" I looked at my cousin.

"You ain't even got to say it Cuz."

"On some real, let me ask you a question Mac."

"Shoot."

"Beezer born and raised over here and you ain't have no problem wit him hustling before, so why now?"

"Cuz that work you hittin' him wit is fire; they don't want nothing else but that. Now since I know tha source, I can cop some myself."

"What tha numbers like Cuz?"

"Mac, you might not want to pay tha numbers."

"Shit, I'm paying a stack a ounce right now."

"Oh well, that's tha same price I want."

"You got 9 on deck right now?"

"Hold on, let me make a call." Alexis picked right up.

"Where are you at?"

"Home why?"

"I need you to bring me 9 over 22nd Street."

"Ok, just call me when you get close."

"Is 15 minutes too long?"

"Nah, let me run up tha street to get tha money."

"Heem, I didn't know Mac was ya kin."

"Yeah, now go put that pistol up." He was back in seconds.

"Now everybody around here gon' have tha same work. As long as you keep treating ya customers right, they gon' stay loyal, believe that."

"Yeah, cause Mac and his squad sell bags, I break off."

"Imma put you in position where Mac coppin' off you."

"That's what I'm talkin' about Heem; let's get this paper Baby." My phone went off.

(chirp) "Where you at Lexis?"

(chirp) "Coming up 22nd."

(chirp) "I see you; park behind that red van."

(chirp) "Gotcha."

Mac came back as she was parking; he handed me tha money.

"Hold up, let me walk down tha street."

(chirp) "Do you want me to bring it up tha street?"

(chirp) "Nah, Imma have Mac walk down there."

(chirp) "Our cousin Mac?"

(chirp) "Yeah."

(chirp) "A'ight.

"Mac take this and give it to Lexis; she parked behind that van and tell her to drop you off where you need to go."

"You talkin' bout our cousin Alexis?"

"Yeah. I probably won't be here when you get back so be safe."

"What's ya number so I can call when I'm done."

"Just get at Beezer."

"A'ight, let me get down here."

I watched as he walked down tha street and got into Lexis' car. When she drove past, she winked and I winked back.

"Ya cousin bad as shit."

Lexis was 5'10" with brown eyes, long hair, caramel skin and a booty like the singer Fantasia.

"Beezer, you too young for her."

"Heem, I'll be 15 next month."

"Yeah, Lexis is going on 20 in two weeks."

"Aaliyah said it first; age ain't nothing but a number."

"Yeah whatever, hit me when you almost done. Don't wait til you run out. You want to always have work, so never wait to you run out."

"I'll hit you when I get down to my last two or three onions."

"If you have any more problems, call me first."

"Heem, I respect you, but I can handle my own."

"I know you can, but if we can nip it in tha bud, then that's all it is."

I knew that Beezer wouldn't hesitate to bust his gun at anybody. He reminded me of myself at that age. The only difference is nobody looked out for me except me. Now don't get it fuck'd up. I'll still push a nigga shit back; I'm just smarter and wiser. That 3 years made me open my eyes, not to mention Swerve schooling me. Had he not been in my ear, I wouldn't even be on my grown man get money shit!

"I'm outta here; remember what I said and make tha money, don't let tha money make you."

I did a little more runnin' around, then went home to fly Swerve a kite and let him know it was on.

CHAPTER 22

Count Down

"Mail call."

I came out to see if I was loved enough to get mail.

"Nigga you got 30 days left and you still getting mail."

Tha CO called my name four times. I had a letter and flicks from Jade, a letter from Killer and Tiz.

"Oh shit, Heemer wrote me," I quickly opened it up to see what he was talking about.

Swerve,

Asalamu-Alaikum

First, all praise due to Allāh what's good wit you? I know it took me a minute to write, but I'm tryin' to get right, so you come home already in position Insha-Allāh. I know you anxious wit less than 30 days left. As for me, I'm still on my Deen hard even though I'm in tha streets it's every man for themselves. Unless you know somebody, unfortunately for me, I didn't know anybody, so everything I got was from tha muscle. And I'm proud to say that I've been home close to five months and I'm able to bake two pies. I know I said I would have half a pie well; I tripled that and hope to have three by the time you hit. If I don't,

I'll still have a pie for you tax-free; I don't want anything in return. Swerve, you already paid for it wit that year worth of knowledge you sent me out here wit. No amount of money could ever equal that. Well, I'm not going to hold you hostage 'cause I know you want to read wifey's mail.

Asalamu-Alaikum

Heem

I had to read Heem's letter a few more times. I was proud of him cause I thought that he was going back out there on tha same dumb shit. Oh shit, that's who Killer was talkin' bout when he said the young boy H. He just earned a spot on tha roster. I know if he up wit no help, I could just imagine where he'll be wit me to guide him. I kept telling him that there are two types of niggaz not to be in tha way and taking up space nigga. A in tha way nigga is a nigga that's hustling but ain't making no money, so he just in tha way. The other is a Nigga who ain't hustling but stands out on tha corner, so he just taking up space. Heem is what I like to call a move to tha side Nigga. A nigga that tells tha other niggaz to move to tha side so I can get this paper! After reading Heem's letter one more time, I decided to go play some handball. When I walked in tha yard, they were already playing.

"I got winners."

"You after me Swerve."

"It don't matter. I'm not getting off when I get on."

I was one of tha best, if not tha best, in tha prison.

"They playing for money Swerve."

"Well, I don't gamble."

"Yeah, but I do," Pooh said, "I'll put tha money up."

"My winners is next."

"Put tha money up; how much are they playing for anyway?"

"Five dollars a man. I heard you was good but are you that good?"

"Put the doe up."

"Next."

"What you gon' do Pooh, you play'n or what?"

"Imma put up tha dime on Swerve."

"Who his partner?"

"I don't need one, me against both of yall."

"You disrespecting us now."

"I know we wouldn't even take Pooh's money like that."

"I got my own money then and we can up tha stakes if yall can afford it."

"Afford it, we can play drawer for drawer."

"Nah, cause after I win you not going to have nothing to bet back wit."

"We can jus play 10 dollars a man. You lose, you pay twenty, we lose we pay ten apiece."

"It's a bet."

A few people on tha side thought it was easy money and wanted to bet against me. Pooh was tha only one who bet wit me. Since they won tha last game, they served first. They went up six to nothing.

"You know skunk is double."

I looked at Pooh, "11-6 will be tha final score."

Yack served and I hit tha bottom brick. I looked over at Pooh and winked. I served my high teaser shot which Dave missed.

"1 to 6!" Pooh shouted.

"This game over," Yack said wit confidence.

Six points later, I was up 7 to 6. After a few more serves it was point 6.

"Pooh, this shit is too easy."

I served it high Yack killed it, or so he thought. I got low and killed his kill shot. Pooh went crazy.

"All you niggaz go get my money," I told Yack and Dave to do tha same.

"You not going to run it back?"

"Yeah but get my money."

"Naw we had next."

"By tha time yall come back, this game will be over! Do yall got twenty apiece?"

"Yeah, but ain't gon' be no skunk."

"Who like these Niggas?" Pooh asked, "oh, nobody want to bet now?"

"I'm betting wit Yack and Dave."

"Me too."

By the time Yack and Dave came back, it was six to nothing. I aced them.

"Go get my 40 dollars."

Tha next game was closer. I won by two points.

"Yall done?" I asked.

"Nah, I want to play head up," Yack said.

"You don't want to do that."

"I like myself for a dub."

Yack was from Philly and was suppose to have a couple dollars.

"It's a bet skunk still double."

I ended up skunking him. When it was all said and done, I won close to 300.

"Yo Swerve, you got that; you got a nice game."

"So do you; you just got to work on your left."

I went to my cell to see what they had given me.

"I'm glad I bet wit you."

Pooh had gotten moved in my room after Heem maxed out.

"You gon' have a lot of commissary when I leave."

"Huh?"

"I said when I leave, I'm leaving you everything, so don't go to tha store anymore."

He looked at me like I just told him his girl was cheating on him.

"Look, I got damn near 500 worth of shit and I leave next week so why would you waste your money. What you can do is fill out a slip for tha shit I have, then go down and credit it back. What's tha purpose of buying it just to credit it back? Duh, damn Nigga, so you can have the blue slip to back this shit up and you do that for tha next few weeks."

"I'm glad you leaving, but Imma miss you."

"You still got 3 left Imma hold you down Insha Allāh!"

"I'm bout to hop in this pond so I can call wifey."

"She gon' cuss you out; you ain't called in 3 days."

"I know; I was just gonna wait til my visit Saturday to see her."

When I got out tha shower I decided not to call Jade. I turned tha TV off and tha radio on. As I lay back, I thanked Allāh for letting me go home early. I couldn't believe it I was going home in seven days and a wake-up wow. I had a couple of scores to settle, starting wit tha young boy who threw his pack that tha vice found by me. He said he was coming to court to say it was his work. Even though it really was his, I was willing to pay him five stacks just to make sure he came. Long story short, he didn't come, but I did some research and found out that he been in Riverside pumpin' Diesel. Killer had wanted to handle him, but I wanted to do tha job myself.

After my visit, I just wanted to lay down. I was so anxious to go home. I know a lot has changed in 3 years.

"Yo nigga get up ain't no time for sleeping, you sleep when you die."

"I heard that. I wasn't asleep; I was just getting my thoughts together."

"What are you gon' do ya first day since you maxed out on a Friday?"

"I don't know; Jade wants me to go to this party wit her at tha Chase Center."

"Doc B must be having a party. Make sure you send ya baby some flicks."

"Come on, that goes wit out saying. You know I got you."

"So, you coming out to play some handball?"

"Nah, Imma fall back in tha hut."

"You try'n to slide out real quiet."

"Yup, I ain't tell nobody but tha Niggaz I fuck wit that they modified my time."

"I'm bout to play poker; I'll holla at you when I come back in."

"A'ight, but if I'm sleep, don't wake me up."

"Yeah, a'ight."

"Nah, I'm serious; I'm tired as shit."

"It don't matter; I'll be at tha card table until count time."

When he left out, I turned tha TV off in tha radio on.

"Girl, it's ya birthday and I know you want to ride out, even if we only go to my house. Sip some weezy as we sit on my couch feels good, but I know you want to ride out. You say you want passion I think you found it. Get ready for action don't be astounded."

This was my shit, birthday sex before I realized it, I was knocked out.

CHAPTER 23

One Last Time

We had been plotting on this nigga for over a year and because we were all on some other shit, we still were going to handle this last score. We got geared up and took tha ride to our destination.

"Are yall sure you want to do this?"

"We been on this Nigga too long to forget about it now."

"Yeah, not to mention he's worth a lot of money."

We drove by tha house just to make sure he wasn't home yet. Then we parked around tha corner so not to be seen.

"Come on yall."

We went in thru tha back. Once we were inside, we made our way to tha couch to get comfortable and wait. It was 9 o'clock, so we had at least an hour before he came home.

I could hear tha keys being placed inside tha door.

"SHH Here he comes."

I stood behind tha door to catch him off guard when he walked in. As soon as he shut tha door, I was in his face wit tha pistol pointed directly in between his eyes.

"What tha fuck is going on?"

"Don't play dumb you know exactly what's going on!"

"Now, this can end one or two ways tha decision is yours. You need to sit down slowly. Tie him up." Once that was done, I began my questions.

"We already know your net worth, so no need in bullshit'n us."

"If you know all that, then why do you need me?"

"Where is tha money and what's tha combination to tha safe?"

"I don't know what you're talking about."

(Smack) "Wrong answer!"

"Tha money is not here. I keep it in Delaware."

(Smack) "Stop lying."

"AAAA Shit, I'm not lying; I keep it at my peoples spot."

I pulled out my phone.

"Tha number and this better not be a game!"

When he read tha number off, I couldn't believe it.

"Call, she'll tell you that tha money is there."

"Why would you keep your money at some broad's house?"

"I know, then tell us where it is; how do you know we not going to off her once we get tha money."

"I could care less if you do or not."

"Wow, that's some shit to say."

"Fuck her; she ain't my bitch."

"You know what, you sorry ass Mafucka."

"Oh shit, what the fuck is going on!"

"You a dumb ass," Turk said, snatching her mask off, "I was using ya ass anyway; that's why you never got none of this pussy." Me and Bre took our masks off as well.

"I'm going to kill you snake ass bitches!"

"You're not going to do a damn thing Nigga."

I screwed on my silencer.

"Now let's play a little game called shot or not. If you tell us where tha money is you don't get shot. If you don't tell us, you get shot. Remember, it's all up to you how many times you get shot."

"You bitches might as well kill me because I'm not telling you a Mafuck'n thing!"

"I had a feeling you would say that."

Turk lit a cigar and then walked over to him. Without hesitation, she put tha cigar against his cheek, causing him to scream out.

"AAAAAAAAH SHIT AAAAAAAAH!"

"To kill you would be too easy. I'd rather torture you to death first. You gonna wish you were dead. Bre put that tape on his mouth; we wouldn't want you to wake tha neighbors."

Turk put tha cigar on tha tip of his nose, causing him to scream again. Only this time, it was muffled, thanks to tha tape over his mouth.

"Hold on, he's try'n to say something."

"It's upstairs in tha back room."

I motioned to Bre to check it out. She was back in tha matter of minutes.

"This bag feeling real light."

As soon as she opened it, I shot him in tha knee.

"So, you want to play games, huh?"

"AAAAAAH Fuck, that's all I got."

"Did you not know we laid on you for a whole year? You make this in a week so let me ask again. Remember we're playing shot or not," Bre said wit a smile, "where's tha money?"

Before he could answer, my phone went off. I looked at my watch; shit, I need to answer this; it's tha last call of tha night. I let tha message play through, then talked to my baby for tha 15 minutes tha call lasted for.

I couldn't wait; he would be home in two days.

"Tell him we said hi."

As soon as tha phone hung up, it was back to biz-ness.

"Now that you had 15 minutes to rest, are you ready to talk?"

"I told you…" (SPT)

Before he could finish, I shot him in his other knee.

"You must be a freak for pain. Just tell us where the money is so we can be on our way," Turk said, relighting tha cigar.

His eye got big as golf balls. He was try'n to say something, so I snatched tha tape from his mouth.

"OK, OK, there's $1 million in tha basement behind tha fake wall. Tha combination is 34–22–09." This time I went down to check; I moved tha wall and punched in tha numbers. And like magic tha safe came open. I put all tha money inside tha duffel bag I had wit me. Before I went back upstairs, my gut was telling me to look around, so I did. After a few minutes of spotting this old video game. It seemed out of place, so I checked it out.

"WHEEEEEEEW!" I screamed at the top of my lungs.

"Jade, is everything a'ight?"

"Sure is, couldn't be better throw those two bags down."

After about 15 minutes, I had all tha money inside tha bags. I carried them upstairs one at a time.

"That was a nice stash spot tha average person would have never found it. But you see, I'm far from average. Come on, ladies let's get out of here and go have a drink."

"You two go ahead let me say something to him."

"A'ight, but don't be long."

After Bre and Jade walked out, I took tha tape off his mouth.

"Turk, how could you betray me? I will find tha three of you if it's tha last thing I do!"

I pulled out my gun and put it in tha middle of his forehead.

"Goodbye," I said as I pulled tha trigger and watched him fall back into tha chair.

I walked outside as if nothing ever happened. Tha ride back to Wilmington seemed like it took forever, especially since we were all anxious to count our take. Once we got to Turks, we started counting up tha money. 3 hours had gone by when we finally finished.

"Bitch we never have to work again."

"I know, we ended up wit close to five mill. I knew that he was holding but damn."

"He had more than that."

"Well, why didn't you get it?"

"That's all he had there."

"I'm not mad at all."

"Who can be wit 1.5 mill to go along wit our already fat bank accounts."

We all agree to invest tha odd 500 grand into some type of legal bizness. We decided to go to tha cash bar to celebrate our fortune as well as our last hit.

CHAPTER 24

Free At Last

"Jones bag and baggage!" tha CO yelled out, but he didn't have to tell me I was already ready.

A lot of people didn't know I was leaving so when they seen me leaving they were surprised. "What you do wit all ya stuff?"

"I left everything wit Pooh."

"Damn nigga you could have left me wit something."

"Ask Pooh."

"You know that tight ass nigga ain't breaking no bread."

"Jones, if you want to go you better come on or you'll be staying, CPL Meslow said.

"Yeah right, ain't nobody stopping me from going home."

"Keep talking and you'll be here until at least 11:30 tonight."

"Man, that doesn't mean nothing you gotta let me go today. I've been down for three years."

"Swerve just chill."

"No fuck him, he's been try'n to book me for tha past two years."

LT Jasp came on tha pod.

"Jones, you ain't left yet?"

"No, Cpl Meslow giving me a hard time as usual."

"Come on, I'll take you to booking myself, 'cause ya girl done called a thousand times."

By tha time I got to booking P had my stuff already waiting for me.

"Damn, they letting tha lion back into tha jungle, huh," P said.

"You know they can't hold a good nigga down wit out letting him loose."

"Jones, I don't want to see you again unless it's in a club or at tha barber shop."

LT Jasp was down to earth; he still did tha club thing. I heard he was handling all tha bad COs in here.

"You'll definitely see me; you might even see me tonight if you go to tha Chase."

"I'll see you 'cause I'm definitely in the building."

"First round on me Jasp."

I gave him some dap as he walked me out tha gate. As soon as I walked out tha gate, Iciss ran up to me.

"Brother," she said, giving me a big bear hug. I picked her up and swung her around.

"Will yall come on I'm hungry."

"I'm not going nowhere looking like this."

"Boy, you look better than half these Niggaz out here."

I had on a pair of black True Religion jeans, a white and black V-neck True Religion shirt and black ACG boots.

"Look at all that hair; you should let me braid it up."

"You can braid?"

"Nobody in tha city can touch me."

"You talk a good one."

Jade looked at me and then said, "She can back it up too."

"Let's go to Mom Jeans 'cause she got the best food in town."

"I heard. After that, I need to go to King of Prussia to grab something to wear for tonight."

Iciss and Jade looked at one another and then yelled, "Shopping!"

"I see what you two love to do in your spare time."

"Ain't nothing wrong wit that, is it?"

"Not at all; I love to shop too."

4 hours later, we were on our way back to Wilmington from doing some shopping.

"I'll make sure you get that 6 stacks back tonight."

"Swerve, please don't disrespect me."

"What? How do I disrespect you?"

"I don't want ya money, you my man I'm suppose to make sure you straight."

"Jade, you've been holding me down for tha last two years."

"As I should!"

"Brother, you're not going to win."

"I know, but it was worth a try."

"Are yall going to move in together?"

"When the time is right," I told her.

"Iciss, are you still stay'n wit Chas tonight?"

"No, she staying over my house."

"Do you want me to take you anywhere Baby?"

"Nah, I'll see everybody tomorrow; today is just about me and you."

"Let me drop Iciss off; then we can go to my house."

"I need Iciss to do my hair."

"Oh yeah, well she can do it at my moms."

"Yeah, cause mommy wants to meet him anyway."

We pulled up in front of Jade's moms' house. Tha funny thing was I had a stash spot not too far from here.

"What's wrong?"

"Nothing, I was just thinking."

"Thinking what?"

"What if your moms don't like me?"

"I know she will, besides she's not the one who has to, I am!"

"Don't worry, brother I told her all about you."

When we walked in, Jade's mom was coming downstairs.

"Hey Mom."

"Well, hello Jadeen and who is this handsome young man."

"Mommy, that's Swerve."

Umm, so you're tha one who is my daughter all in love."

"I extended my hand and Jade didn't tell me she had an older sister." My mom started blushing.

"Unh Unh Sweety, I'm tha mother."

So, this is where they get their good looks from. If you didn't know any better, you would have thought they were all sisters.

After Iciss finished my hair, she told me to go in tha bathroom to look at it. I had to admit she definitely put it down. I normally just get straight backs, but this design was off tha chain.

"Do you like it Brother?"

"Yeah, we locked in now once a week. How much?"

"I wouldn't charge you."

"Swerve, you ready it's 9 o'clock?"

"Come on."

"It was nice meeting you Ms. Sady."

"You too; I'm sure I'll be seeing a lot more of you in tha future."

"Yes, you will," I replied wit a smile, "unless Jadeen gets tired of me.

A half-hour later, we were at Jade's house. When she pulled up in her garage, I was surprised to see her 600 and her bike.

"Wow, you have really good taste."

"Thank you."

"What time does tha party start?"

"Now, but we'll be there by 11:30."

My phone was ringing. I knew from the ringtone it was Killer.

"Hello."

"Hey, Jade, is he wit you?"

"Yeah."

"What time yall leaving?"

"I am bout to get dressed now. I should be there by 11:30."

"A'ight, I'll see yall there."

"Yes, I will be there by 11:30. Bye."

"Why are you looking at me like that?"

"No reason, just admiring ya beauty, that's all. I'm about to get in tha shower."

"Tha towels are in tha hallway closet."

I walked up tha steps hoping that she would join me. Damn, it felt good to be in a real shower. I closed my eyes and let tha water run over my face. I felt a pair of hands on my shoulders, so I opened my eyes.

"I didn't hear you come in."

"I know; I hope you don't mind."

"Not at all; this is tha first of many showers together."

"I know that's right."

She wanted to get it on, but I told her I wanted to wait until we came back home.

"You gonna make me wait? I've been waiting for two years."

"I know, so a couple more hours won't hurt. But just to hold you down," I pushed her back on tha bed and then rolled my tongue over her breast causing her to let out a soft moan.

"Oh please, don't tease me Baby."

I ignored her and continued to caress her breasts wit my tongue. When I got down to her vagina, I stopped and admired tha clean-shaven area. I planted a soft kiss on her lips before slid'n my tongue inside. It's been a while, but judging from her body movement, I still had it. As soon as I hit tha man in tha boat, she said, "Oh My God, Daddy I'm about to cum."

That's when I softly sucked on her clit, bringing her to an instant orgasm. I kept going until she had finished her multiple orgasms.

"Now, that should hold you down until later."

I didn't say a word; I just took his face into my hands and kissed him.

I went into tha bathroom and washed my face while Jade washed up.

I've never met a man that could make me cum, especially by eating me out.

"Not bad huh?"

(Ha! Ha! Ha!) "You crazy Boy, let's get dressed; it's getting late."

By the time we got dressed, it was 11 o'clock.

"Unh, Unh, Unh you look good as shit Baby."

"Thank you and so do you."

Jade had on a black Gucci dress with match'n sandals. She had a diamond necklace, bracelet and earrings to really bring it out. All I had on was a pair of white Gucci capris wit a white and brown Gucci shirt and brown Gucci slip-ons. My Gucci frames were killing 'em. Even though I didn't get a shape-up, I was still play'n.

"Here, put this on," she said, handing me this iced-out David Yurman watch.

"Jade, you're too much."

"I'll take that as a compliment and say thank you, thank you."

We jumped in her S-600 and made our way to tha Chase Center. I just stared at Jade tha whole ride there. When we pulled up, it was jampacked wit cars and people everywhere. What a way to make my re-emergence then tonight at this party tha whole city is at. Jade pulled up to V.I.P, where tha valet took my keys and replaced them wit a ticket.

"Swerve, welcome home! Hey Swerve! Swerve you looking real good! Swerve what up Baby Boy? You glowing!" that's what the people in line for yelling as we walked straight in to be greeted by Killer, Tiz, Maze and my squad.

"Oh shit, I didn't know you niggaz was going to be here."

"Nigga like we're gon' to miss ya coming home party."

"Huh?" I said, turning to look at Jade, who was now smiling from ear to ear.

"That's right, Baby this is ya party; welcome home."

I was just overwhelmed by all this; Jade really went all out on me. I grabbed her by tha waist and planning a kiss on her lips.

"Oh, so that's why you stop me from visiting tha last two years, huh?"

I stopped kissing Jade only to see Rayna standing there wit her hands on her hips. Now don't get it twisted; Rayna was bad, 5'8, with brown eyes, brown skin, shoulder-length hair and a nice apple bottom to top it off. But she didn't have shit on Jade. Not to mention all she wanted was my money.

I didn't want any problems, so I said, "How are you doing Rayna?"

"Good, now that I've seen you."

"Man, get outta here wit that bullshit. Shouldn't you be home wit ya son?" Killer and Tiz both said.

It was no secret neither of them liked her, especially after they caught her creeping.

"Fuck both of yall! Yall need to mind your business."

"Swerve is our business trick."

"Yo, what's tha problem?" some big dude said.

"Ain't no problem Baby; I was just saying hi to an ooold friend."

I didn't like the way dude walked up, but before I could say anything, Jade said, "Let's take some pictures."

Once we were done flick'n it up, we made our way to where tha party was at.

"Here, Baby take this couple dollars and enjoy ya self." She went to reach in her Gucci bag but was stopped by Killer.

"No, you've done more than enough."

He went into his pocket and pulled out a whopper, then peeled off five hundred dollar bills.

"That should hold you down for a few." Everybody else did tha same thing.

Jade turned to leave, "Excuse me, Miss where are you going?"

"Imma let you have fun wit ya boys."

"You better get back over here, you wit me all night."

"I know that's right," Bre said wit a smile.

"Damn, you real popular in this town," Turk said.

"I used to be."

"Boy, stop it, every couple minutes people walking up giving you dap and money."

"That's niggaz that owe me."

"Yeah whatever. Hey everybody, I want to take this opportunity to say welcome home to Swerve!" Everybody started clap'n then tha music came back on.

This is my jam right here, Jade said. She hit tha floor and started partying.

"ATL Club see her do her thing might wanna rap but she'll make you sing I was on her she was on him."

Yeah, that was tha shit before I fell; I went out there to do my two-step. By tha end of tha night, I was buckled.

"You a'ight Baby?"

"Yeah, I'm just grooving, that's all."

By tha time tha party was over, I was pissy drunk. Everybody was going to tha Thunder Guards, but I was too drunk, so I let them know I would see them tomorrow.

As soon as we got to tha house, I went straight to tha bathroom to piss. When I came out, Jade had tha stereo on wit tha sounds of Jermain's

Birthday Sex play'n. If that wasn't enough, she had on tha sexiest teddy.

"Don't keep me waiting. I've waited long enough."

She didn't have to say another word; I stripped down to my boxers and was next to her in tha bed wit in seconds. I started caressing her breasts wit one hand and my tongue wit tha other. A series of soft moans escape Jade's mouth. I took her soft body and massaged every spot possible. After about 30 minutes of foreplay, Jade was ready for tha real thing. I slid my hand down in between her legs where she was more than welcome them. I could feel her juices running down my fingers. I put my fingers in my mouth, tasting her. I then slid off my boxers and slowly entered her.

"UUUMMM be gentle; it's been a long time."

And I could tell because she was as tight as a virgin. Once I had tha tip in, I took my time wit tha rest; I was in no rush; we had all night.

Damn, he was holding; it hurt at first, but once he got majority of it and started feeling good. Five hours and 9 orgasms later, we both lay there panting, sweaty and out of breath.

"Damn Boy, you put it down fo' real."

"You da truth Mama!"

Before long, we fell asleep in each other's arms.

CHAPTER 25

Finally

I have been home for three weeks and still no site of Cam. He must of heard I was home and went underground. My probation officer was cool, especially since Tiz was twisting her back out. She let me know that I could do me and if I was out past curfew to stay away from Safe Street. I took that and ran wit it I only had a year. She told me to pay my fine off and she would discharge me in six months, seven tops. Now, what more could I ask for? Truth be told, she was flirting wit me. I always acted like I didn't pick up on it because tha moment I smashed, it would all go downhill. Not to mention I couldn't and wouldn't do that to Jade. I had just come from the motor vehicle getting my license back when I spotted Cam.

"Jade, follow that car right there!"

"Which one Babe?"

"The blue Lexus. But don't get too close. I don't want him to know we're following him."

I thought to myself, *"This is a piece of cake if you only knew."*

"Jade, Jade!"

"Oh, huh."

"Damn, you was in another world."

"I was just think'n about something, that's all. Why are we following this car?"

That's that tha young boy Cam who drugs they charge me wit."

"You talk'n about tha young boy Cam from Riverside?"

"Yeah."

"Why didn't you say that."

She pulled out her phone, looked through her phone book then put it to her ear. I laid my seat as far back as it would go.

"Hello, Cam." She put it on speaker, so I could hear.

"Who this?"

"Damn, you don't know my voice?"

"Nah, who dis?"

"It's Jade."

"Oh shit, what made you call me?"

"I was cleaning out my phonebook and came across ya number, so I called to see if it was still active."

"Damn, I gave you my number damn near two years ago."

"Yup, you did and up and every time you seen me."

"So, what made you call me? You finally gon' give a nigga some play or what?" I looked at Swerve, who was shaking his head yeah.

"Yeah, I'm gon' give you one shot at tha title."

"Where are you now?"

"On my way to tha Jects."

"A'ight, I'll be through in about a half."

"Don't be bullshit'n!"

"I don't play games."

"Take me by tha park so I can grab a whip."

"Look, you go over there and talk to him, then I'm gon' come through."

"A'ight, but make sure you call me so I can let you know where we at."

"Gotcha," I said gettin' out.

I hit Killer's phone to see if he was close by so I could get one of his pistols, but he didn't pick up. That's when Tiz pulled up. "What tha biz Swerve?"

"Yo you hold'n"

"All the time; why what's up?" I informed him on what was going down.

"Let me roll wit you."

"Nah, I got this; I just need some heat in case something pops off." He handed me his .45.

"This my baby, so make sure I get her back."

When I got close, I called Jade.

"Hey Turk," she said when she picked up.

"I'm over Bower Street hollering at Cam. Yeah, I finally gave him some play. No, he ain't got no friends wit him he by hisself."

I hung up; she told me everything I needed to know not that it mattered who was out there wit him. I pulled up on tha corner and parked; when I started walking down tha street, I could see him trying to touch on Jade. He had his back to me, so he never seen me coming.

"Yo, what tha biz is Cam?" When he turned around, he looked like he seen a ghost.

"What up Swerve? I heard you was home."

"Oh yeah, so why didn't you come to court and take ya charge like you were suppose to?"

"I forgot about tha court date."

"Mafucka, I called you tha night before and you assured me you would be there. Nigga I wasn't ask'n you to take a charge for me. All I wanted you to do was man up and take ya weight. That was ya shit that they found. I did three years for you."

"Whoopee doo, you did three years what tha fuck you want from me."

I turned around to see six niggaz walking through tha cut. I grabbed Cam by his collar. "Nigga do you think I give a fuck about them."

"Yo, what tha hell you doing my man!" one of them shouted.

I pulled out tha .45 Tiz had given me.

"Jade, get out of here!" I told her.

She got in her car and got right out holding a chrome 9mm.

"I said get outta here now!"

"I'm not going nowhere." One of tha dudes went to move.

"Don't even think about it," Jade said wit a serious look on her face that said try me.

"Oh Shit Swerve," one of them said. I turned in his direction wit Cam in one hand and my .45 in tha other.

"P.K.?"

"Yeah, Damn, Cuz when you come home?"

"Three weeks ago."

"Why you ain't hit me up?"

"I gave aunt Sue my number."

"I ain't been home. So, what's tha deal wit you and Cam?"

"Tell 'em Cam!" Cam didn't say shit.

"I heard he tha man over here."

"Yeah, he got tha best D and his numbers are fair."

"You hustling for him?"

"I cop 5 logs and he throws me 5."

"Well, he a snake. The three I just did was because of him."

"Huh?"

Tha police rolled up on tha block; he threw his shit; they found it by me, end of story."

"So why didn't he just man up."

"I called him tha day before tha trial to make sure he was still coming. His bitch ass assured he was, but he didn't. I would've been cool if he would have held me down, but he did not send me one dime. So check this out, Cam, you gonna pay me $500 for each month I spent in jail; so wit that being said, I did 36 months, so that's 20 grand."

"Nah, that's only 18 stacks."

"Tha other two is for pain and suffering."

"A'ight, I'll have it in a couple of days."

(Ha! Ha! Ha!) "You must be joking; you'll have it in one hour or they'll have a picture of you on a T-shirt in memory of."

"I'll be right back."

"Nah, you better get on tha phone and have it brought here in one hour."

One hour later, a white Honda pulled up.

"That's tha money right there."

"Jade, go get it. If they try anything funny, ya brains will be all over tha sidewalk."

Jade came back wit a Gap bag. "Baby, this don't feel like 20 grand."

"Sit in tha car and count it."

Tha look on Cam's face let me know it wasn't the full amount.

"Save me tha trouble Cam; how much is it?"

"I told her 20; you heard me." Jade got out.

"It's 6 stacks short."

I cocked tha .45, "Why you try'n to play me? You did it once, never again." I aimed tha gun at his chest.

"Hold up, hold up, I got about six in my car."

"Where in ya car?"

"Under tha driver's seat."

Jade went to get it. She hit me wit tha thumbs-up. P.K. and tha other dudes let Cam know he could no longer sell his work in tha Jects. Right when he was about to say something, I hit him square in tha jaw wit tha butt of my gun breaking it instantly.

"You lucky I'm letting ya bitch ass live. Oh, don't let me ever hear you try'n to holla at my wife. Are we clear on that?"

Since his jaw was broken, he just nodded his head yes. I hit P.K. wit my number and told him to holla at me.

"I'll meet you back at tha house. I need to take Tiz his pistol back."

I stopped at tha light on 8th and Spruce; when I looked to my left, I seen Heem on 8th and Bennett. I went to tha next light, made a left, then came around. I rolled my window down.

"This is where you get ya money at?" He was trying to figure out who I was.

"Asalamu Alaikum."

"Oh shit, Walaikum Asalam. When you touch?"

"Couple weeks ago."

"Why didn't you call me?"

"You got time to take a ride wit me?"

"Why, what's up?"

"I got a pie and a half for you."

"Nah, I don't need it tha nigga you been buy'n ya work from."

"Oh Yeah, my man Killer."

"Yeah, he's on my team."

"All that work is mine and you have proven that you bout this money, so I'm in position to hit you wit whatever you think you can handle."

"You never said you was tha man in tha bing."

"I didn't need to expose my hand. I wanted you to take tha knowledge and feed off of that.

And I can see that you did. So what was Killer charging you?"

"24 flat."

"That's a good number, but I'll give them to you for 21 and 23 on tha front."

"Damn Swerve, that's good shit. I'll be ready in a day; let me get rid of these two birds I got."

"Take ya time tha work ain't going nowhere."

"Man, I'm glad you finally home."

"By tha sounds of it doesn't look like you need my help."

"I could always use some help."

"Let me get outta here before wifey start blowin' my phone up." Just as I said that Jade hit my phone.

"Yo."

"Where you at?"

"I made a stop over Eastside, but I'm on my way now."

I made a hand gesture for Heem to call me. Then it dawned on me that I didn't give him neither of my numbers. He handed me his phone, so I could store tha numbers in there. Once that was done, he Salaamed me and got out. By tha time I made it back to Jade's, she had fallen asleep. She looked so peaceful sleeping I didn't bother to wake her. My phone rang, but I didn't know tha number. I didn't answer, but whoever it was called right back. This time I picked up.

"Hello."

"I see you still don't answer numbers you don't know."

"Who dis?"

"So now you don't know my voice?"

"I looked at Jade; she was still asleep or so I thought.

I knew he was too good to be true. Let me play sleep so I can hear what he has to say.

"Rayna, how did you get my number?"

"Does it matter?"

"Yes it does matter."

"Why do you sound so hostile Baby?"

"Please don't call me baby what do you want Rayna?"

"I want you back in my life Baby."

"What did I just tell you? And you can't have me. I have a girl!"

"She's just wit you for ya money."

(Ha! Ha! Ha!) You funny, nah you was tha one wit me for my money. Jade has her own money and unlike you she doesn't depend on no man! Besides, where is dude you was wit at tha party?"

"At work."

"Well, you need to call him and please don't call my phone anymore. What we had is over! Please don't forget that and just in case you're on your dumb shit, Jade will know about this phone call."

"Fuck you and ya bitch!" she screamed before hanging up.

All I could do was smile, hearing my baby let her know tha deal.

"Is everything okay?" I asked.

"Oh Shit, you scared me. I thought you were sleep."

"I was until you got all loud on tha phone."

"I'm sorry that was Rayna." I screwed my face.

"Don't worry; I let her know not to call my phone anymore."

"I know she had something to say about that."

"Yeah, but I also let her know that I was wit you and she needed to respect that."

Jade leaned forward and kissed me passionately. One thing led to another and we were butt naked gettin' it on.

CHAPTER 26

Played

"Yo, ain't nobody gon' be disrespecting me. Where is this Nigga at?"

Pop, Pop, Pop, Pop, we all dropped to tha ground. I looked up to see where tha shots came from. When I did, all I saw were two kids lighting firecrackers. I put my pistol back in my pants.

Pop, Pop, Pop, Pop.

"Lil Troy, come here."

"What up Maze?" I smacked him in tha back of tha head.

"OOOW Why you do that?"

"Boy, you could have gotton yaself killed lighting those damn things," I said, pointing to his firecrackers he was still holding in his hands, "give me the rest of 'em."

"Awe man."

He reluctantly gave them to me; I reached in my pocket in came out with a 50-dollar bill.

"Here," I said, passing him tha money, "and you better not buy no more."

"Good looking, Maze Imma go get that new Madden now."

"A'ight, when you get ya game up, come see me so I can bust dat ass."

"Yeah what ever, give me a week."

I laughed as Lil' Troy turned and walked away.

"Yo, that young boy crazier than a Mafucka."

"I know, but on some serious shit, what up wit Trench? If he disrespectin' me I need to handle him a.s.a.p."

"I overheard him say that he was tired of hustling for you and that he was going to front like somebody robbed him so he wouldn't have to pay you."

"Is that right? Well, I got a surprise for him."

"Maze, let me send him to tha boneyard!"

"No Sly, I'm a handle this one myself."

Three hours had went by and we were standing on C.B.W when Trench walked up.

"What up yall?" Nobody said shit; we just nodded.

"Yo Maze, can I holla at you for a second."

"What's up?"

He looked at Sly and said in private. So, I walked off to hear this bullshit game he was about to try and run.

"Niggaz ran up in my spot last night."

"OK and."

"They hit me for everything."

"OK and."

"I don't have ya doe."

"So, when will you have it?"

"Didn't you hear what I just said?"

"I'm gonna need some more work so I can pay you. I'm fucked up Maze."

"I don't know what to tell you Trench."

"You not gonna look out for me?"

Trench you in tha hole 25 grand and you ask'n me to hit you wit more work? Tell you what I'm gonna do; meet me on Guyer Street in about half an hour and I got you." I seen him smile as he walked away.

Damn, that was easy. I should have been did that.

"What that nigga talk'n bout Maze?"

"He said what you said he was gonna say. He also had tha nerve to ask for some more work."

"I know you not giving him none."

"I told him meet me on Guyer in a half hour."

"Man, you can't be serious."

"Dead serious," I said while laughing.

"Well, what's so funny?"

"Nothing, it was an inside joke."

"Sly, shoot to tha stash spot on Church, put this up, then meet me on Guyer."

"Gotcha."

Trench had no ideal what he was in for, but he'll soon find out! When I walked around to Guyer, it was pitch black.

"Good, tha streetlight is still out."

I stood in tha cut as I watched Trench pull up in his Lexus and hit tha lights. I stepped out of tha shadows so he could see me. Sly also pulled up, but he stayed in tha car.

"So, what you bring me Maze?"

"Listen, before I give you this, I need you to understand one thing."

"What's that?"

"I don't like to be played!"

"What you talk'n bout?"

"Stop wit tha bullshit," I said, pulling out my .357.

"Hooold on Maze, I don't know what you think is going on, but I assure you."

Boom! Tha sound of my .357 echoed in tha night. I watched as Trench laid there shaking. When I was sure his existence was no more I casually walked down tha street past Sly's car. I didn't want to get in just in case anybody was looking out tha window. Once I got around tha corner, I sat on Ms. Barb's steps to wait for Sly. My phone started to ring.

"Hey Babe."

"Hey you."

"Are we still going to tha club? "Yeah, I'm bout to come home and get dressed."

"A'ight."

When Sly pulled up, I jumped in. "Drop me off to my car."

"Did you get tha shell?"

"Didn't need to," I said, pulling out Thelma.

"I need to get one of those; that thing sounded like a canon. You parked on Sherman Street, right?"

"Yeah. I'm bout to go get dress me and wifey going to Plush tonight."

"Word, I'll probably see you 'cause my girl wants me to go wit her and her cousin. I wasn't going, but since you gonna be there, Imma slide thru."

It had been a long time since I popped anybody's top. I have to admit it gave me a rush, like it was my first time. I just hope I didn't wake tha beast that lives within me.

It was 10:45 when I finally got dressed. Bre was already dressed when I got there. Sitting on tha loveseat blow'n some Sour Diesle.

"I hope you rolled enough to hold us down for tha night."

"I rolled 3 up. That's all we'll smoke dat on tha way up."

"Well, I guess you better roll some more then."

I twisted another 5 then we headed out tha door.

"Oh, can you stop and pick up Turk and Fresh?"

"Yeah, but Fresh ain't old enough to get in and you know how Plush be on that dumb shit."

"I know, I told Turk and she said she had a fake ID."

"That's all it is then."

15 minutes later, we were pulling up to Turk's house. I honked tha horn to let them know we were out front, even though I know they heard us pull up. Fresh got in dapped me and spoke to Bre.

"Hey Fresh." As soon is Turk got in, she lit up her weed.

"Girl, I hope that ain't no dirt you lighting up."

"Bitch pleeeeease you know I only smoke Kush or Sour D."

"Just making sure."

"Damn, it's packed tonight."

We pulled into tha parking lot, so we could get valet parking.

"It's 20 to park in here, 40 to park up front."

"Park my shit up front."

I pulled out my white own white Bentley sittin' on dub-deuces. I bring it out every now and then and tonight was one of those nights I wanted to stand out.

"Come on, we ain't standing in this long ass line."

The V.I.P. line was even kinda long. I remember tha bouncer from tha last time I was up here, so I got his attention. As soon as he noticed me, he motioned for us to come to tha front. I reached into my pocket and pulled out 2 100 dollar bills. As we went pass, I slid tha money in his hand wit out anybody noticing.

"Me and my girl had some problems. I needed time to breathe, so I made my way to the club straight to tha V.I.P.," were tha sounds we heard as soon as we stepped through tha door.

"This my shit right here," Turk said, moving to tha beat.

"Let's hit tha bar Fresh."

"Gray Goose and pineapple!" Bre yelled. I hit her wit tha thumbs-up.

"Damn, I forgot what Turk wanted to drink."

"Bombay and cranberry."

"Excuse me, can we order?"

"I'll be wit you in a sec."

She finally came back after 10 minutes.

"Sorry, how can I help you?"

"Let me have a bottle of Bombay and Grey Goose."

"And you?" she said, talking to Fresh.

"A bottle of Bombay and Remy."

"Will that be all?"

"Two cups of pineapple wit ice."

"Turk wanted cranberry."

"My bag Shawty make that a cranberry too."

"Is that together or separate?"

"Together," we both said.

"$250.00."

"Damn yall killing 'em but it ain't bout nothing," I said, pulling my money out.

Fresh pulled his money out, "Nah Maze, first round on me."

"If you insist."

When we got back to tha table where Bre and Turk were, two guys was try'n to spit their best game.

"What's up yall lose something?" Fresh asked.

"Nah, playa just saying hi to tha lovely ladies, that's all."

I set tha bottles on tha table and then sat opposite of Bre. These two niggaz had the nerve to finish talk'n. I just sat there about to say something when Brie said it was nice to meet yall. I guess they got tha hint because they stepped off. One of them tried to be slick and wink at Bre. I wasted no time getting on tha phone to call Sly.

"Yo where you at?"

"Pulling up, why?"

"Two niggaz on deck as we speak."

When Sly came in, I saw he had his C.B.W chain on wit his wifey on his hip. He walked up to tha table and dap me and Fresh while speaking to Bre and Turk.

"Bre, Turk, this is my girl Dina." They all spoke.

"Dina, what you want to drink?"

"Baby, you can get me a Long Island Iced Tea, strong."

The music stopped and the DJ's voice came over the speakers.

"If everyone would refrain from leaving tha club, it would be highly appreciated."

Before anybody could ask why he announced that two people had been shot out front; by tha time we were finally let outside, they had bagged up tha bodies of the two dudes that were spittin' game at Bre and Turk earlier. Nobody had to see anything because we all knew what happened to them. The ride home was silent, besides Ne-Yo telling us he was so sick of love songs. After we dropped Turk and Fresh off, we decided to shoot to Wawa for sandwiches.

"Maze, I love you; you do know that, don't you?"

"Of course I do. Why did you ask me that? Bre, there's nothing I won't or wouldn't do for you. As far as those dudes, it wasn't about nothing at first. That's why I didn't say shit. I know you can handle yaself."

"I had told them from tha door we were both spoken for."

"I know you did. It was tha fact that he disrespected me by winking at you like I was a sucka or something."

"Baby, you know no matter what, I'm wit you and I got ya back."

So, wit that being said, we ate and went to sleep.

CHAPTER 27

Young Jawn

"What tha biz is Beezer?"

"Same ol' same ol'. I need you. Are you around?"

"I will be in tha next half hour."

"Mac hit me wit that change too."

"Ok, that's what's up. I'll hit ya phone when I want you to meet me."

"No doubt."

I couldn't believe how Beezer was running through tha work I was hittin' him wit. It was only 54 ounces, but he was dumpin' it every 5 days. Since I was grabbing 3 and Swerve was hittin' me wit 4 it was time to hit Beez wit more work. Alexis picked up on tha first ring.

"You must be wait'n on a phone call, damn."

"Boy shut up. I was try'n to call somebody."

"Yeah they said you would say that."

"Who's they?"

(Ha! Ha! Ha!) "Never mind, I need you, though."

"I'm listening."

"Grab 2 ½ and go meet Beez for me."

"At the same spot?"

"That's up to you. He's going to give you some money; put that up minus ya nickel."

"A'ight, what's his number?"

"275-4395 or do you want me to call him and give him ya number?

"Naw, I'll call him in a few minutes."

"Make sure you call Lex."

"You think I'm not gonna make that nickel? Boy stop play'n."

"Well, hit my phone as soon as you're finished."

I called Beez anyway to let him know that Alexis will be calling and meeting him. I was in Philly doing some shop'n wit my young jawn. I was only 21, but she was 18, so that gives me tha right to call her my young jawn.

"Heem do you like these on me?"

Did I like them hell Nah, I loved them on her. Madi was Spanish and Dominican. If you didn't know it, you would think she was black wit pretty hair. Her skin was bronze as she was 5'8, with hazel eyes, wavy shoulder-length hair and an ass like Jackie O, maybe a little fatter. I caught her at tha Dominican café on 4th Street. Actually, she caught me. I walked in and ordered my usual steak, red rice and fried bananas. When I walked outside, she was leaning on my car, talking to her friend. I hit the automatic start startling her.

"I'm sorry I didn't mean to scare you."

"It's OK. I guess I should not have been leaning on it in tha first place. You're cute Papi. Do you have a girlfriend?"

"Nope."

"Are you looking for one?" she said wit a seductive smile.

"It all depends on who's asking."

"I am Papi!"

"Well, in that case, Unh, Unh."

"Here's my number."

"Naw, take my number and you call me when you want to talk to me."

"Hold up," she said, pulling out her iPhone.

I gave her my number which stored instantly. And it's been on ever since.

"Papi, Papi, Papi."

"Oh huh."

"I said how about these?"

"Madi, whatever you put on you look good in."

"Stop you makin' me blush."

Madi was also a ride-or-die chick. Not to mention tha sex was off tha chain. After she was done trying on her clothes, I paid tha bill then we headed to tha Gucci store.

"Papi, I want to tell you something, but I don't want you to think that it's because you're buying me nice clothes either."

"Madi, for tha past six months, you've been my peeps and I haven't spent a dime on you until now."

"I know and I wanted to say this to you before, but I didn't want to scare you off."

"I hope this is not where she tells me she has herpes or some incurable disease," I thought to myself, *"that's probably why we have not had sex yet."*

She grabbed my hands, stop walking, looked me in tha eyes and said, "I understand if you choose to run after I say this." I know my face showed a look of concern.

"Papi, I love you and I have for a minute."

"Is that all you wanted to say?"

"Is that all? Do you know what it took for me to tell you that?"

She must have noticed tha look on my face.

"What did you think I was going to say? I had aids or something?"

When I didn't say nothing she said, "Pleeeeease yeah right! Papi, I've never even had an STD that alone aids." She said dead serious.

"I wasn't try'n to offend you, but when you said you didn't want to scare me off, what was I suppose to think?"

"Papi, you crazy, I said that because when you say those three words, men who are afraid of commitment normally run for tha exit."

"Madi, I have to be completely honest wit you."

"Is this tha part where you tell me that you're not ready for a relationship or that you have a girl?"

"Nah, this is tha part where I say that I really like you a lot, but I don't know if I can honestly say I love you."

"I didn't think you would Papi, which is fine by me. I'm not try'n to rush you into anything."

She started to say something else when my phone went off.

"Hold that thought. Talk to me."

"Everything is tooken care of."

"That's what's up, thanks Lex."

"I know, I know, Boy what would you do wit out me."

"Let's hope I never have to find out."

"How long are you gonna be up top?"

"I don't know, why?"

"Just asking; if you see something, I might like pick it up and I'll reimburse you."

"Lexi, I didn't come up here to shop for you. I came to bring Madi."

"Boy, you heard what I said; I love you, bye."

"Love you too Cuz. I'm sorry you were say'n."

"Umm I forgot."

"I bet you did."

"What's that suppose to mean?"

"Nothing. I don't know about you, but I'm hungry."

"So am I Papi."

We walked over to this Italian eatery to get some food.

"I think I want tha Parmesan shrimp and chicken wit garlic bread but can I have spaghetti noodles instead."

"Yes and you Ms.?"

"Umm, let me have tha shrimp and beef Alfredo wit garlic rolls and an ice tea."

"Oh, I'll take a bottle of spring water, please."

We talked while we ate our food. Wit tha decision that we would be a couple. After we finished shopping, I headed back home to handle some biz. My phone has been blowing up all afternoon.

"I'll be by later," I said as I was pulling up to her building.

"Okay, I'll be here; I'm not going nowhere Papi."

I called Swerve to see what was going on wit him. He let me know that he was sittin in tha park and to come thru…

I pulled up to the park 30 minutes later. It was J-Peed outside people everywhere. It was only 7 o'clock and they had tha grill blazing.

"Yo Heem over here."

"Asalamu Alaikum."

"Walaikum Salam. Yo you want a bite to eat or something?"

"Naw I'm cool, I just had some Italian."

"Yeah we had a bar-b-que for tha kids today."

"That's what's up. I'm going to need to holla at you in tha morning too."

"No doubt. I seen that Dominican Mami that you be talk'n to yesterday."

"Oh yeah."

Yeah, you need to put her on the team if you haven't by now."

"Why you say that?"

"Cause I knew she was ya peoples, so I tested her loyalty. I went at her she kept it 100; she said she didn't have a man, only a friend, but she was hoping that they would be a couple. I let her know that she could have more than one friend, she told me she don't get down like that. Long story short, you better snatch her up before somebody else does."

"Funny you said that I made it official today. So, what tha money lookin' like on ya end."

"You already know. You see how I've been gettin' at you every couple of days."

"Yeah, I noticed. That's why I'm upping your shipment to 10 bricks instead of tha 3 and 3. You don't have to buy any; I jus want you to stack ya paper."

"I need to come to tha table wit something."

"Heem, all you need to come to tha table wit is your loyalty and honesty. One thing about me is I make money. I don't let tha money make me!"

Well, I guess that's one other thing we have in common. Jeezy said it best when he said, "Look up in tha sky tell me what you see clouds nah nigga not me, I see Opportunity. I'm an opportunist; you heard what I said? I'm an opportunist, soft or hard. I get this cream; all these free agents better build ya team." I looked at Swerve's face; he was serious as a heart attack.

Heem, you have a lot of potential and wit me behind you, there's no way you won't make it to tha top."

After another 30 minutes, I told Swerve to hit me when he was ready.

"I'm ready right now if you ready. Let me call my peeps to see where she is at." It just so happened she was on 6th and Tatnall.

"I'm ready."

"A'ight Imma have somebody bring it around here."

I told Lexi to come down to tha park and to park on 6th and Madison. 10 minutes later, she was walking over to tha park.

"Lexi over here."

"Oh shit, Alexis, is your peoples?"

"Yeah, you know her?"

"Alexis, what's up," I said giving her a hug. No wonder my letters has been coming back tha last few months." I looked at both of them like what is going on.

"Heem, this is my baby. Heem, why didn't you say this was ya plug?"

"You didn't need to know."

"Boy, this is my best friend."

"Hold up, Swerve this is tha best friend you was talk'n bout when we was down?"

"Unh Huh."

"Talk about a small world. I tried to call you when I came home, but you changed your number."

"When Heem came home, he made me change my numbers."

I'll make sure to make a mental note of tha two things Heem did that was on point. When my man pulled up, I hit his phone and told him to put it in Alexis's car. Before she left, I made sure to get her number and give her mine. I couldn't wait to tell Jade I found her. She knew about her since I was in jail. I wanted her to know so she wouldn't think there was nothing going on between us.

"Swerve, I did not know you were talking about my cousin."

I moved her to a spot and told her not to bring nobody there. "Imma hit you when I'm ready, Insha Allāh it will be in a week if not sooner."

"Just take ya time and be safe."

No soon as I got in my car, a few shots rang out. I looked to see where they were coming from. I could tell it was coming from up on Jefferson because I could see people running from all directions.

CHAPTER 28

Knocked Up

It had been a whole year since Swerve had been home and we were happy as ever. Just think we had made a pact to never fall in love. What were we thinking about? I couldn't be happier, we weren't robbing niggaz anymore and my bank account was on swole. I ran to tha bathroom; I barely made it before I threw up. I think I had too much to drink last night. Shit, I still had to jump in tha shower and my doctor's appointment was in less than an hour.

I arrived at Dr. Jone's office wit five minutes to spare. I almost called and rescheduled. I feel sick as hell. I checked in and waited for my name to be called. I've been coming to Dr. Jones since I was a little girl.

"Jadeen, Dr. Jones will see you now," Nurse Taylor said wit a smile that would light up tha darkest room, "you know tha routine; Dr. Jones will be in in a minute."

I went into tha bathroom to put on tha gown.

"Hello, Jadeen."

"Hey, Dr. Jones, how are you doing today?"

"I'm doing fine and you?"

"I feel a little under tha weather today."

"Yes, and you look like it too."

Dr. Jones gave me my yearly exam and pap smear.

"I'll be back in a few," he said while walking out.

I went back into tha bathroom to put my clothes back on. I sat in tha chair and closed my eyes. "Jadeen, Jadeen."

"Huh, oh, I'm sorry, I must have dozed off."

"That's alright, everything came back fine. I also found out why you're feeling tha way you are."

"Please tell me it's not tha flu in tha middle of tha summer."

"No, it's not tha flu. Jadeen, you're 11 weeks pregnant."

"Pregnant!" I said at tha top of my voice, " I can't be. I haven't missed a period."

"Sometimes you don't."

"You said I'm 11 weeks?"

"Yeah, that gives you a due date of January 16. You are planning on keeping it, right?"

"Of course I am," I said wit a smile.

"Well, I want you to stop at tha desk so you can get an appointment for next week."

"A'ight," I said, heading for tha door.

Once I got in tha car, I just couldn't stop smiling. I just hope Swerve is as happy as I am. I called my mom to give her tha good news. She was more excited than me.

"I thought I would never be a Nana. What did Swerve say?"

"Mom, you're tha first to know."

"I'm tha first to know?"

I could hear Iciss asking first to know what? My mom wasted no time telling her she was going to be an aunt. I could hear her scream I'm bout to be an aunt! "Mom, I'll call you back. I need to call my baby's daddy."

When I called Swerve, he didn't answer but called me back in 15 minutes.

"Hey Babe, sorry I was handling something."

"That's okay. Are you still busy?"

"No, why, what's up?"

"Just wanted to hear ya voice."

"Jade, you hungry?"

"Yeah, I was about to go to TGI Fridays."

"Wit who?"

"By myself."

"Come pick me up at tha park. If I'm not here, I'll be on 8th."

I pulled up, bumping that new Jay-Z "It Is Wht It Is."

He motioned for me to pull over. Some girls walked in front of my car and then stopped. I turn my music down. I could've sworn I heard one of them say yeah, that's his bitch. Then they had the nerve to sit on my shit.

I got out, "Excuse me," I said.

They acted like they didn't hear me, so I walked up to them.

"Excuse me, but could you get off my car." Neither of them moved.

"I tried to be nice bitch; if you don't get ya dirty ass off my car."

"Who are you talking to?" tha one wit tha messed up weave said.

"Both, you dusty bitches."

"I'll fuck you up."

By now, Killer had came across tha street.

"What tha fuck is going on?"

"These two broads gon' sit on my shit like I wasn't in there. When I asked them nicely to move, they ignored me. So, I told them to get tha fuck off my car." The next thing I knew, one of them hit me in the back of my head.

"Oh Bitch you got tha right one," I popped my trunk and took my air max out.

Swerve came running down tha street.

"What tha fuck is going on?"

Killer filled him in while I put my sneaks on.

"Who hit her?"

"I did."

"Jade, just get in tha car."

"You got me fucked up."

"Bitch you better listen and get ya pretty ass in tha car."

"Jade fuck this bitch up," Killer said.

"Oh, believe I am."

Swerve never seen me fight, so he probably assumed I was just a pretty face. Long story short, I beat tha bullshit outta her.

Her friend said, "You lucky I'm pregnant."

"Bitch, what does that mean? So am I."

Swerve looked at me and said, "What?" I was still pissed and I let him know it.

"Mafucka, you heard me; I'm 11 weeks pregnant! You must be fucking that dirty bitch for her to be acting like that."

"Yeah right, Jade, don't disrespect me. I've been nothing but faithful to you. That's tha problem. I won't fuck her or none of tha other ones for that matter," he looked at her and then said, "if anything is wrong wit my seed, you'll be on tha back of a milk box."

"Are you threatening me because I have my cousin…" (Smack)

Before she could finish Killer smacked tha shit outta her.

"Bitch tell ya cousin that."

"Nigga and you gon' get dealt wit," she said, calling somebody on her phone.

"Nitty, this Mafucka Killer just smack me."

"Nitty that bitch ass nigga he no what tha deal is."

"He know me, fuck that nigga. Matter a fact, tell him I'm on my way over there."

As soon as she hung up, Killer's phone went off.

"What Nigga?"

"If you want to get this started Nigga we can."

"Mafucka, you know my work."

"Bitch you better try another cousin."

"You gon' get yours," she said, walking off.

"That bitch scratched me on my face."

"You a'ight, you can barely see it. So, I'm bout to be a daddy," he said wit a big smile.

"Yup."

"Why didn't you say something?"

"I was at lunch."

"So, do you still want to have lunch?"

"Yes I do."

"Yo, I'm bout to go to lunch; I'll hit ya phone when I'm done so we can handle that."

"A'ight, aye Jade."

"Yeah."

"You got hands too."

"I know you thought I was just a pretty face wit no fight game."

"You ain't never lie. If I would have known you was knocked up I would never let you fight her."

When we pulled up to TGI Fridays, there wasn't that many cars in tha parking lot.

"Maybe I should buy you a minivan."

"For what? I'm only having one child not four."

"Hello, table for two?"

"Yes please," I said not giving Swerve a chance to speak.

"Smoking or Non?"

"Non please."

"Ok follow me." She took us to a nice, secluded table.

"What would you like to drink?"

"I'll have a bottle of spring water."

"Me too, please. Actually, I already know what I want. I'll take the Jack Daniel's steak and shrimp."

"You can give me tha sizzling chicken and shrimp."

"OK, I'll be back."

"I'm sorry, how do you want ya steak?"

"Well done."

"So, when did you find out you were pregnant?"

"Today, when I went to get my yearly checkup. I didn't think you would be as happy as you are."

"Why not?"

"I don't know. I just thought maybe you didn't want any kids."

"Jade, I'm 28 wit no kids. This will slow me down; I'm thinking about getting out of tha game anyway. I have more money then I can spend in a lifetime. So, what do you want?"

"I don't even need to ask you want a boy."

"Actually, I want a girl."

"That's a first; most men want their firstborn to be a boy."

"Not me, I want a little diva."

"Well, I want a son."

We talked while we ate about everything.

"I know between tha both of us this child is going to have everything. I want to go to all your doctor's appointments wit you. I need to know everything that's going on."

"Well, I have one next Wednesday at 10 o'clock."

"Don't you mean we have an appointment at 10 o'clock."

"I'm sorry baby daddy." We both busted out laughing.

"Baby I love you."

"And me you Ms. Jadeen."

There were all types of police when we pulled back up. They had tha middle of tha block taped off.

"Baby I'm going around tha block."

As soon as I turned tha corner Killer jumped off tha steps. Jade unlocked tha door so he could get in.

"What tha fuck happen around here?"

"That Bitch had somebody come through here shootin'. All they did was shoot a few innocent bystanders."

"Where were you at?"

"Sittin' right here."

"You don't know who it was?"

"I'm not 100% sure, but it look like that nut ass nigga Wisher."

"Babe ride thru tha hill real quick."

"Where, by tha park?"

"Yeah."

When I rode through Killer told me to pull over right in front of them. I hit what needed to be hit and my secret compartment opened up revealing to twin 9's.

Swerve took one and handed Killer tha other one. They both got out and walked toward tha crowd.

"Swerve, what up Baby Boy?"

"I can't call it Casey. Yo Wisher, let me holla at you for a sec."

"What's up?"

"Yo, Candice ya peeps, right?"

"Yeah and?"

"A few people saw you earlier when you came thru and shot tha block up. First of all, if you got a problem then deal wit tha problem. Two people who didn't have shit to do wit it got hit."

"Man, ain't try'n to hear that shit!"

"Nigga you a bitch always have been always will be. You accidentally shot a nigga now you runnin' around like you some killer." (Ha! Ha! Ha!)

"Yeah right," Killer said.

Wisher went to reach for his pistol.

"Don't even think about it," Swerve said wit his pistol already pointed at its chest, "nigga you shouldn't have put ya hands on her. When you rode by you seen me sittin' on tha steps you should have shot me or at me. All Imma say is tha only reason Imma let you live is because it's too many witnesses out here."

Casey and tha rest just looked on.

"Swerve let me Holla at you real quick."

"Killer take his pistol just in case he try some funny shit."

After he got his gun he emptied tha clip and tha chamber then handed it back.

"What up Casey?"

"Listen we ain't got shit to do wit that. I told that nigga don't bring that dumb shit up here."

"Casey I don't got no beef wit yall but ya boy he crossed tha line. So get a good picture and go ahead and get ya shirt made."

"What shirt?"

"Ya in memory of shirt. He's outta here like yesterday."

Hey man handle yours, but on another note I need two pies."

"When you need 'em?"

"A.S.A.P. but I only got 45 stacks."

"I gotcha Imma call ya phone in 30 or 40 minutes."

"No doubt, Swerve, no doubt."

"Killer come on we out of here. Imma see both of yall niggaz."

POP, POP, POP , BONG, BONG, BONG, POP, BONG, POP, POP, BONG, BONG.

We all hit tha deck not knowing what was going on.

"Oh My God somebody call an ambulance!" one girl said holding wishers head.

"Pleeeeease Somebody Heeelp Meee!" she wailed.

That was my cue to get outta there. We got in tha car just as tha police were pulling up.

"Put those guns back. You can drop us off back on 8th."

"Somebody saved us that time of having to kill that faggot."

"Well, they can't put that on us."

"Yo I need you to holla at Casey he needs two pies for 45."

"A'ight, what was he talkin' bout anyway?"

"Just that they didn't have nothing to do wit it. I will shoot to tha spot for a while."

"Right spend some time wifey."

"Baby, where you parked at?"

"Killer came and picked me up. I need to get some rest I'm tired as hell."

CHAPTER 29

R.I.P.

"There they are right there. Slow down."

POP, POP, POP,BONG BONG, BONG, POP, BONG, POP, POP, BONG, BONG.

"I hit him, pull off."

The only sounds you heard where that of screeching tires.

"Follow that stop sign we don't need to draw no attention to ourselves."

"What did Wisher do?"

"I don't really know we'll find out later. I need to start going back to the range."

"For what?"

"I only hit him five times."

"Bitch please, you only let off six shots."

"Yeah, six shots that should have hit him. Let's dump this car and grab something to eat."

"That's tha best thing you said all day."

"Let me make this call. Hello, Mission accomplished. OK we're going to get something to eat. I'll call you when we're done."

"Did you remember to fill tha gas can?"

"Stop asking questions you already know tha answers to."

"I'm just making sure."

"Shut up and drive."

CHAPTER 30

Engaged

It was 6 o'clock when I woke up. I decided to run to tha mall and pick Jade up a nice gift.

"Jade, I'm going out. I'll be back in a few. Do you need anything while I'm out?"

"No, but if I do, I'll call you on your cell."

I went to tha Concord Mall first but didn't see anything I wanted, so I went to Whitehurst in Christiana Mall.

"Wow, this is exactly what I'm looking for. How much is this?"

"4500, its worth every bit of it." I was going to use cash but decided to use my debit card instead.

"Would you like me to gift wrap this?"

"No that's a'ight, thanks anyway."

"No thank you and please come again."

On my way home I called Jade to make sure she didn't want anything since she didn't call.

"Hey Baby."

"Hey Sweety, was you sleep?"

"Yeah but I was about to get up."

"Do you want something to eat?"

"Baby I got a taste for some KFC."

"OK."

"Get me two piece breast and wing spicy wit a soft chicken taco. I don't need nothing to drink I have water here."

"Gotcha, be there in a few love you."

"And I you."

Jade was definitely a keeper and now that she was giving me tha most precious gift in tha world she definitely was worthy of this gift I was going to give her tomorrow over a romantic dinner and evening. I'll called Turk and Bre to tell them what I had in store. They were more then willing to help me pull this off.

"Jade."

"I am upstairs."

I walked into tha bedroom to find Jade naked on tha bed putting lotion on. She finished up then put on one of her sexy nightgowns.

"Here's your food."

"Where you going at?"

"To take a shower."

"You not going out tonight?"

"Nah, I'm staying in wit my wifey."

"Wow, what do I owe this?"

"Can't I just stay in wit you because I love you?"

"Yup, you sure can."

We watched Obsessed wit Beyoncé and my favorite movie Scarface until we fell asleep.

Tha next morning I woke up feeling a little tired. Jade was already up and dressed. I looked at tha clock on tha nightstand and it read 11 o'clock.

"I was just about to leave you a note."

"A note saying what?"

"Just that I was going out wit my girls for tha day."

"Okay, enjoy your day and I'll see you later. Oh yeah, don't eat too much; I'm taking you to dinner tonight." (Beep, Beep)

"That's Turk and Bre, I'll see you later," she said giving me a hug and a kiss.

As soon as she was out tha door, I called Turk to thank her and Bre.

"Anytime, you just handle your end."

It was a hot day outside. I went to Thriftway to get everything I needed for dinner. I decided to cook Jade's favorite meal fish, shrimp, crabcakes and fried potatoes. I was doing so much running around that I had lost track of time.

"May I help you Sir?"

"Yes, let me get this in a medium if you have it."

"Let me go in tha back and see."

She returned holding tha same exact thing but in peach and pink.

"We only have it in this color, but it's a medium."

"I'll take it."

"Will that be all today?"

I walked over to tha other section and looked until I found what I was looking for.

"That will be all."

On my way to tha counter, I grabbed two bottles of body spray. By tha time I finally got dinner started, it was close to 6:30.

"Friends, how many of us have them, friends, one we can depend on."

"What up Turk?"

"Are you almost done? She keeps on say'n that she needs to get home."

"You can bring her."

"A'ight, oh and congrats on tha baby."

"Thank you."

I had it set up as romantic as I could get it.

When we pulled up it was dark, had it not been for Swerve's car in tha driveway I would have thought he had left.

"Enjoy your dinner; call us tomorrow."

"I will."

I opened tha door to tha soft sounds of Mary J. Blige. Tha dining room was dim wit candles burning on tha table.

"I see you made it home."

"What smells so good in here?"

"Dinner, I decided to cook instead of going out."

"You cooked?"

"Yup, that's one of my hidden talents. Before you eat go take a warm bath, tha water is already ready for you. When you're done put what's on tha bed on."

I got upstairs and went straight to tha bathroom. I slipped my clothes off and eased into tha warm bubble bath. It felt so good I dozed off only to wake up 20 minutes later. Once I dried off I headed to tha bedroom.

"Unh, Unh, Unh, my baby really went all out."

I opened tha Victoria's Secret box to find tha prettiest nightgown and matching panties, bra and robe. I quickly put everything on after I put cucumber melon all over my body. I was going to make sure I didn't get fat and out of shape after I have tha baby.

"I was about to come check on you. I thought you drowned. Wow, that looks good on you."

"I'm loving it."

"I didn't know whether to get you a thong or bikini panties so I just got both."

"I noticed and I put these on," she said, standing up, lifting her robe and nightgown, exposing her fat ass.

As if that wasn't enough, she made it bounce like a ball, giving me an instant erection.

"Sit down and eat before you get yaself into trouble."

"Wheeew this shit is banging; damn Baby I did not know you could burn like this."

We sat there and talked when we were done eating.

"Baby, I love you and thanks for this romantic evening."

"Your very welcome, but on some real shit. Jade these past 3 ½ years have meant a lot to me."

"Me too Baby."

"Jade, I've never loved another woman tha way I love you."

"And vice versa."

"I could see spending tha rest of my life wit you."

"They say great minds think alike."

I got up from tha table and walked around to her.

"Jadeen, I love you more than words could ever show," I kneeled down and took her hand, "before you all tha other broads never love me only my money. You've show me tha true meaning of love and I don't want to lose that."

"Neither do I Swerve."

"Jadeen will you marry me?" I said reaching in my pocket and pulling out that huge rock.

"OOOOOH MY GOD," she said wit tears in her eyes, "YEEEES, YEEEES, YEEEES I WILL MARRY YOU."

I slid that ring on her finger.

"If he like you then he would've put a ring on it," she said standing doing Beyoncé's dance.

That night we made tha best love we ever made.

When I woke up I had to look on my finger to make sure last night wasn't a dream. I couldn't believe it I was engaged. I looked over at my fiancé and kissed him on his forehead. I picked up tha phone and called my mom.

"Good morning Mom."

"Same to you Jadeen."

"Mom guess what?"

"You hit tha Powerball."

"Mom."

"Can I make a joke?"

"Swerve proposed to me."

"I know."

"You know?"

"Yes, he called to get my blessing. That's a pretty big rock you got."

"You seen tha ring too?"

"No, but hey told me how much he paid for it, so I assume it's big."

"Mom it's huge."

"Well, we had to set a date and all that good stuff."

"I know it won't be til after I have my baby, that's for sure."

I looked over at my future husband who was smiling wit his eyes closed.

I tapped him on his side, "You ain't sleep."

"I know I'm just laying here listening to you. Tell Ms. Sadie I said hello."

"Mom Swerve said hi."

"I heard him and tell him from now on drop tha Ms. Sadie and call me mom."

"She said from here on out call her mom."

"Ok Mom," he said loud enough for her to hear him.

"It's been a surprising week for you. First a baby and now an engagement."

"Where's Iciss?"

"She stayed wit Chas last night. I'll make sure she knows tha good news when she comes home. Well, she is too old to be a flower girl."

"She can be a bridesmaid wit Turk, Bre, Chas and Alexis." Me and Alexis had gotton real cool since she was a big part of Swerve's life.

"Jade, let me let you go. I'm bout to go to tha market."

"I'll talk to you later Mom."

"How you gonna ask my mom for permission to marry me?"

"It was more like her blessing."

"Did Turk and Bre have something to do with this?"

"I plead the 5th."

"I bet you do. Baby that dinner you cooked last night was tha bomb. Especially those homemade shrimp crab cakes."

"Why thank you My Lady."

"I told my boss that when I get seven months I would be taking maternity leave. I just want to lay in bed all day today."

"Sounds good to me."

"Boy please, tha minute any of those phones go off, you'll be up and out tha door."

"I'm not even going to cut my phones on."

"Yeah right."

"Tha only one that's on is my emergency phone, so as long as that don't ring, you're stuck wit me today."

She looked at me seductively and said, "That's not a bad thing."

Next thing I know we were at it again. This went on for most of tha day. It felt good not having to run around all day.

"Baby we need to do this more often."

"What, make love all day."

"No not just that, I'm talking about us spending time together."

"I think you're gonna get tired of me in tha next six months."

"I doubt it."

"Do you want to go over moms house for dinner tonight?"

"What is she cooking?"

"I don't know but I'll find out."

She picked up tha phone and called her mom.

"Hello."

"Hey Mom, what you cooking for dinner?"

"Just some beef and chicken yack, nothing major."

"Is there enough for two?"

"You and tha baby coming over?"

"In that case three."

"Three."

"Yes me, tha baby and my future husband," I said, rubbing his chest.

"What time are you guys coming?"

"We'll be there by 8 o'clock."

"A'ight I'll see you when you get here."

"Let's jump in the shower."

"After you," I said looking at her flawless body.

I smiled to myself because since she knew I was watching her she made her ass jiggle when she walked. When we finished in tha shower we were both exhausted. We laid across tha bed in each other arms. Before we knew it we were fast asleep.

CHAPTER 31

Pay Me My Money

"Mafucka, where is my money?" (Smack)

"Imma pay you Nigga." (Smack)

"Who you talking to? You got two hours to have my money or you can kiss da baby!"

I knew tha minute I let him go he was not going to be found.

"Listen, I would advise you to call who ever you got to call to get my money here in tha next hour."

"I need more time." (Smack)

"Mafucka wrong answer!" (Smack) (Smack) Boom, Boom Two shots, one in tha middle of his head tha other in his chest.

"Now all of this could've been avoided If he would've just gave my money back."

"Come on let's get outta here before tha police come."

"Ain't nobody going to call tha cops. Hell, they all applauded when you pumped that hotness in his punk ass."

"It's crazy how that one nigga was shakin' down tha whole town like he was Omar from tha Wire."

"That nigga won't be doing shit now!"

"Yo Fresh ya girl ain't got no friends?"

"Yeah, but they spoken for."

"I need me a thurl broad like yours."

"Man, it's plenty of them out there you just have to find her."

"Man fuck that dumb shit I'll just keep knocking 'em off until I find tha right one."

"Shotz you crazy as shit. Did Lil' Gene hit you wit that paper yet?"

"Nah, but he told me he would be ready today."

"He better, he's been on that same pack for tha past two weeks."

"I know it don't take that long to knock off a big eight. We ain't play'n wit Niggaz no more. So, what's th deal wit ya young boy from tha hill?"

"Which one?"

"Nigga you know who I'm talking bout."

"Ain't nothing up wit him; he's bringing in that money."

"I don't know what it is about him that I don't like."

"Shotz you don't like nobody. If it was up to you tha whole Wilmington would be in tha boneyard."

"Fo' sho my nigga."

Shotz was my ace he just came home from beating an attempt charge. The DA knew she didn't have a case but you know how them crackers uptown play. Shotz sat for nine months, I made sure his books was stacked. I also had a trap so he was tight on tha weed. Me and Shotz were like brothers there's nothing and I mean nothing we won't do for one another. Just as we walked into tha park Turk pulled up.

"There go wifey."

"I know, she's gon' get out." When she did she was hurting that Dior Homme dress and she knew it too.

"Hey, you," she said walking towards me wit tha prettiest smile.

I couldn't resist I had to grab her butt when she hugged me.

"Soft ain't it," she whispered in my ear.

"Aye, Turk not to be ignorant but are those your real eyes?"

"Yeah."

"You don't have no sisters?"

"Nah sorry. Shotz you probably got broads all over you."

"Yeah, but they not thurl like you."

"I'll take that as a compliment and say thank you."

"You're more than welcome. Fuck!"

"What's up Shotz?"

"That's tha chick I was telling you about."

"Where?"

"Right there," he said pointing to the Acura that was parking on tha corner.

"Damn playa that happens when you don't keep tha lion tamed."

"We ain't had sex and we not. Could you imagine how she would act if I hit that."

"Hey Shotz."

"What's up Nye?"

"Why you ain't been answering ya phone?"

"Which one?"

"Tha 5042 number."

"I got that changed a few weeks ago," I was lying, but she didn't know.

She pulled out her phone, pushed a couple buttons, then put it to her ear. I felt my phone vibrate, I almost answered it until I realized that it was Nye calling me. I played along.

"Damn you gonna get on tha phone while I'm right here?"

"No, I was actually calling your phone to see if you really lost it or not."

"Yo you crazy for real."

"So, are you going to give me tha new number or what?"

"Nye Imma keep it real wit you. I don't want to get involved wit you."

"I'm not good enough for you?" It wasn't that; Nye was bad as a mafucka, 5'6, brown eyes, bronze skin, hair to tha back of her neck and an ass that Delicious from Flavor of Love would be jealous of.

"It's tha way you be, uh, let's see, what's tha word I'm looking for?"

"Stalking," Fresh said.

"Yeah, that's the word I was looking for."

"Hey, I thought guys like that type of attention."

"Some do just not me."

"I know now, well take my number and when you're ready give me a call."

Shotz took her number and let her know he would indeed call her.

"She's pretty Shotz."

"I know, I never said she wasn't. I just said she was a stalker."

"Well, now you know why."

"Fresh Imma hit ya phone I gotta handle something."

"A'ight," I said walking wit her to her car.

"We are supposed to be having dinner wit Jade and Swerve tonight."

"I know he called me earlier to tell me."

"Did he tell you he proposed to Jade?"

"No, he didn't tell me that one."

"I'm hungry."

"I could use a bite to eat myself."

"Let's go to Minato's I got a taste for some shrimp fried rice wit crab meat."

"You better call and order now 'cause you already know."

We got our food and decided to go to Battery Park and have a picnic.

"I know your birthday is coming up. What do you want?"

She looked at me and then said, "Whatever you get me, I'll be OK wit."

What do you get a person that has everything already? For tha past year me and Turk have been going strong. I've never dealt with a female on her level before; all tha other broads I dealt wit were young and immature. My phone went off but I didn't answer. Then it started to ring again.

"Baby, it must be important they keep calling."

"This is our time right now; they can wait," I said, wit more attitude than attended.

"Well excuse me."

"I didn't mean to come off on you like that, I'm sorry."

"Apology accepted."

We finished our lunch and then headed back in town.

"What time is tha dinner tonight?"

"8 o'clock Jade said but you know Black people ain't neva on time."

(Ha! Ha! Ha!)

"Ain't that tha truth. We don't have to get all dressed, do we?"

"No," Turks phone went off, "talked her up, hold on. Hello. Hey, Unh, Unh, sure no problem at 9 o'clock see you there. Well, I've just been informed that dinner will be at tha Hotel DuPont instead of their house."

"So that means I have to get dressed up."

"Do you have anything to wear?"

"Yes I do. You gonna ask that?"

Baby for tha past year I've neva seen you in a shoe."

"I just don't like wearing them."

"Well, I'm gon' shoot up top to Blondies to get some shoes."

"Do you want some company?"

"Now why would you asked me something like that, of course I do."

"Take me by my house so I can grab a few dollars."

As I was about to get in tha car, Teddy walked up.

"Aye Fresh."

"What up Teddy?"

"Yo did you hear about Eva?"

"Nah."

"She was fighting some dude."

"Fighting a dude?"

"Yeah, that is what Shell told me. She said that tha dude came up talk'n bout she set his brother up or something like that."

"A'ight, good-lookin' Teddy."

When I got in tha car Turk wanted to know if everything was OK.

"Yeah, let's go."

I called Shotz, who told me the same story Teddy did.

"Shotz find out what's going on then hit me back."

"You still wit wifey?"

"Yeah, I'm about to go up top."

"Cool, I'll hit you if I find out anything."

An hour later we were try'n to find a parking spot on South Street.

"Hold up, hold up right there."

"Were Baby?" I pointed to show her where somebody was pulling out.

"Good thing you spotted this because I was about to turn up there."

"Here's some change for tha meter."

I put in as much change as tha meter would take since I knew we would be up here for a while. We walked two blocks to Blondies.

"I'm going next-door while you're in there."

Sal was a fat Italian who had a nice collection of shoes. I had something already but I wanted to grab a few pair of shoes to add to my arsenal. I ended up wit three pair of shoes that cost a pretty penny. Turk was coming out at tha same time I was.

"Did you buy enough shoes?"

"I was going to ask you tha same thing," I said, wit a smile. We drop tha bags off at tha car so we wouldn't have to lug them around wit us. By tha time we finished shopping it was close to 6 o'clock.

"We better get going so we don't be late to tha dinner party."

Turk dropped me off home, I let her know that I would pick her up by 8:30.

CHAPTER 32

Dinner Party

I was so excited to be having this dinner party. Everybody that was in tha wedding would be attending. My stomach was getting big, instead of 6 ½ months I look like I was due any day. I found out we were having a boy. There was no secret he would be a junior. Swerve wanted to name him Aziz which meant mighty. I let him know my sons name would be Ahmad Jones just like his daddy. He eventually left it alone because he was in a no-win situation. We had planned our wedding for April. I wanted a spring wedding. We did agree that tha colors would be ivory and pink.

"Babe, I'm home."

"It's about time you better take a shower and get dressed."

I know I have been really getting on his nerves. My doctor told us it was normal to have mood swings. My sex drive has really increased. Even though wit my big stomach we were limited in positions Swerve didn't mind doggy style since it was his favorite anyway.

"What time did you make tha reservations for?"

"9:30 but I told everybody 9 o'clock; you know Black people ain't neva on time anyway. It's only 8 o'clock," I said as I looked at him seductively.

"You know they say great minds think alike," he said, removing his towel and exposing all 10 inches of his manhood. Just tha sight of it had my juices flowing.

"Shit, we going to be late to our own dinner," he said while still pumping all 10 inches inside of me.

"OOOOOH BBBBABY, I'm CUUUMING!"

"Damn me too."

"UUUMM, AAAAHH," we both said releasing at tha same time. We both collapsed on tha bed breathing hard. By tha time we got dressed and made it to tha hotel it was 9:25.

Everybody was already there when we walked in.

"We thought we were going to have to send out and APB on yall." We looked at each other and busted out laughing.

"EEEEEL yall so nasty," Bre said.

We spoke to everybody and then sat down.

"So how is tha pregnancy going?" my aunt asked.

"Moody," Swerve said. Everybody included me busted out laughing.

"Yall laughin', but yall don't have to deal wit it."

"Boy you a'ight," Chas said still laugh'n."

We had a nice time everybody said who they wanted to walk wit down tha aisle. I wasn't surprised because that's how I pretty much paired them up. Bre and Maze, Turk and Fresh, Chas and Tiz, Iciss and Heem, and Alexis and Killer. My wedding was going to be tha wedding of tha century.

The next few months was tha same ol' thing. My mood swings calm down but my hormones were in overdrive. Dr. Jones said it was good for me to have sex. I didn't gain too much weight; I don't know if it's because I still worked out during my pregnancy. The few pounds I did gained went to my hips and ass. Swerve said he loved me better wit tha added weight. I didn't even have stretch marks thanks to tha cocoa butter Swerve constantly rubbed on my stomach. I was a few days overdue and I was more than ready to have my son.

"Baby I have to go to Philly to check on something."

"Can you drop me off at moms?"

"Yeah."

"Let me know when you're ready."

"I'm ready when you are."

"Give me a few minutes to use the bathroom."

When I got downstairs Swerve was rolling up some Sour D.

"I can't wait to blow some of that."

"I bet you can't."

Iciss was out front talk'n to two girls when we pulled up.

"What tha deal Lil Sis?"

"Nothing. Look at you look'n like you bout to explode."

"Shut up; where mommy?"

"In tha kitchen cooking."

"I'll call you when I get back." "OK love you."

"And me you."

"Brother, where are you going?"

"None of ya biz-ness."

"Philly to handle something."

"We haven't been shoppin' in a while."

"I know; we can go next weekend."

"OK, Imma hold you to that."

I looked at my watch.

"Matter fact, tell mom you going wit me."

"Unh, Unh," I said. She came back out in a flash.

"Can my friends come?"

"As long as their parents know."

They both pulled out their cell phones after a couple minutes they said, "Let's roll."

"Swerve, don't smoke that wit them in tha car."

"Jade go in tha house," I said, pulling off.

As soon as I got on tha highway, I lit my weed up.

"Let me know if tha smoke bothers yall." They all started laugh'n.

I looked at Iciss, "I know you ain't smoking."

"I'll be 18 in a few months. Mommy knows I'll be smoking."

"No, she don't; stop lying."

"Call her then, better yet," she pulled out her phone and called. "Mom, hold on; Swerve want to ask you something."

"Mom. Do you know Iciss smoke weed? Oh OK." I passed her tha phone back.

"I told you."

"Yeah, you sure did."

She turned to her friends, "Light it up."

"Hold on, hold on. Where yall get that?"

"Some boy."

"Let me see."

I lit it, then smelled it, "Iciss this shit dirt." I rolled down my window and threw their blunt out.

"Why did you do that? You didn't have to smoke it."

"Yeah, yeah, but yall not smoking that dirt in my car."

I took a couple of pulls and passed them the weed.

"Now, this is what you call fire." Iciss started choking.

"Oh My God, what kind of weed is this?"

"Sour D," I said wit a big smile.

After her girls hit it, they were high as shit.

"This tha best weed we ever smoked."

"And tha most expensive you ever had also. What are you going to get?"

"A few more things for A.J."

"You don't think he has enough stuff already?"

"He could never have enough, plus they called to let me know they just got a new shipment in this morning."

I lucked up on a spot right in front of Unica For Kids.

"Here, take this and do what you can wit it. Before you say anything, I know it's not a lot, but you will make it work." I watched as she counted it, walking down the street.

"How much did he give you Iciss?"

"Hold on, let me finish counting. Imma make it work; he gave me $1,900."

"He said that's not a lot."

"It's not; I normally get at least 3,500."

"Girl, I'm lucky to get a nickel."

"A nickel, huh I'm lucky to get 200."

"Well between mom, Jade and Swerve they kinda spoil me."

"Kinda, Iciss I haven't seen you wear tha same outfit twice not to mention all tha high price name brand stuff."

"I know that once they have A.J. I won't be getting too much from them."

"Girl, yeah right; if that was tha case, you damn sure wouldn't have gotton that," she said, pointing to tha money in my hand."

"Time will tell." I had gotten A.J. everything new they had in.

"You're going to be giving a lot of tha stuff away."

"Why do you say that?"

"Because your son is going to outgrow most of tha stuff before he even has a chance to wear it."

"That's why I got all different sizes, so he should be straight for his first year."

"You going to see other things you like and buy them."

"Yeah you're probably right."

"Ain't no probably, I am right and that's not including what me, Mommy and Jade buy."

An hour later, we were back at Ms. Sady's.

"Unh, Unh, Unh, I knew you was going to come back wit a lot of bags."

"This is not a lot of bags."

"Well, did you bring me back anything?"

"As a matter of fact, we did."

"What and where is it?"

"Baby clothes and they're in tha car."

"I said me not A.J."

"It is for you, Iciss," said wit a big smile.

"Swerve, I know you didn't buy that baby no more clothes. He already has more than enough. You gonna spoil my grandbaby rotton."

"Like you can say anything Mom."

"I know I'm starving like a hostage."

"Me too."

"Yall didn't eat while yall was out."

"Evidently not if they are hungry."

"Don't defend them Mom."

"Baby, I know you ain't mad because we did a little shoppin'?"

"You damn right I am!"

"Why?"

"What do you mean why?"

"First off, you knew I wanted to go shopping."

"Jade, you still can go shopping this weekend."

"AAAAAH Shit!"

"What's wrong?"

"Your son just kicked tha shit out of me."

"He ready to come out of there."

"You think."

A few minutes passed and he did it again. Next thing I knew, my leg was wet.

"Oh My God, I think it's time."

"AAAAAH!"

"Yeah she's having contractions."

"AAAAAH, AAAAAH SHIIIIIIIT get me to the hospital now!

CHAPTER 33

A.J.

I pulled into tha emergency exit at tha hospital.

"Sir, you can't park there."

"My wife is in labor."

"AAAAAH, It feels like he's coming out.

By now, a few nurses and Dr. Jones were out wit a gurney. Ms. Sady had taken tha liberty to call Dr. Jones. By tha time they got Jade into one of tha maternity rooms, A.J. was more than ready to make his world debut.

"Jadeen, give me one long hard push." I took a deep breath and pushed as hard as I could.

"Oh My God, I'm not having no more children."

"Babe, keep pushing. I see his head."

"I am pushing!"

"Remember what they taught you in Lamaze class 1, 2, 3, Breathe."

"That's easy for you to say you're not tha one wit ya legs spread open!"

"Jadeen, one hard push should do it."

"UNHHHH!"

When I seen my son come out wit all that hair, I was in awe. I know it was his job, but when Dr. Jones smacked him on his ass, I almost lost it.

"Mafucka, don't you ever put ya hands on my son again."

"Baby, that's his job to do that." A.J. was crying real loud.

"I'm sorry Dr. Jones."

"It's OK; you're not tha first and you definitely won't be tha last to snap."

Once they had all tha blood and white stuff off I could see my firstborn. He looks just like me wit tha exception of those gray eyes like Jade, Iciss, and Ms. Sady. As soon as Iciss and Ms. Sady saw him, it was love at first sight.

"Look at Mom-Mom baby; he is so precious. All this pretty hair looking just like your daddy, yes you do."

"Well, at least he has our eyes," Iciss said.

"Mom let me hold him. Hey, you Aunty's little man, yes you are."

I couldn't take my eyes off him. My first child and he was a bonafide dime wit out question.

"Baby, when you bring his outfit, make sure you bring something tight."

"Don't worry, I got tha perfect outfit. I'll be back in a hour or so."

"Mom, I had A.J. natural, no sedatives or nothing."

"How much did he weigh?"

"7 lbs. 6 oz."

"Are you serious?"

"Yup."

"That's how much you weighed."

Most babies come out light and A.J. came out bronze.

"Mommy, little man is going to be a lady killer."

My mom and Iciss took turns holding him.

"Yall not going to spoil him."

Swerve came back a few hours later.

"Unh, Unh, Unh look at you that don't make no sense."

"I had to have a smoke."

"Well, did you remember to bring our clothes back wit you?"

"Shit, I knew I was forgetting something."

"That was tha whole purpose of you leaving, wasn't it?"

"I forgot it in tha car, not at home."

"Oh, I thought you meant home."

"Naw, I'll be right back."

When he came back, he had A.J.'s Gucci diaper bag and car seat.

"Let me see what you got him to get his first pictures taken in."

He had bought him a pair of Gucci jeans wit a Gucci button-up and loafers.

"Wow, I didn't know they made Gucci this small."

"Yeah, they got this store up top called Gucci For Kids. They got it all and so does A.J."

"I'm feeling this," my mom said, holding up tha jeans and shirt.

"Well, we're leaving, but we will be back tomorrow."

"OK." They both kiss A.J. and then left.

"Baby, you know we got to get a family portrait taken."

"I'm already ahead of you."

"I'm only going to be in here for two days."

"WAAAA, WAAAAA," A.J. started to cry.

"It's time for his bottle, do you want to feed him?"

"Yeah, let me start getting my practice in now."

"Yeah, 'cause we going to be taking turns doing this."

"You said that like I got a problem wit it."

"I don't know, you might."

"Anything that has to do wit my son I don't have a problem wit it."

"Remember you said that."

"Home Sweet Home, I can't wait to smoke me a blunt and take a hot bath. Baby, we going to need a bigger house," I said, looking around seeing nothing but A.J.'s stuff.

"I know, but for now, we straight."

I already had a house being built from tha ground up, which would be ready in another 6 or 7 months. A year ago, I had asked Jade to describe her dream house; what she didn't know was tha house was being built. Insha Allāh, it will be done by tha time we get married. I was in A.J.'s room, putting his clothes away when tha doorbell rang.

"Ahmad, can you get that? I'm putting my clothes on."

Jade has started calling me by my government tha last few months. By the time I got downstairs, tha front door was coming open.

"I know yall hear tha doorbell, Bre said, walking in.

"If you give somebody a chance to get downstairs."

"Boy, where is my godson?" Just as she was asking, Jade was coming downstairs wit A.J.

"All of that hair, Oh My God." Turk put her hands out to get him.

"He's sleep." As soon as she said that he opened his eyes.

"Bre look at his eyes."

"Wow, yall not going to be able to keep tha broads off of him. He looks like a Dominican wit gray eyes. A.J. if you don't look just like your daddy wit ya mom's eyes."

"Hello," Ms. Sady said, walking in wit Iciss on her heels.

"There go, Mom-Mom baby."

"Hey Aunt Turk, Aunt Bre."

"Hey Iciss. Where's Chas?"

"Home, I think."

"I tried to call her, but it keeps going to her voicemail."

"Mom let me take his picture so I can put it on my Facebook page and use it as my screensaver on my phone."

Iciss got a good picture; it was like he knew he was getting his picture taken because he opened his eyes.

"I know yall getting a family portrait taken."

"Saturday."

"Well, let me call Tish so I can make an appointment for her early tomorrow morning."

"Ahmad, I know you're going to tha barbershop."

"I do that every Friday anyway."

"Well, I'll braid ya hair tonight if you want me to."

I looked at Iciss, then said, "Nah, Little Sis about to hook me up."

"Excuse me."

"Jade, you know I do his hair every week. Jade, does he have a bottle already made?"

"Yes, it's in tha fridge."

"How you want it?"

"Straight back."

"No, get something exotic for tha pictures."

"Don't worry Brother I have just tha design for you."

It took her two hours to hook me up. When I looked in tha mirror, all I could say was wow. She had really done her thing this time. I went in my pocket and pulled out a $50 bill.

"I don't have no change."

"I don't want any change."

"Thank you Brother."

"No thank you Lil' Sis."

"Your hair jus keep growing and growing."

"I know; I was thinking about cutting it off."

"No, you not," Jade said.

"How you gon' tell him what to do wit his hair," Ms. Sady said.

"Because he told me that A.J. wasn't gonna get no haircut and neither is he."

"Yeah Brother, if you get it cut yall won't be twins."

"You know I'm not going to cut my hair this is seven years' worth of hair."

"You got more then enough of it."

"I was thinking about cutting it down some."

Jade looked at me then said, "Yeah whatever." All I could do was laugh.

"You don't look like you gained a lot of weight."

"I gained 20 lbs. but I'm only going to drop 10 off it."

"Did you get one of those pouch stomachs?" I lifted up my shirt up to show her.

"I see going to tha gym while you were pregnant paid off. I know that little bit of stomach won't take no time to get rid of."

"You don't have to tell me. I'll be ready by tha time I walk down tha aisle."

"You don't even look like you just had a baby. How many people you know can say that after giving birth?"

"Ungh, Ungh," my mom said, clearing her throat.

"Well then, it runs in tha family."

"Jade, I need to handle a few things. I'll be back later."

"We startin' this shit already."

"Startin' what?"

"Leaving me wit A.J."

"You have more than enough company to keep you company. Plus, I want A.J. all to myself."

"I knew it."

"You knew what Iciss?"

"I knew he wanted A.J. all to hisself."

"Look at Mom-Mom baby, can you blame him."

"Nah, yall go head and get ya time in."

"Don't be gone all day and night."

I looked at my watch, "It's only 2 o'clock."

"You heard what I said."

I pulled up and Mr. Marlarky came over to the car.

"I didn't think you were coming."

"My bag, but my fiancé just had my son."

"Oh, she finally dropped tha load?"

"Yeah."

"Well, I guess congrats is in order."

"Thanks."

"Well, looks like the house will be done by tha time you say I do. Come on let me show you around."

There was no fronting I was impressed Mr. Marlarky had it down to tha tee. I would actually be able to say I own a million-dollar home. I couldn't wait to move in. Jade is going to love this; there was no doubt in my mind. This house had 6 bedrooms, 2 ½ bathrooms, a weight room, game room, den, living and dining room wit a kitchen wit all state of tha art stuff. I had a floor safe built-in tha basement it was something special. Once I get married, I plan on retiring from tha game. There is no need to keep going; I have enough money to last me a lifetime.

"Mr. Marlarky, I'm really feeling this house."

"I gave you exactly what you asked for."

"I'll be in touch wit you in tha next few weeks."

I got back in my car and pulled off, headed back in town. When I pulled up to tha park, it was packed for it to be January and it wasn't all that warm out.

"Swerve what tha biz is?"

"You know, same shit, different smell."

"I guess congratulations is in order on ya baby boy."

"Thanks."

"Here, light this up."

He must've noticed a look on my face because he said that's Kush. I ain't say shit.

"You didn't have to ya face said it all."

While I was busting it up wit Fresh Heem had pulled up.

"Asalamu Alaikum."

"Walaikum Salam."

"Why you ain't answer ya phones?"

I look down, "Oh shit, I left 'em in tha car. I was wondering why nobody was calling me."

I went to get my phones. I had 37 missed calls on one, 25 on tha other, and 52 on one. And about 30 were from Jade. Just as I was about to call her back, my phone went off.

"Hello."

"Why are you not answering ya phones?"

"I left them in tha car and I didn't realize it until Heem just pulled up and asked tha same question."

"Well, what time are you coming back?"

"I don't know why?"

"Cause I want you to come home."

"Everybody must have left."

"No, they still here; I just want you to come home."

"Awe, let me find out you missing a nigga." She responded wit something terrible.

"It is wht it is then, me and tha fellas was going to go out and celebrate tha birth of Ahmad."

"Why don't yall just come here?"

"Did I just hear you right? Ms. every time ya friends come over yall always leaving a mess for me to clean up!"

"Ahmad, can't you see I miss you?"

I could hear everybody in tha background say'n boy bring ya ass home.

"I'm on my way."

"Damn Nigga you just got here."

"Wifey on that miss a Nigga shit. Why don't yall come to da crib and we can get it in while I bust yall ass in Madden."

"Now you're talking my language," Fresh said, I'll make the LQ stop."

"I got tha trees."

"We out then."

Everybody got in their cars and headed to my crib.

15 minutes later, I was pulling up to tha crib. Looks like they already having a party. When I walked in along wit tha people that were already, there were my mom, aunt, and a couple of Jade's cousins.

"Hey Mad," my mom said giving me a hug.

"Hey there nephew."

In a few seconds, Fresh and everybody else was coming through tha door.

"Hello, everybody," they all said.

"Come on yall," I said, leading tha way to my game room.

Jade gave me tha look as I walked past.

"I got winners," I said as a stopped to sit next to Jade.

"Nigga wifey got you in her web you ain't play'n."

"Yes, I am, plus I need to holla at yall about something important."

My aunt was holding A.J.

"Aunt Mel, do you think I can hold my son?"

"Boy, you got all day and night to hold him!"

"Swerve, you play'n or not?"

"I'll be back," I said, kissing her on her forehead.

"Damn, that was quick."

"You know I had to 21 him it ain't bout nuffin'."

"That's right, talk that shit."

Turk and Bre came in why we were play'n. Fresh was play'n wit tha Eagles while I was play'n wit tha Packers.

"That's right, Baby bust his ass!" He had just kicked a field goal and went up 3.

"He better do something 'cause Imma run Grant down his back this last quarter."

Jade walked in, "Baby, I know you ain't down."

"Don't worry, I got this."

"Why you ain't run wit Payton?"

"I want it to be a game."

I decided to run a half-back draw. Fresh was all over it.

"You ain't gettin' that shit off."

2nd and 14, I went back wit tha same play.

"AAAAAH Nigga that run shit ain't working, not today."

3rd and 18, This time, I went wit tha short screen pass. Grant broke a tackle and ran for 52 yards. I didn't say nothing I just kept play'n I knew I was going to win. Jade gave me harder games than this.

I'm a stop; you get the ball score and when by 10. (Ha! Ha! Ha!)

Jade was laughing, "No, since my Baby don't want to talk shit Imma talk it for him. He gonna run Grant up tha middle two straight times to get in tha end zone. Then wit five minutes left, you might try to hold tha ball thinking you're going to run tha clock out and score. If you do that, he's going to make you fumble. Now, if you choose to score quick and throw it, interception run back game over."

I looked at Jade, who had her lips puckered for a kiss, which I gladly gave her because she called it on tha money.

Turks said, "All that sounded good, but you got to score first."

"I say that's right," Fresh said, giving her dap.

My first play, Grant up tha gut 17 yards gain.

"Try that shit again, I got something for that."

I seen he was blitzing, so I audibled at tha line and he did too. I knew he would so I audibled back to my original play. When I hiked tha ball, he came wit tha corner blitz; I ran up tha middle and scored wit less than 4 minutes in tha game.

"Way to 52 fake 'em Baby," Jade said laugh'n.

I kicked tha ball down to tha 1-yard line. He returned it to tha 10.

"You think you can go 90 yards in 3 minutes?"

His first play was a run play for 5 yards; then he passed for another 7.

"You're never win like that."

Tha clock stopped for tha 2-minute warning. I knew he would have to go deep, so I took a chance and sent in an all-out blitz, which worked. Fresh ran a no-huddle; I didn't bother to audible. He got tha pass off just in time, but it was incomplete.

"You got a minute left; what you gon' do?"

"Playboy."

He threw a short pass, got tha first then called time out. 40 seconds, he gotta pass. Imma pick this shit off.

"This game is over, little cousin."

He threw tha ball and Charles Woodson came across tha middle, picked it off, then ran it back wit no time to spare.

"You put up a good fight."

"Nigga you can't really beat me."

"What ever."

"Bet a hundred."

"You know I don't gamble."

"But I do, bet a hundred on me."

"Jade, I'm not going to play you that wouldn't be fair."

"If you're scared just say you scared." He looked at me.

"I don't think you can beat her."

"Baby, her money spends," Turk said wit a smile.

Heem said, "I like her a nickel."

"Nigga you crazy?"

"Nope not at all."

"It's a bet."

Before you knew it, everybody had their bets on; some for Fresh, some for Jade, most for Fresh.

"I like myself, another stack," Jade said.

Fresh took tha bet and then said, "I'm not giving you ya money back and if I 21 you, it's double."

"You said that to say what!"

Fresh ran wit tha Eagles again while Jade took Pittsburgh. Jade told Fresh not to take it personal. Jade won tha coin toss and chose to kick off.

"You must really want to lose," Killer said.

"Hold on before I kick it off." She got up to check on A.J.

"He's alright go on back in there," my mom said.

"Let me put Jeezy on so I can get into my zone," Jade said.

She kicked it off and it was on. Fresh ran it back to tha 40.

"This is gonna be easy."

Fresh went wit a running play to Westbrook but Jade was on it made him fumble and picked it up and took it in for tha touchdown.

"Yeah, this is going to be easy," Heem said langh'n.

"Damn, Jade must of been practicing," I thought to myself.

When she set up for tha sidekick, I thought she was bluffing and so did Fresh.

"That's right, Baby don't fall for that!"

"For what? Imma kick this on the side, get tha ball back and score."

"Oh, you think it's that sweet, huh?"

I'll be damn, she kicked it on tha side and recovered it.

"Ahmad, I don't see how you let this bum give you a game, ya game must be falling off. I'm not going to play wit 'em."

Her first play was a flea flicker yet. She had me fooled. Willie Parker came up tha middle and then pitched tha ball back to Rottenburg, who hit Santonio Holmes in tha end zone for another score.

"I hope yall got tha double money," Heem said.

Next possession, Fresh moved tha ball all the way to tha 1.

"Heem, you talk'n that double money bullshit."

"Oh shit, he got a voice," Jade said.

"You can't beat me Girl."

"Now see, you just fucked up. I was going to let you score but not now."

"You can't stop me."

"Watch this." As soon as he hiked tha ball, they were on McNabb.

"Oh shit, he fumbled!" Heem yelled.

Jade recovered and ran it to tha 10.

"I told you if you wouldn't have talk that shit, I would've let you score, but it's over now."

Sure enough, she scored, then got up and looked at Fresh and said, "Don't take it personal Kid."

"Damn peeps, she bust ya ass."

"I ain't gon' front she good."

"I know she stepped her game up. I wish my girl knew how to play Madden; it would be on and poppin'"

"Yall can finish. I'm going out here."

I went straight to my aunt and pick my son up.

"OOOH Mom, as soon as he picked him up, he opened his eyes and smiled."

"That's cause he knows that daddy got him, don't you Lil' Man."

After about another hour, everybody went their separate ways leaving me, Jade and A.J. to enjoy one another's company

.

CHAPTER 34

Tha Nite Before

I couldn't believe I would be a married man in less than two weeks. A.J. was now four months and moving fast. My mom and Jade's mom asked if she was pregnant again. They said when a baby moves fast like that it normally meant he was making way for anotha one. We didn't plan on having anotha one until A.J. was at least 4.

We were having tha wedding in tha same place as tha reception at the Chase Center. Jade had given out over 100 invitations, which meant that there would be at least 200 people in attendance. Instead of having tha Chase Center serve that bougie food, we decided to have what all Black people eat soul food. And who better to cook it than my mom, aunt, grandma and Jade's mom, aunt and grandmom?

"Baby, are you a little nervous?"

"Nah, to be nervous would be to say I'm not sure."

"Are you sure?"

"Jade, I've neva been more sure of anything in my life. We were destined to be together."

Over tha next few days, I was finish'n up last-minute details. Jade didn't want me to have a bachelor party and truthfully, I didn't care if I had one or not. Tha funny thing was she wanted a bachelorette party which didn't bother me one bit.

It was tha night before my wedding and me and all tha ladies were staying in tha Hotel DuPont. We were all sittin' back, remembering how years ago, we all made a pact to never fall in love. Now look at us all in love and I'm 24 hours away from being married. There was a knock at tha door.

"Oh, that must be room service," my mom said wit a smile.

Sure enough, it was room service; three guys came in pushing carts.

"Did yall order enough food?"

The next thing I knew, music came on and tha three waiters were dancing around in G-strings. One of them came over, shaking his shit in my face. Before I could say anything, he was in my lap, giving me one hell of a lap dance. I couldn't believe it, my mom and Ms. Joan were having more fun than me. The one guy who had tha elephant trunk G-string was packing every bit of 12 inches and his shit wasn't even hard. My cousin Tanya was all over him. When it was all said and done, we were all drunk. I think I fell asleep before tha strippers left.

Across town or should I say a few blocks down at tha Sheraton, Maze and tha crew we're waiting on Swerve to arrive.

"Aye, Fresh what time are tha broads suppose to be here?"

"Do you mean strippers?"

"Strippers, broads, it's all tha same thing."

"Somebody's at tha door."

"Must be tha broad's cause Killer is going to call when they on their way up."

When we opened tha door, there were 5 beautiful women stand'n there.

"Come in ladies, make yourself comfortable tha guest of honor hasn't arrived yet."

"Do you mind if we have a drink and smoke?"

"Not at all, do yall."

"Well, we're going to go in tha back and get changed."

Killer bust through my phone, "We on our way up."

"On second thought, yall go back there until we say come out he's on his way up now."

"A'ight, when you ready just put this on," she said, handing me a CD.

"Damn, we didn't think yall was coming."

"Man, who got tha Sour D, fuck what you talk'n bout Nigga."

After about 30 minutes I put the CD on. "I'm in love wit a stripper; she ridin' that thing."

Two of tha girls came out and put on a hell of a performance. Everybody had their money out. When tha song switched to "She Got a Dunk," tha other three came out shaking them fat asses like their life depended on it. Niggaz was going crazy throwing money. I had my mind on my big day tomorrow. One of tha broads jumped on my lap and started grinding on me something serious. I felt my nature rising and so did she. It was like she was try'n to sit on it through my jeans. I told her to get up, which disappointed her, but I did put a buck in her thong, which put a smile on her lovely face. As bad as I wanted to fuck I just couldn't do that to Jade. I wonder what they're doing?

"Yo yall ball out; I'm going in tha back and get some sleep."

When I stood up, I had to catch myself tha Sour D and Bombay had me on smash.

"Nigga I know you ain't calling it a night already?"

"I just need to lay down for a sec."

"Yo yall this nigga trip'n, it's only 12 o'clock."

"Naw, we was gettin' it in before we got here," Killer said in my defense.

Fresh grabbed me by tha arm and said, "Naw, man ain't no laying down up in this Mafucka. Swerve you getting married tomorrow we gon' party like rock stars."

Maze screamed out, "Totally dude!"

"Fuck it then, let's hit tha club," I said.

"What about them?" Tiz said, pointing to tha strippers.

I pulled out my money and peeled off $1500, "Here you ladies go."

That wit tha money they already made was more than enough for one night. They wasted no time taking tha money and getting dressed.

"It was good doing business wit yall; here's my card if you ever need us again," she said wit a smile.

"A'ight yall, let's roll."

"Where are we headed?"

"Philly."

45 minutes later, we were pulling up to Palmer's on 6th and Spring Garden.

"Damn, look at the mafuckin' line."

"Nigga, since when we start waiting in lines."

"True dat true dat."

Niggaz was staring as we walked past to get in tha cut line, is they called it.

"Oh shit, look what tha cat drug in. What up, Swerve where you been?" Muhammed asked.

"In tha cut like a band-aid."

"How many?"

"8."

"Just give me a buck."

Maze pulled out a Benjamin Franklin and handed it to him. Once we got inside, we went straight to tha bar.

"First round on me," Maze said as we all placed our orders.

"A buck sixty," tha bartender said.

Maze gave her 180 and told her that tha extra dub was for her since she was cute.

"Thank you," she said, blushing.

We made are way to tha second floor.

"God damn, it's hot in this bitch!" Tiz yelled over the music.

We stood over by tha bar, which was crowded from everybody try'n to order drinks. I got Melissa's attention and winked at her. She smiled and mouthed tha words where you been at? "Damn playa, you sure you want to get married tomorrow?" Maze asked.

When Malissa came over a few people yelled, "Yo, we was next!"

She paid them no mind and asked, "Double shot Bombay on tha rocks wit a splash of cranberry?"

All I could do was smile, it had been 5 years and she still knew what I drank.

"Yup, plus," and I told her tha rest of tha orders.

Fresh pulled his money out and peeled off 10 twenties. I passed it to Malissa and I told her to keep tha change.

"Still a big tipper, I see. Hold up, let me serve them; I'll be right back."

"Shorty must like you," Heem said.

"I was knock'n her off before I fell."

"Oh word."

As soon as she came back, she asked, "So, where have you been hiding?"

I explained it all to her, including tha fact that I was getting married in less than 24 hours.

To my surprise, she held her hand up and said, "Me too."

Malissa was a bad chick; she was 5'8, with brown skin, brown eyes and hair that had grown to her shoulders; she used to rock tha Anita Baker look and she had a fat soft ass to top it all off. I told her I would be back and headed to tha third floor. It was much cooler on tha third floor, this is where all tha sophisticated and dimes hung out. Everybody was gettin' their talk on when we came through tha door.

"Who got tha next round?" I asked.

Heem let us know he had it. Heem was really on his grind. He was runnin' thru bricks like Carl Lewis in tha 100-yard dash. I still haven't told everybody that at tha end of tha year, I was officially retiring from tha game.

"Swerve, Swerve."

"Yo, what's up Heem?"

"Damn Nigga you was in La Land."

"Nah, I was just thinking about some shit."

"Don't tell me you having second thoughts."

"Hell no!"

For tha rest of tha night, we partied and had a ball.

CHAPTER 35

Wedding Day

When I woke up this morning, I couldn't believe I would be getting married today. After we were all up and dressed, we went to breakfast. After breakfast, we got our hair, nails, and feet done.

"Jade, after today, you'll be a married woman."

"I know who would of thought, huh."

"Ahmad said he has a surprise for me after tha wedding. I wonder wht it is?"

Don't look at us; we don't have any ideal," Iciss said.

"I know and even if we did, we wouldn't tell you, my mom added.

After we were all finished, we had about 2 hours before showtime. I hadn't seen Ahmad in 24 hours and I really was missing him something terrible.

"Iciss, did you remember to get my diamond necklace and bracelet from tha house?"

"Duh, of course, I did."

"How did you do my baby's hair?"

"You'll see it when you get to tha altar."

We headed to tha Chase Center to get ready.

After Iciss strapped my hair, I made my way to tha barbershop so Skills could do his thing. "Swerve, I never thought I'd see tha day you tie tha knot."

"You and a lot of other people."

"I know this is going to be tha most talked about wedding for years to come."

"Skills, this shit cost me 80 grand, it better be!"

"Wheew you spent out Baby Boy."

"Hey, she deserves it and much more. Not many people would have done what she's done."

"I know you definitely got a rider, not to mention that you're tha only nigga in tha city she ever gave tha time of day."

"A'ight you good to go; this is on me; I'll see you later."

When I looked in tha mirror, I knew I had tha best Barber in tha city. Skills hit my shit tight, but tha pink outline really set it off. I decided to get dressed at tha crib instead of tha Chase Center. By tha time I did get dressed, I had a half an hour until it was time. Maze and everybody else was blowing my phone up. They told me they were all out front waiting on me. Of course, I had to smoke me a blunt before I left. When I opened tha door, I saw tha prettiest white on white Rolls-Royce sittin' on a pair of 22-inch Halachi's.

"Damn, where yall rent this from?"

"Rent, nigga don't disrespect us! This is a wedding gift from all of us."

"What, this my shit?"

"Hell yeah nigga, it's only right wit out you; we wouldn't be where we at."

"Speaking of that, at tha end of tha year, I'm retiring outta tha game." I could tell by tha look on their faces they were tha least bit surprised.

"We had a feeling you were; we just didn't know when.

"Oh yeah."

"Yeah and we decided to all be partners."

"We better get a move on it before Jade thinks you're bailing out on her."

"I know, my mom just two-wayed me asking where I'm at."

"We rolled out and everything from my Rolls to Maze Maybach.

"Shit, I know all these people not here for tha wedding?" Heem asked as we pulled up.

"Nah, it's probably something else going on too."

Little did I know they were here to see me and Jade tie tha knot. We all went in and went upstairs, where there were way more than tha 200 I anticipated coming.

"Swerve, good thing you had it here; there's no way all these will fit into a regular hall."

"Nah, it's a good thing I got enough food for 500 people."

I ended up hiring this Soul food catering so that our moms and aunts wouldn't have to miss tha wedding to cook. We all took our places. I came walking down tha aisle wit my mom on one arm and Ms. Sady on tha other. Once they were seated, Musiq Soulchild came out and sang "Love" as tha bridesmaids and groomsmen came down tha aisle. There were so many cameras flashing you would have thought it was an award show. Of course, I had a professional photographer and cameraman to get it all. As soon as the music stopped, Jesse Powel stepped up.

"You, You, You, let's call today our anniversary tha day I put my heart in ya hands and said it was yours to keep, from this day forward you'll always be mine I'm gonna give my love to you and there's only one thing on my mind Jade is you."

As Jade walked down tha aisle, everybody was standing. I smiled as I saw my lovely wife-to-be stand before me. When I pulled her veil back, I could see tha tears in her eyes which I wiped away. She had no ideal that I would have Musiq and Jesse perform live; in rehearsal, it was tha CDs. I looked at my mom and Ms. Sady crying; while tha song finished up tha photographer was doing what I paid him to do.

"Baby, you look so beautiful," I said to Jade.

She smiled and said, "You showing off."

I knew she was referring to my pink outline. When they got to tha part about tha vowels, they informed them we have written our own.

Jade looked me in my eyes and said, "Ahmad, I knew there was something special about you tha first time we met. And even though we didn't have tha chance to get to know one another, you came back around like a boomerang. I said I would neva fall in love, but you changed that; not only did I fall in love wit you, but I can't see myself wit out you."

Next, it was my turn.

"Jadeen, let me first say that tha love I have for you is never-ending. You have given me what no other woman has given me and that is my firstborn son. When I look into your eyes, I feel like there is nothing you won't do for me. Despite everybody telling you not to get involved wit me, you still took a chance. So, I don't know what's in my future but I do know that I don't have one unless you're in it."

Tha next thing I did was put tha ring on her finger. When Killer handed me tha ring, everybody was in awe. I heard people say'n, damn look at it that thing. Wow, do you see that rock? I neva seen a ring like that. I had paid damn near 20 stacks for this custom-made ring. Once that was done, he said I could kiss my bride and pronounced us Mr. and Mrs.

Jones. Musiq and Jesse hit us wit tha Stevie Wonder classic "Ribbon in tha Sky" as we headed out. They escorted all tha guests to tha ballroom so everybody could get their eat and party on.

"Baby, is that tha surprise you had for me Musiq and Jesse?"

"Nah, do you want it now or later?"

"Wow!"

"A'ight." I got tha whole wedding party together.

"Come on, I want everybody to see my wedding present to my wife."

"Man, you got all those people waiting for yall."

"Let 'em wait!" I told Jade to close her eyes; when we got close.

"OOOH Baby, is it tha car I wanted?"

"You bout to find out as I stopped tha car in front of our new house.

Once everybody was out of their cars, I put my hand up to tell them to be quiet.

"Open your eyes."

"Baby, AAAAAH, AAAAAH, AAAAAH!" Jade couldn't stop screaming.

"Welcome to ya new house Baby."

I handed her tha keys and she ran to tha door. We all walked to tha house.

"This is nice Baby," my mom said.

"Damn Swerve, I'm feeling this," Bre said.

"Oh My God, Baby this is my dream house."

"I know that day you told me what your dream house would look like, I went and got it built from tha ground up."

When everybody was done wit their tour, Iciss said, "You could put this on MTV Cribs."

"Nigga you had to spend at least 1 million for this."

"Try 1.5."

"Daaaaaaamn," Turk said, "you went all out."

"Sky is tha limit for my baby."

"What yall gonna do wit tha other spot?" Iciss asked.

"It's yours when you graduate."

"You hear that Chaz?"

"So what."

"Bitch you know you gonna be my roommate."

"I know you better watch ya mouth!"

"Sorry Mom."

"Come on yall, let's go; I know everybody's hungry."

"I don't want to leave," Jade said.

"Girl, you better come on; you got tha rest of ya life to enjoy this house."

By tha time we got back, everybody was more than ready to eat and party. They introduced tha wedding party and then us. We had our own little table on top of tha stage. Everybody came up to congratulate us and drop cards which I'm sure had money in them in Jade's bag. When we finished eating, we had our first dance as husband and wife. We danced to "Always and Forever" and after that it was on. We both had brought a change of clothes, so we decided to change.

"And where are yall sneaking off to?" Ms. Sady asked.

"Just to get in something more comfortable."

Jade had put on a pink and cream Dolce & Gabbana dress that she had made wit a pair of cream sandals. I went wit these cream Gucci capris, pink Gucci shirt and pink Gucci loafers; you couldn't tell us we weren't sharp.

"Baby, don't forget ya shades."

We got back to tha ballroom every body was on tha floor dancing as Doc. B played tha latest jams.

"Hear they go, ladies and gents," Doc said on tha mic.

"We thought yall left ya own party, but I see yall wanted to get a little more comfortable. I don't blame you, we here all night.

"ATL club see her do her thing might wanna rap, but she'll make you sing. I was on her, she was on him, she all up in my thing wit that thong on her hip."

"Come on, Baby this my shit," Jade said, pulling me onto tha floor.

We hit tha floor and cut up. By tha end of tha night, I was exhausted and we had to be at tha airport by 7 in tha morning to catch a flight to the Dominican Republic.

CHAPTER 36

Back

We came back from our honeymoon after spending two weeks in the Dominican Republic. I really look like a Dominican now tha sun had turned both of us a shade or two darker. When we stepped into our house, Jade acted like it was her first time seeing it.

"OOOOH WEEE look at this place tha people that own it must be holding."

We looked at each other and busted out laugh'n. Everything from tha Italian furniture to tha Gucci curtains was well coordinated. My son's bedroom was all Louis Vuitton, including his crib.

"Wow, Baby you really did this house to tha tee."

"So, does that mean you like it?"

"No, I love it."

I explained to her about tha two alarms. Once you came in and turned off tha first one, you had 5 minutes to go to tha kitchen to turn off tha second one; it was located in tha pantry. If you didn't tha police would automatically be notified. Just in case anybody tried to break in. I also showed her how to work tha underground tunnel in tha basement, which led to tha backyard.

"Ahmad, I am really impressed; I love this house."

"I know; you told me already."

She punched me in tha arm and told me to stop being smart.

"I don't know about you, but I'm tired as shit."

"Baby, you psychic now."

We went into tha bedroom and Jade was amazed.

"Now, how did I miss this? I didn't see this bedroom before. You know I'm loving this canopy bed." She plopped down on it.

"OOOOH, it's SOOOOO soft."

I had our room done and all white Gucci.

"I want you to feel like you're in Heaven every time you step in this room; that's why I had it done in all white."

She didn't say nothing; she just grabbed my face and put her tongue down my mouth.

I've pulled back, "You betta stop before you start something."

"My point exactly," she said, undoing tha straps on her dress.

"Mrs. Jones, you so nasty," I said, noticing she didn't have on any panties.

"Now Ahmad, you know I haven't worn any panties on tha whole trip."

"I know, but we are back now. I don't know about you, but I'm ready to see A.J."

"Me too, but you need to handle ya biz-ness first."

All I could do was take my clothes off and handle my biz like a true champion.

Two hours later, we were both getting out tha shower. My cell phone were ringing nonstop since we got in tha shower.

"Somebody must really want to talk to you."

Just then, my phone started ringing again. I looked at tha caller ID and seen it was Ms. Sady.

"Hello, hey Mom. Nah, we just got out of tha shower. He has. Tell him that Da-Da is on his way to get him. Ok, see you in a little bit."

"Who was that, ya mom?"

"Naw yours."

"What did she want?"

Just to see if we made it back safe and to let me know A.J.'s been calling my name. It's amazing how all babies' first words are Da-Da."

"I know; I think it's cute, though."

"She also said make sure we bring her gifts wit us."

"How she know we brought her anything back? Neva mind don't answer that. Well, so much for getting some sleep."

"I know it's all good. Come on, let's go."

On our way out, I looked at all tha gifts sitting in tha dining room and tha money bag on tha table.

"We can open those when we get back."

Since it was nice and hot, we chose to drive tha droptop 59 Impala that was cranberry on white, sitting on 26s. When we got in town, I let tha top-down and rode through tha hood to see what was jumpin' off. I pulled up to tha park; it was jam-packed. I had my boy Plies banging so loud that everybody was watching us when we pulled up.

Look at them," Jade said, pointing to Bre, Turk and Lexis. As soon as they seen Jade, they came strolling over.

"Well, hello Mr. and Mrs. Jones; how was tha honeymoon?"

"Girl, I didn't even want to come back. If it wasn't for A.J. we would have stayed another two weeks."

"I know that's right," Turk said.

"Hey best friend," Lexis said to Ahmad.

"What up Lexis?"

"Boy you look tired."

"I am; I didn't get any sleep."

(Ha! Ha! Ha!) "I bet you didn't."

"Where is my godson?" Bre asked.

"Wit my mom, we bout to go get him."

Fresh and Tiz walked over, followed by Heem and Maze.

"Why don't yall get him and come back here?"

"A'ight, you better not did!"

When Jade slid over and grabbed tha wheel, Fresh said, "Damn, you try'n to blind a mafucka."

"Must be nice," Turks said, looking at Fresh wit a smile.

"Bye, see you when we get back," was all he responded wit.

"Damn nigga you got Black."

"Fuck dat; what did them Dominican bitches look like?" Heem wanted to know.

"All I can say is you'll see in a few days."

"Nigga I know you did not take no flicks of bitches."

"Jade know, I let her know I was sending 'em to my peeps in tha Bing."

"Oh shit, you just reminded me I got to put some more minutes on my cell so that nigga can call."

Come on, Heem you 'posed to keep money on there."

"It's money on there; I just need to put more on. That nigga be calling me all day every day to do 3-ways."

"I know you ain't talkin' as much as you used to play tha phone."

"It is wht it is. But on some real, I did meet this nigga who said he got them things for tha low."

"What's the low?"

"Yeah, since we only paying 12.5 right now."

"8."

"8 stacks?" Maze questioned.

"Yeah."

"That shit can't be no good."

"We gon' to find out."

"You brought some back?"

"Nah, he got peoples down here. Imma holla at them tomorrow."

"So, if it's good, you gonna cut tha connect off?"

"Imma real nigga so Imma let him know I got somebody that's willing to let them go for tha 8. Nine outta 10, he's not going to want to lose tha money I be spend'n, so he'll come down on his number also. Right then, tha bidding war starts and when it's all said and done Insha Allāh, we'll be paying around 5 or 6 grand."

"Yo, that's a crazy flip since we'll be letting them fly for 21. Swerve you da only nigga I know to go on ya honeymoon and come back wit a potential sweeter connect."

"I gotta make sure yall niggaz is straight since I'm out in another six months."

"So, you really retiring from tha game, huh?"

"Yeah, I got to think about my wife and son now; plus, I have more than enough money to last me a lifetime."

"You gon' have a lot of free time on ya hands."

"Actually, I plan on buying tha corner store."

"What corner store?" Tiz asked.

"The one on 5th."

"Malik and his peeps ain't going to sell that."

"How do you think I even got tha ideal in tha first place?"

"Shit, you gonna kill 'em wit that?"

"I'm a change tha whole shit."

"How?"

"See, Imma buy tha building from Rev; then I'm going to have tha grocery store in tha front and tha steak & sub shop in tha back. Now I'll be gettin' tha legal swop."

"When this gon' happen?"

"I'm waiting for tha paperwork to be finalized. So Insha Allāh, it should pop off in another week or two."

"Are you going to have to close tha store down why they do tha work?"

"Yeah, but money talks, so tha crew I got doing it said they can have it done in 30 days, 40 tops."

"No wonder Malik ain't been really having shit in that mafucka. What you gonna call it."

"I haven't figured that out yet."

"Been in tha game since I was 16. Little young mafucka try'n to get cream."

We all turned around in tha direction tha music was coming from. I didn't really need to turn around because I knew it was Jade. All she wanted to listen to was Meek Millz or T.I. When she parked, I walked over to tha car to see my son. When he seen me he said Da-Da.

"OOOOH did you hear him," Lexis said, "he know who his Da-Da is."

"He should; he look just like that nigga," Fresh said.

We stayed in the park for another hour and then headed home so that Jade could cook dinner.

CHAPTER 37

Another Engagement

"Listen Nigga didn't I tell you not to play wit my money? (Smack) Didn't I? I told you if you couldn't handle it not to take it. (Smack) Didn't I?"(Smack) (Smack)

"Imma pay you ya money Maze," Ron said through swollen lips, "I just need a little time."

"Nigga how tha fuck you gon' pay me my money?"

Sly looked at me and I nodded my head. "Boom" was tha sound of tha .357 knockin' Ron out of his chair killing him instantly. Tha hole in his head was tha size of a 50 cent piece.

"Throw that nigga in tha grinder so we can be out."

After everything was cleaned up we made our way back in town.

"I know you ain't feeling bad about what we did?"

"Hell Nah!"

"Cause you been quiet tha whole ride back."

"Sly I been thinkin'."

"Awe shit, here we go."

"Nah seriously, I've been thinkin' bout askin' Bre to marry me."

"Damn Swerve got everybody wanting to get married."

"It's not even that, it's just I don't plan on being wit nobody else so why not married tha one I love."

"I hear you and I can definitely feel you on that. Truth be told, Maze I was thinking tha same shit."

(Ha! Ha! Ha!) "That's why you said what you said about Swerve got everybody on some married shit."

"Fuck it, It's only 7 o'clock let's shoot to Foley's."

"You got enough paper on you?"

"I should, I don't plan on spending out."

2 ½ hours and one diamond ring later I was pulling up to tha house nervous as hell. Not nervous to ask but nervous she would say no. I walked into tha door to tha smell of steak, shrimp, fried potatoes, and corn.

"Damn Baby what's the special occasion?"

"Why it gotta be a special occasion?"

"Because you cooked my favorite meal. Uh Oh"

"What?"

"You leaving me," I said wit a smile.

"Boy please I ain't going nowhere you stuck wit me."

That brought a smile to my face and instantly took away my nervousness.

"Baby you must of felt me cause I was just about to call you."

Bre looked so damn good standing there over tha store wit her boy shorts and half shirt that said taken on it.

"A couple more minutes and we can eat so go wash your hands."

By tha time I came back downstairs Bre had dinner on tha table wit a bottle of Grey Goose for her and Bombay for me.

"Wow, you must be about to ask for a new car or something."

"No, I'm not, I just wanted to have dinner and spend tha evening wit my baby. Is there anything wrong wit that?"

"No not at all, so did I that's why I came home."

My phone started ringing and from tha ring I knew it was Sly.

"I knew it was too good to be true," Bre said.

"It's Sly, I need to get this. Hello. Yeah, that's what's up But I'm having dinner wit Bre I'll hit you in tha a.m."

I looked a Bre who had her lip poked out.

"I'm turning my phones off except my emergency phone."

That quickly brought a smile to her face. We finished up dinner then I decided it was time to pop $1 million question. I stood up and walked around to her side of tha table. I kneeled down and let her know that dinner was delicious.

"Bre did you mean it when you said that you were going anywhere?"

"Of course, I did."

"Well in that case," I reached in my pocket then asked her to marry me by pulling out tha ring.

"AAAH, AAAH, AAAH, OOOH MY GOD, OOOH MY GOD, OOOOH MY GOD!" I thought she was having a panic attack.

"Are you a'ight Baby?"

"YEEEES, YEEEES!"

I didn't know if she was saying yes she was OK or yes she would marry me.

"Yes I will marry you!" she screamed while fanning herself.

She jumped up and ran to tha phone. Next thing I know she said hold on when she clicked back over she screamed, "I'm getting married!" She must have called Turk and Jade.

"Right after we ate dinner. Yes girl and you know it is," she said looking at her ring.

All I could do was smile knowing I made her tha happiest woman alive. While she was on the phone I decided to call my boys and let them in on the good news. Mom said she was wondering what we were waiting on. But she was definitely happy for us. By tha time Bre got off tha phone I was playing Call of Duty on my Xbox 360.

"I'm sorry Baby but you know how Turk and Jade is."

"It's cool," I said not taking my eyes off tha game.

She sat down next to me and put her head on my shoulders.

"Imma let yall handle all tha details."

"Well, you can pick tha colors."

"That's easy, white and peach."

"How did I know you was going to say that?"

"Maybe, just maybe you know me."

She punched me in the arm and said, "Maybe I do know you."

"Bre I told you I wasn't letting you go this time and I meant it."

That night we made love as if it was our last time.

CHAPTER 38

Grand Opening

It has been three months since I had gotton married and I was loving every minute of it.

"Hey Mom."

"Hey Jadeen, hey mom-mom baby."

"Mom-Mom."

"Oh my God did he just say mom-mom?"

"Yeah he too damn grown. You know he trying to walk too."

I put A.J. down and he just stood there then took a step and plopped down.

"Hey Jade. Hey there nephew you miss you aunty." He shook his head yes.

"Oh, did yall see that he said yeah. Boy you growing up fast wit ya cute little Gucci set on. Wanna go wit aunty to tha store? Jade where yall get these Gucci frames from?"

"I don't know his dad bought them."

"Did he open up his store yet?"

"Next week."

"Cause he said I can work in there, I need some more money I'm try'n to buy a car."

"I told you I would give you some doe."

"I know but I want something real nice not no hoopty."

"Girl you better be thankful for whatever you get."

"Well, I'm taking my nephew to tha store." I reached into his diaper bag and handed her one of his body bibs and some wipes.

"Jade we gon' have to change his name to Gucci cause that's all he wear."

"You sound like Bre."

"I FINALLY FOUND THE NERVE TO SAY GOING TO MAKE A CHANGE IN MY LIFE STARTING HERE TODAY."

I smiled knowing it was Ahmad.

Jade if you don't snap outta it and answer that phone.

"Hey husband of mines."

"Hey Sexy, what you doing?"

"Nothing, over moms."

"Were you busy?"

"No, just talking to mom."

"Where is A.J.?"

"Iciss took him to tha store. You know he said mom-mom."

"Did he?"

"Yup."

"You sure you ain't pregnant?"

"Yes I'm sure."

"He's doing a lot for seven months old."

"He's about to be eight in a few weeks."

"Well, when you get a chance come by and see tha store. I'm going to have tha grand opening tomorrow."

"I thought you said it wouldn't be ready for two more weeks?"

"That's what I thought but I was wrong. Tell Iciss Imma need her tomorrow if she still wants to work in tha store."

"Yes she does, she was just say'n something about that. She's trying to save up for a car."

"I thought you was gon' give her some money?"

"I am but tha hussy just told me she wants something new and not no hoopty."

"I mean, hey she takes after her mother and sister."

"What's that suppose to mean?"

"Nothing, just it she likes tha finer things in life."

"She's supposed to. How long are you gon' be at tha store?"

"All day, I ain't going nowhere."

"A'ight, give me about an hour."

"OK, love you."

"Love you more."

I doubt that he said, hanging up not giving me a chance to respond. Iciss and A.J. came walking back in.

"Unh, Unh, Unh, I'm glad I gave you his body bib. Oh, did Ahmad call you?"

"No why?"

"He said he needs you to start tomorrow."

"I thought you said."

"I know what I said, but he's just called and told me tha grand opening got pushed up to tomorrow. I'm bout to go by and check it out."

"I'm going wit you.

"Me too but Imma drive 'cause I have to meet somebody."

"Let me find out you got a friend on tha low, Mom."

"And if I do, I'm grown, thank you very much."

An hour later, we were pulling up in front of tha store on 5th and

Madison. I had to call Ahmad so he could let us in. Tha whole store looks totally different. It was like a miniature grocery store; he even had a plasma TV so whoever worked behind tha counter could watch TV if they want it.

"Come on, let me show yall tha steak shop."

We walked through tha door in tha back of tha store, which took us inside tha steak shop. I was really impressed it was big enough that he had five tables in case you wanted to eat there. I looked at the menu; they served everything from cheesesteaks, subs, and hot wings to pizza. The only thing they didn't serve was pork; he even had Ms. Pac Man. There was no doubt that it definitely would be a profitable biz-ness.

"So, who's gonna work for you besides Iciss?"

"I got that all taken care of. Iciss, do you want to work out front or back here?"

"You already know I'm working out front."

"I'm paying you $12 an hour; anybody else 10. Imma have two people back here and two up front. I'm putting you in charge when me or Jade isn't here."

"Oh yeah, Baby, you can quit ya job at tha bank, 'cause before you know it we're gon' have a chain of A.J.'s."

"So, you finally came up wit a name, huh?"

"Yeah I figured why not name after my son."

"Don't you mean both of yall," she said wit a smile.

"I wasn't thinkin' bout myself when I came up wit that name."

"Baby I know you wasn't." I looked down and seen A.J. walking.

"Oh Shit."

"What?" Ms. Sady said.

I pointed to A.J. who was walking pulling everything off tha shelves he could get his hands on.

"Oh My God my baby is walking. Wow just earlier he was only taking one step now he's walking."

"Nah that little Nigga was playing us. A.J." He stopped and looked at me.

"Come here," I said wit my hands out. He dropped tha soap he had and made his way over to me.

I scooped him up, "Little Nigga you knew how to walk you was playing daddy." When he shook his head no we all started laugh'n.

"I'm telling yall we gon' to have to put him in a smart school; that baby gifted ain't he," Ms. Sady said.

We went back outside Tiz and Fresh was out there.

"Damn nigga when you gon' open this shit up. I know mafuckas tired of walking way over 7th giving them Indian Mafucka our money."

"After today you won't have to."

"Well, it's about mafuckin' time!"

"Hey man, I wanted my shit to be right Imma shut tha steak shops down. Shit, I might even shut Thriftway tha fuck down."

"Ya shit like that, I can't wait til tomorrow."

"You'll see."

Today was a grand opening but instead of opening at 7 I opened at 12 o'clock. Iciss and Mamy ran tha front while my two old heads Johnny and Redz ran tha steak shop. I knew both of them could cook plus they had gotton laid off Chrysler a few months ago. They were more than willing to work in tha shop getting paid to do something they loved to do. Everything was going better than I expected. All tha older people were happy that they finally had a grocery store in tha hood as well as a steak shop. A few days went by and biz-ness was going extremely well. I was standing out front when a couple came out tha steak shop.

"Baby, tha food was delicious."

"I know I'm glad ya sister told us about this place. We might have to move in town to be closer to this place," they said smiling.

When they got by me they stopped then said, "You lucky to live around here."

"Nah, I don't live around here."

"Oh, you waiting for ya food?"

"Nah, I own this spot."

"Peeps you on ya way to tha top."

"You sure are, everybody's talking about this place and now I know why."

"Thank you and I do hope you come back again."

"Oh, you don't have to worry about that." Maze and Sly had pulled up.

"What up Brother?"

"I can't call it, what's good wit you?"

"Same shit just a different smell."

"Hold up let me order something to eat."

"I got you, what you want?" Sly asked.

"Get me that chicken and shrimp platter. So, what's tha deal on them numbers?"

I was gon' call yall today and let yall know that we'll be pay'n 6,500 from tha original connect. Ya Dominican boy wasn't try'n to come down off 8? He said tha lowest he would go was 7. But Fiacco said 6.5 so I went wit that. So tha next shipment that's tha number."

"I'm probably gon' keep my shit at 25. You know what they say if it's not broke don't fix it."

"Well, everybody need to be on tha same page."

"I'm pretty sure they won't have a problem wit it. Speaking of tha devils," I said pointing at Killer, Tiz, Fresh and Heem walking down tha block.

We all said our what's up then got straight to biz-ness. I told them what I had just told Maze. They were all more then happy and agreed to keep tha price at 25 a bird. Everybody said they would be done by tomorrow morning. I also let them know that we were going to have a sit down with Flacco in tha morning at my house over breakfast and they should be there by no later than 8.

"Aye man, this is what yall been waiting on, ain't it?"

"You better believe it ain't no turning back now. It is wht it is."

When Sly came, everybody spoke. Even though Sly was Maze's right hand, he was at all our disposal because he was a stone-cold killer. As long as tha money is right, he would murk ya mother, no questions asked. I believe every team needs somebody like Sly. Now don't get it fucked up my whole team will slump anybody, but wit tha money we seeing why not pay somebody else to do it.

"Oh yeah, Maze, me and Jade are thinking about getting Iciss a Maybach or Bentley for her when she graduates."

"Say no more; just let me know how much yall need me to put in. Will give up 25 grand a piece; you know she's like a little sister to us too," Tiz said.

"Uh Oh, who done did something 'cause if all yall out here that can't be good," Iciss said stand'n in tha door wit her hands on her hips.

"We gon' see you in tha morning, Swerve."

"I'll probably see you later. I think ya wife invited me and Bre over for dinner."

"Cool, I'll see you later then."

I walked back into tha store behind Iciss, who had this car magazine on tha counter.

"That's tha kind of car Imma get when I finish college."

I picked tha magazine up and it was a picture of a BMW 850.

"But once I get my bar and get my law firm off tha ground, I'll be pushing a Bentley or Maybach. What you smiling for you don't believe me?"

"Actually, I'm smiling because I know you gon' do it. Iciss you can do anything you put ya mind to. I'm just glad to know you plan to go to college and be a lawyer."

"Yeah, you might need to retain me one day."

"I doubt that I'm done wit tha game in four months Insha Allāh."

"That's good you have more than enough money."

"I know that's why I opened this store plus I have to think about Jade and A.J."

"See, Brother I knew you was a smart family man."

"Yo, you gonna be a'ight I'm about to bounce?"

"Yeah, I got my mom's car, so I'll lock up and put tha money in tha safe."

"OK, see you tomorrow."

"OK, kiss my nephew and tell him aunty loves him."

That night Maze and Bre came over for dinner; we talked about their wedding that they planned to have next spring. Maze also let me know how he respects tha fact that I was getting out of tha game.

"You know Swerve; I'm giving tha game up tha end of next year."

"I feel you because this shit ain't promised. So tha best thing is to get out while you ahead and on top."

"It's not about me anymore; it's about my wife and my son now. That's what I want to be able to take care of my family and live comfortable."

"Since Jade turned me on to you I've been really stackin'."

"I really appreciate that and now wit this new deal coming into play by tha time I get out I'll be set for life."

After Maze and Bre left we put A.J. to bed and did tha same.

CHAPTER 39

Tha Meeting

Jade cooked a big breakfast and as soon as she was done everybody start coming. Flacco was tha last to arrive, he had one of his bodyguards wait out front and tha other stand by tha door. Once everybody was formally introduced we all sat down to eat.

"So, these are the 5 guys you've told me so much about?"

"Yeah Flac this is my team."

"Well let's get down to biz-ness," Flacco said while shoving some eggs in his mouth.

Maze spoke up, "At this new number we decided to spend 1.9 and some change to get 300."

Flacco's eyes got big like a deer in headlights. He was only use to Swerve coppin' between 100 to 200.

"I figured between tha 6 of us we can easily dump 50 joints apiece."

"Well, since you going to spend that much I'll let tha 300 go for 1.8. Which means 6 grand a bird."

By tha time tha meeting was over everybody was happy. Flacco left wit tha money and said tha product would be waiting on us at tha usual spot. He even said that it was a notch up from tha usual product.

Later that night, I decided to see how good tha new product was. I couldn't believe it to say that tha new product was better would be an understatement. I got back 54 ounces off a brick and it was top of tha line. My old head said he hasn't had coke this good since tha 70s. Over tha next two months, biz-ness was doing extremely well on both ends. We were offing tha coke faster than we could get our hands on it. My store was tha talk of tha town; everybody from far and near came to eat at tha steak shop. I would be retiring from tha game in 2 months; even though I was making major money off tha new product, I was still getting out.

I had just come from picking A.J. up from daycare. I decided to stop by tha shop to grab a bite to eat.

"What's up Sis?"

"I can't call it, just pick ya bad ass nephew up."

"He's not bad, where is he?"

"Out front wit Maze."

"Hold on, let me go order us something to eat."

"Hello Jade."

"Hey Mr. Redz."

"Didn't I tell you about calling me Mr.? You make me feel like a old man," he said wit a smile.

Mr. Redz was damn near 50 and still dressed like a young boy.

"Can I have tha chicken finger platter and a cheese steak gyro please."

"Coming right up."

"I'll be in tha store."

"Where is tha little man at?"

"Next-door."

"Make sure he stops by before you leave."

"OK."

As I was about to go back next door Rayna walked in. I didn't have anything against Rayna but she didn't like me because of Ahmad.

"So, this is tha place that has tha city in an uproar?"

"Can I help you?" Mr. Johnny asked.

"Yes, let me have tha chicken and shrimp platter. Um Mrs. Jones how are you?" Rayna said in a smart tone.

"I'm good," I said walking back into tha store, "Iciss why are you giving him all that candy? He's not gon' want to eat his food now."

"Well, he said aunty candy."

"Unh, Unh, Unh, he got you wrapped around his little finger."

"So, this Aunty's baby," Iciss said kissing A.J.'s face.

"Jade remember I said I needed three credits to graduate."

"Yeah."

"Well, it turns out I only need 1 ½, which means I'll be done by late February early March."

"Aren't you co-op?"

"Yeah, I go from 8 to 12 every day."

"Iciss I'm so proud of you."

Rayna walked in, "Can I get two purple haze wraps? Look at you looking just like ya dad," as she was saying that Ahmad walked in.

"Da-Da."

"What up Little Nigga?"

"Hello Swerve."

"Hey Rayna."

"You still looking good."

"Thank you, I see you put on a few pounds," he said referring to her stomach.

"I know I'm six months."

"Well, it was nice seeing you."

"You too but you don't need those," he said pointing to tha wraps in her hand.

"Oh, they not for me but nice to know you cared."

After she left out Ahmad asked me if I was cooking dinner.

"I didn't have any plans on it, why?"

"Why don't we go to TGI Fridays?"

"Well in that case, I'm not going to eat my food I just ordered. I'll let A.J. eat his platter."

"If yall want I'll keep A.J. tonight so yall can have some alone time." We both looked at each other.

"I guess we could use tha time alone."

"I'll call mom and have her come pick him up. We don't need no clothes he has plenty at tha house." Ahmad looked at Iciss.

"Boy he don't have to wear Gucci all tha time."

"That's all my son wear if not that then Prada or Ralph Lauren."

"Well, we got Ralph Lauren."

"Oh Ok."

"Brother you a piece of work."

"You already know how he is about A.J.'s clothes."

"You buy as much Gucci as I do."

"Yeah, that's because I don't want to hear ya mouth."

"My motto is if you can afford to buy it." Tha young boy Das came in.

"What up Iciss?"

"Hey Das."

"Let me get 3 Dutches and one those Bic lighters."

"Is that it?"

"Yeah unless you want to give me ya number too."

"I told you, you got too many bitches for me, and I refuse to fight over a man."

"Didn't I tell you that I will drop all of them for you?"

"Boy pleeeeease."

"I'm dead serious!"

I just sat back and listened as Das shot his game. He reminded me of myself when I was that age. I couldn't front he got at a dollar and he was in his last year of school.

"Well, let me give you something to think about to let you know I'm serious."

"And what might that be?"

"Would you do me tha honors and go to tha prom wit me?"

"Boy tha prom ain't for another six months."

"I know that way you have time to think about it."

I have to give it to him he was definitely on his "A" game.

"A'ight, I'll think about it."

"That's all I ask."

"Aye Yo Das let me holla at you outside."

"Awe shit, here he go on some big brother shit."

Once we were outside I went straight at him.

"Listen Swerve, I know Iciss is your little sister and my intentions are good."

"I don't doubt that but that's not what I wanted to talk to you about. I know you doing ya thing and I just wanted to know who you be dealing wit?"

"I be Fuckin' wit tha nigga Black from tha hill."

"Oh yeah, what his numbers like?"

"I'm not going to front I'm only coppin' 4 ½ to 9. He be wanting 4,500 and 9,000."

"Shiiiit, that's kind of steep."

"I know but I don't have no other plug."

"Check this out, I can let you get it for 3,600 or 7,200."

"You serious."

"Dead."

"If that's tha case, you ready now?"

"Hold up, that number is if you what it soft. If you want it already done it'll cost you 6,750 for tha 9 and 3,375 for 4 ½."

"Is tha work official for tha number?"

"One thing for sure, two things for certain it's tha best on tha East Coast hands down!"

"So, for tha whole pie it's 27 grand?"

"Nah, if you come in like that you can get it for 25. Do you know how to cook?"

"Hell yeah!"

"Well, I would advise you to get it soft because you can turn 36 into 54 easy."

"Fuck it, let me get tha whole pie."

"Imma plug you in wit Fresh. Let me make the call. I called Fresh and within minutes it was done.

"Take his number and call him when you're ready."

"This is good lookin' to Swerve."

"It ain't bout nothing just keep it 100."

"To me Swerve loyalty is everything wit out loyalty you don't have any trust. I was loyal to Black even though his numbers were high."

"Now you can sell Black weight."

"Let me go get this money so I can holla at Fresh." He gave me dap and hopped in his 745I.

"So, what was that about?" Jade asked.

"Biz-ness."

"My biz-ness?" Iciss asked.

"Actually nah."

"But I do think you should go tha prom wit him."

"Whaaaat, you think I should go to tha prom wit him? Let me feel ya forehead."

"Baby are you feeling Ok."

"Will yall stop it."

"If you're about to get out of tha game in two months why are you still networkin'?"

"I'm retiring but my team ain't."

Mr. Redz came through tha door wit A.J. and our food.

"Here you guys go."

"Thanks Redz," Swerve said.

"No problem."

"Mr. Redz can you make me a cheesesteak gyro?"

"Here you can have this one."

"Never mind Mr. Redz."

"What, you want something else?"

"Unh, Unh Ahmad's taking me to dinner."

"Mom-Mom!" A.J. yelled as he ran into my mom's arms.

"Hey Mom-Mom's baby, yes he is," my mom said smothering him wit kisses, "I just came by to pick A.J. up Imma take him to Chuck E. Cheese." A.J. got really excited hearing that.

I decided we will go to A.C. to see Jamie Fox perform.

"Baby you need to put on ya good shit, not those jeans."

"Why?"

"Because we are going to Atlantic City to see Jamie Foxx."

"Are you serious?"

"Yup, sure am."

An hour later, we were both dressed and ready to go.

"Damn, Jade you look good in that Monique Hueller dress."

"Thank you Baby."

"I'm just glad you're married to me."

"I'm tha one that should be saying that as good as you looking."

I had on a pair of Gucci jeans wit my brown Gucci blazer, white button up and brown Gucci loafers.

"You ready Ahmad?"

"Yeah, let me just grab my frames and we out."

An hour later we were pulling up at tha Bogada. I let the valet park tha car and then headed in. Tha show had already started by tha time we sat down. Tha waiter came to see if we were ready to order.

"Yes, can I have 16 oz steak well done, wit tha bake potatoes and shrimp."

"And let me have tha same thing."

"Would you like an appetizer?"

"Yes, one order of tha boneless hot wings and grilled chicken salad. Oh, and a bottle of Bombay wit two cups of ice please."

After Jamie finished "You just like me" tha waiter was back wit our appetizers and drink.

"Baby this was really nice."

"I know, we haven't been out in a few weeks. Do you want to stay the night up here?"

"Sure, why not? A.J. is staying wit mom and Iciss."

After tha show was over, we got a room and then headed to Kiss Kiss.

Tha next morning, we had breakfast, then hit tha highway and headed home. Once we got back to Wilmington, I decided to turn my phones back on.

"Damn, they must have been waiting for you to do that." I handed my phone to Jade.

"Why you," She stopped midsentence once she looked at the call ID.

"Hello."

"You can answer ya husbands phone but not yours. Wow."

"Bitch please, I turned my phone off last night."

"Umm Oochie Coochie la, la, la."

"No, we were in A.C. at tha Jamie Foxx show."

"Are you serious?"

"Girl Jamie snapped."

"I know he did. Look tha reason I called you is because I need to go over a few things about tha wedding."

"A'ight, I'll swing by later."

"Make sure you call me before you come."

Here Honey.

"That must of been important for Bre to call my phone."

"Not really, she wants to go over some wedding stuff."

"Lucky you."

"Shut up."

"Jade just in case nobody's told you lately or you just need to hear it, I love you."

"Awe that was so sweet and I love you too."

Iciss was coming out wit A.J. when we pulled up.

"Hey where yall headed?"

"We about to go to the mall, I'll call you when we get back."

"Is mom in tha house?"

"No, she left wit her friend."

"She's been hanging out wit her friend a whole lot lately."

"I know, I said tha same thing to her. You know what she told me."

"What?"

"I'm grown, don't worry about who I'm spending my time wit."

"Hey that's Mom for you. A'ight, just hit one of our phones when you're done." We went home to shower and change clothes.

"Baby I'll see you later, I'm headed to Bre's."

CHAPTER 40

Pay Ya Debt

"I can't believe these mafuckas."

"Niggaz think shit sweet since we been on some money shit!"

"I think mafuckas think we going soft or something."

"We been getting so much paper that we haven't really been concerned about tha small change niggaz owe us."

"All that is about to change as of right now!"

I sat there listening and looking at tha team that I had put together. I waited for them to finish before I spoke.

"If you ask me I say fuck 'em," Everybody looked at me as if I just lost my mind, "listen, yeah you could kill 'em but tha best thing to do is cut 'em off. Don't sell 'em shit and let any and everybody else know if they sell them anything they will be cut off too."

"I feel you but when a mafucka is broke they get desperate."

"Yeah Swerve, ain't no telling what they might do."

"Shit, if they on that type of time they should have neva been on tha team anyway."

"Well looking at it like that, that changes everything. Do what you need to do."

Wit that being said we all got up and went our separate ways.

"Sly I don't know about you but I'm hungry as shit."

"I'm wit you on that let's shoot to Suki Hana in tha mall."

I jumped on 95 headed to Christiana Mall.

"Damn they ain't done remodeling this shit yet? Man, this line is always long."

"I know, order me that steak and shrimp wit tha noodles I have to use tha bathroom."

"You want extra meat?"

"Yeah both."

On tha way to tha bathroom, I thought I seen that nigga Kwan. Nah, that nigga said he was fucked up, so that couldn't have been him. When I came out, I looked around tha food court until I spotted him standing in line wit some broad and a whole bunch of bags.

"Damn Nigga what you do fall in?"

"Nah, that nigga Kwan in here splurgin' on some broad."

"Word, where he at now?"

I pointed to where he was sitting wit his back to us.

"Well, we gon' sit here and wait for his bitch ass."

We let them leave out the mall, then followed 'em. They must be in her car and sure enough, she was parked on tha other side of us. Once they pulled off we ran to my truck to follow them.

"See, Sly Niggaz always try'n to get the fuck over!"

"I told you not to give his bitch ass shit in tha first place. Everybody ain't cut from tha same cloth we cut from."

She got off at tha New Castle exit. 10 minutes later they were pulling up to a nice house in Old New Castle. We parked down tha block and waited what seemed like forever until Kwan finally came back out. He got in his car and pulled off wit no knowledge of us following him. He led us right to his house where he took two bags and then came out and switch cars. "This Nigga keep frontin' when he living it up. He's probably on his way to tha block let's meet him there."

After making a few drop-offs and pick-ups, we were pulling up on 30th. Tiz walked up.

"What's good wit yall?"

"Same shit different smell."

"I heard that, I ain't doing shit just came to check on my money."

"Tiz what's up wit Kwan?"

"I don't know, he asked me for some work. Said he was fucked up."

"That nigga owe me some money. Yo what's up Maze?"

"You."

"I wish, I'm down on my luck try'n to get a buck."

"Yo Kwan cut tha bullshit, we know you holding!"

"This faggot ass nigga always in somebody's biz-ness; I neva liked him anyway, " Kwan thought to himself.

"Yo what you talking bout?"

"Don't you own that pretty ass 850 on 22's?"

"Oh shit, how do he know about my whip? "

Playing it cool, Kwan said, "Nah, that's my uncle's shit. I just use it when I'm try'n to get some new pussy."

"Yeah, I bet you do," Sly said lookin' at him.

"Maze, what's up wit ya mans?"

"Nigga you was up!" Sly went back to tha truck.

"Listen, Kwan I ain't neva been one to play games and I'm not going to start now."

"What's that suppose to mean?"

"Where's my money and I don't want to hear that bullshit about you fucked up either."

"I am." (Smack)

"Nigga stop playin' wit me and my paper."

By now, Sly was standing there wit his pistol in hand.

"I saw you at tha mall spending out on that broad. I also know you went home and changed cars."

"Listen Maze... (SPTT, SPTT)

Before he could finish, Sly had shot him twice in tha face. Tha silencer Sly had on his gun came in handy; nobody knew what happened until it was too late.

Meanwhile across town Killer and Heem were riding around in a stolen Honda from Philly.

"Pull over right here Heem."

"Where are you going?"

"I need to holla at my young jawn real quick I'll be right back."

"Don't be all day Nigga! Oh, shit there go Chip right there. Aye Yo Chip."

He turned around just as Killer was coming back around tha corner.

"What up Heem?"

"Damn nigga you been M.I.A."

"Nah, my grandma passed and I was down south for a while."

"Well, well, well, look what tha wind blew in."

Chip turned around to be standing face-to-face wit Killer.

"You got that money you owe me?"

"Damn all tha money this nigga making and he really sweatin' me for 30 grand," Chip thought to himself.

"Yeah, I got it but you got to give me a ride to get it."

"A'ight get in." Chip was about to get in tha back when Killer told him to ride up front.

"I need to lay down I'm not feeling well to go," Killer said looking at me.

On cue I said, "Nigga you been back to sleep all day."

"Yall gon' have to bring me back up here, is that cool?"

"Sure."

Shit if Heem wasn't wit us I would push his wig back. When we got to where he needed to go he was in and out in 5 minutes.

"Here you go," he said handing Killer tha bag he came back wit.

I looked in tha rearview and caught tha look on Killers face when he looked in tha bag.

"Heem before you drop Chip off stop by tha stash house so I can drop this money off," he said while winking at me.

10 minutes and we were pulling up on this secluded block.

"Chip you a funny dude," I said while pulling out my pistol.

"Why, what I say?"

"It's not what you said, it's what you did."

He was about to say something when (boom) brain matter was all over tha dashboard and window.

"Make sure you wipe tha car down."

"For what?" Heem said holding up his hands exposing his gloves."

"A'ight, pop the trunk so I can get tha gas."

We poured both cans inside and out of tha car, lit a match and watched tha car go up in flames. By tha time we got around tha corner to my car there was a loud boom.

"Oh shit, you left tha money in tha car."

"That shit was fugazy Heem."

"Oh, so that's why you put his brains all over tha dash?"

"And they said you were stupid." (Ha! Ha! Ha!)

"Yeah what ever Nigga."

They had Jefferson between 5th and 6th taped off.

"What happened up here?"

"The young boy Miles just got killed." As soon as they said Miles already knew who was responsible.

"Do they know who did it?"

"Nah, they said whoever it was had on all black and a mask."

"That narrows it down."

Fresh walked up to me and asked what happened as if he didn't already know.

"Come on, let's walk down to tha store."

"Yo I know you heard about Chip and Kwan?"

"Nah, I ain't heard shit what happened?"

"They in tha boneyard just like Miles."

"Niggaz don't play no games."

"Man, ain't no more chances for Niggaz. If you owe you either pay or die, shit maybe both."

CHAPTER 41

Girl Talk

"Bre, did you ever think that you would be getting married?"

"Girl, hell no."

"Turk, your next."

"I'm not getting married no time soon."

"Why not?"

"Truthfully, I'm not ready."

"I can honestly say I didn't think I was ready either, but I knew I loved Ahmad and didn't want to be wit anybody else."

"Don't get me wrong, I love Fresh, but I'm just not ready to get married yet."

"Well Maze said he wants the colors to be peach and white."

"That's pretty colors."

"Imma have my bridesmaids wear peach and Imma have my dress made like yours Jade. Well, a different style but white wit peach stitching."

"Yall will never guess who called me today."

"Who?"

"Remember Malik from DC?"

"Tha one wit all tha money, right."

"Yeah."

"Well, what did he want?"

"He claimed he was thinking about me a lot lately and decided to call. I kindly let him know I was involved wit somebody. He told me to store his number and if things didn't work out not to hesitate to call him."

"Well, you got a backup if it doesn't work wit you and Fresh."

"Bre please, Fresh ain't going nowhere."

"I know, it just sounded good." (Ha! Ha! Ha!)

"Do yall miss what we used to do?"

"I do at times when I'm sitting at home bored outta my mind," Turk said.

"Not really I think about if one of those jobs would've went wrong we wouldn't be where we are now."

"I was just wondering cause at times I do, but then I agree wit you Jade."

"Even wit out Ahmad I'm financially secure for tha rest of my life."

"So, is he really getting out tha game next month?"

"Yes and he doesn't know we are giving him a retirement party."

"Maze said you guys were thinking about having him a party. I think it's a good ideal why not go out in style. Are yall going to have it at tha Chase Center?"

"More than likely. I got to call Andy so he can get tha flyers made. We're going to have it on New Year's Eve. Doc B. said he would DJ for us."

"I better get my outfit now."

"Me too."

"We can all go to King of Prussia together. Well, I need to get home so I can start dinner." "Yeah, I need to get going too I have a few things to pick up from tha supermarket."

"A'ight make sure yall call me tomorrow."

"We will."

CHAPTER 42

L.A.

Damn I can't believe in 3 weeks I will be done wit tha game. This is something not too many hustlers have been able to do. Either you get killed or you go to jail. I'm proud to be one of tha elite to retire outta tha game. I'll be able to focus more on my Deen and family who I intend to convert to this beautiful Deen of Islam. Once I'm done I will repent. As it says in tha Surah 110 Ayat 3 (Fasabbih Bihamdi Rabbika Wastaghfirhu Innahu Kana Tawwaba) which means so glorify tha praises of your Lord, and ask His forgiveness verily, He is tha One who accepts tha repentance and who forgives. I just finished making ASR Prayer and was sitting on my rug reading tha Quran when Jade walked in.

"Oh, I'm sorry I didn't know you were praying."

"I was done I was just reading, that's all. Babe let me ask you a serious question though."

"I'm listening," she said after sitting on the bed.

"I love you and A.J. wit all my heart. I say that to say I am going to be raising A.J. on this Deen."

"I knew you probably would and I have no problem wit that, in fact, I have been doing some reading of my own."

"When, I neva seen you reading."

"Ahmad if I convert I'm going to do it because my heart is in it and not because I'm married to you and you're Muslim."

"Jade I totally respect that and I would never force tha Deen on you. But in 3 weeks I will be Deening like you've never seen before and Insha-Allāh so will you."

I didn't tell Ahmad but I have been reading and studying for tha past few months. I even went to a few of Shaheeda's Taslim classes. I figured since I won't be able to wear my clothes, I'll have all my Kemar and HiJabs made. Shit, I'll be tha only one wit Gucci, Prada, D.K.N.Y, Christian Dior, and Liz Hijabs.

After Jade left, I couldn't stop smiling. Tha ringing of my phone brought me back outta my daze.

"Assalam Alaikum."

"Wailakum-Salam. Was you busy Swerve?"

"Nah, Heem what tha biz is?"

"Did you grab something to wear for tha party on New Year's Eve?"

"Nah, but since it's my last party, I'm flying to Beverly Hills to shop on Rodeo Drive."

"Damn, you going all out, huh?"

"Yeah I am."

"Count me in then."

"Call everybody else and see if they want to go too."

"A'ight, I'll hit you back in a few."

15 minutes later, Heem was calling me back.

"Tha whole team is going, even Sly."

"Let me call and book us a first-class flight and a few rooms."

"Don't forget to reserve two rental cars."

"Imma book everything for Friday so we can stay tha weekend."

When I got downstairs, Turk, Bre, Iciss, and Ms. Sady were sitting around talking.

"Bre, Turk let me give yall a heads up."

"Uh, Oh."

"We're all staying tha weekend in Beverly Hills next week."

"Why?" Jade asked.

"Rodeo Drive."

"Let me find out yall going all out for this party."

"It's my last party and I'm retiring why not."

"Well, you better book us a few tickets since yall not going to shit on us," Turk said.

"Yeah and make sure you get Lexis one too."

I wasted no time calling tha airlines and tha best hotel in Beverly Hills to reserve tickets and rooms. Since tha girls were going I reserved 5 suites and 3 rentals.

"Jade come on; we don't want to be late."

"I'm ready Baby."

Everybody met up at Bre's at 9 since we had to be at the airport at 11. By tha time we got to tha airport and checked in we had just enough time to go in tha book shop to get a few magazines.

"Flight 118 boarding for Los Angeles at gate 8."

"That's us yall come on."

It was about 5 o'clock when we finally landed in L.A.

"It's a good fuckin' thing we were in first class because there is no way I would been able to make it in coach," Turk said.

"I am wit you on that," Maze added.

"We need to find tha rental car place."

"That shouldn't be too hard," Lexis said pointing at Hertz.

There was this bad ass chick at tha counter when we got there.

"Hello, reservations for Jones."

She tapped a few keys on her keyboard and said, "Yes 3 luxury cars. Well, we only have 2 Rolls Royce's and a Bentley."

"That's cool."

"We want a Rolls Royce," Jade said.

"Nah, Sis yall got tha Bentley."

Seeing where this was headed I quickly said, "I'll take tha Bentley."

After all the paperwork was done she handed us tha keys, then told us tha cars were in tha lot across tha street. Tha girls got in one of tha Rolls while Maze, Sly, Killer and Tiz got in tha other one. Leaving me, Fresh and Heem tha Bentley.

"Yall follow me to the hotel."

I put tha address in tha Navi system and got to tha hotel wit no problem at all. We all went to our rooms to shower and change. Even though it was tha middle of December it was 75° outside.

"Baby I just want to say thank you for lettin' me have tha Rolls."

"I just didn't want to hear you and ya brother going at it over something petty like a car."

"There was going to be no argument, I knew I would get one."

"Yall are too much alike that's why yall be bumpin' heads."

"You absolutely right about that."

We hit the town up and found tha hotspots. We partied til 3 in tha morning.

Tha next morning we woke up showered and found a nice spot to eat breakfast. After breakfast we all went to Rodeo Drive to shop. My first stop was tha Gucci store. They had so much stuff that I know I would never see again. I ended up spending close to $16,000 in there.

"Damn nigga you almost bought tha whole fuckin' store."

"I probably would have if you Niggaz didn't grab what yall did! Yall don't even rock Gucci like that."

"Yeah but this shit is hot and exclusive."

While they were in Saks I decided to go into Tiffany's to grab my wife a nice bracelet.

"Hello, may I help you?" this old white lady asked.

"Yes, I'm looking for a nice bracelet for my wife."

"We have a nice selection of bracelets," she said opening up one of those display cases.

"Wow, I'm feeling this one right here," I said pointed to this one wit plenty of diamonds in it.

"That's a nice pick; we even have a necklace to match," she said, locking the case back and opening another one.

"Shit," I said looking at tha necklace, "I'll take them."

"Well, these are rather pricey."

That statement almost made me change my mind. If it wasn't for tha fact I wanted my baby to shit on tha competition I would have walked out.

Just to be petty I asked, "How much is pricey?"

"Well, tha bracelet is 10,000 and tha necklace is 15,000."

"Is that all! Put them in a box and ring me up."

"Will that be cash or credit?"

"Which do you prefer," I said handing her my debit card.

"I'm sorry, we don't do debit."

This old bitch was really try'n to bring tha Black out of me!

I pulled out my Visa but decided to just pay cash. She went to reach for it, I pulled it back and I let know I was paying cash. I went into my Gucci bag and pulled out 250 crisp $100 bills.

"That should be about right but count it just to make sure I didn't give you too much," I said wit a smile.

Once she finished counting she put my boxes in tha bag along wit my receipt. As I was walking out I spotted Jade and tha girls going into tha Christian Dior store. I walked down tha street to Designer Frames. They had any and every kind of designer frames; I ended up spending 5,000 or 13 pair of frames. When I was done everybody was out front hands full of bags.

"Nigga you still shoppin'?" Tiz asked.

"Nah I'm good, I just had to grab me some frames."

"Jade ya husband bought tha whole Gucci store."

"I see."

"Then he got mad at us for grabbing like one set a piece."

"Yall know he's strung out on Gucci."

"Like you need to talk, you did tha same thing in Dior."

"Well, you know she all strung out on Christian Dior."

"Shut up Ahmad."

"It was a'ight when you said to me." (Ha! Ha! Ha!)

"You look like you spent a lot of money," I said changing tha subject.

"Not nearly as much as you," she said kissing me on my cheek.

"I need to take a nap, I'm tired as hell."

"A nap, nah we gonna explore L.A."

"Yall go ahead. I'm getting dropped off at tha hotel."

"Me too Honey."

"Unh, Unh yall so nasty."

"Um Hmm."

"Bitch ain't nobody try'n to get sexed."

We had a ball for tha rest of tha weekend. When tha plane landed back in Philly I looked at Jade and told her I love her.

She responded wit, "You better." We both laughed.

I decided I would wait until New Year's Eve to give Jade her necklace and bracelet I had gotton her while we were in L.A. For tha next week I tied up all loose ends. I gave all my peoples Maze's number. They were a little disappointed that I was getting out of tha game. I did assure them that everything would still be tha same they would just be dealing wit Maze. They were familiar with him since I had them dealing wit him tha last few times anyway.

CHAPTER 43

It's Over

I couldn't believe it after tonight I was really officially outta tha game.

"Baby, what's tha matter? You look like you have a lot on your mind."

"Nothing."

"Are you having second thoughts."

"Nah, not at all."

"You might do it a Jay-Z, retire then come back."

"I seriously doubt that when I'm done Baby I'm done. I was just thinking about all the money I made. Baby not too many people are able to leave tha game on their own. So, for me to be able to do that feels good. If it wasn't for Cam I would have gotten out wit out a scratch."

"Look at the bright side; had you not went to jail, there might not be and us or A.J." That brought a smile to my face.

"We better get dress."

"Before we do I have a little something, something for you."

I went into tha closet and came back wit tha Tiffany bag. Jade opened tha boxes and tha tears started running.

"Oh My God!"

"SSSH you don't have to say anything just get dressed.

"Jade you are drop dead beautiful!"

"Wow you got me blushing, help me put these on," she said handing me her jewelry.

Her Christian Dior dress showed every curve she had.

"Are you going to just stare at me or get dress?"

"If you got me like this I hate to see the rest of tha niggaz tonight at tha party.

When I finally got dressed everybody was downstairs. I stood in front of my full length mirror admiring myself.

"Damn I'm gonna have to be on ya side all night."

"That was tha plan anyway."

I put some of my Furdose on grabbed my frames and headed downstairs. I had to admit everybody looked like a million bucks. We all decided to drive our own cars so they wouldn't have to drive all the way back to our house. Since it was my last night I chose to pull out tha Rolls Royce. It was packed outside when we pulled up.

"Unh, Unh, Unh, look at these broads they barely have anything on."

I pulled up to tha valet, who took my keys and handed me a ticket. We went to tha V.I.P. line. I went into my pocket to pay.

"I never seen nobody try to pay to get in to their own party," tha bouncer said. Tha look on my face must of said it all.

"Baby, all these people came to see you," she said, handing me a flyer.

"Oh shit," I looked at everybody who was smiling.

"I should've known yall would send me out wit a bang. How did yall managed to give out flyers wit out me seeing them?"

"We can't even answer that."

"Hey Swerve," some broad said wit barely nothing on.

"What's up?"

"Yeah I'm wit you all night cause I can see Imma have to fuck a bitch up tonight!"

No soon as we got in some dude was like damn shorty fat to death.

"I might be tha one Fuckin' somebody up! Come on yall let's take a few flicks."

We made our way to tha V.I.P. section and ordered a few bottles. I could tell that Jade was getting fed up wit all tha broads coming over try'n to talk to me.

"Baby these bitches are straight disrespecting me."

I did feel her because a few niggaz were holler'n at her.

"Baby girl what's your name. Come here let me buy you a drink, take you to my crib show you where I live. What's tha chance of you rolling wit me."

"Come on, I ain't heard this song in a long time."

Before I could say anything Jade had me on tha dance floor. Bre and Turk were now on tha floor.

"Imma go get some more to drink, I'll be back."

"Hurry up!"

"Hey there Sexy." I turned around to see King standing there.

"What's up, I don't get no hug or hello?"

"Hello King."

"Still playing hard to get, huh?"

"Please don't start tha bullshit."

"So, I don't get no hug?"

"I don't think my husband would like that."

"Yeah, I did hear you got married to some nigga."

"I see you still a stalker," Bre said.

"And I see you still minding other peoples biz-ness."

I went to walk away and King grabbed my arm. I snatched away which caught Maze's attention.

"Yo what tha fuck is going on?" Before I could say a word Bre said, "This stalking ass nigga."

"Fuck you Bit…" Before he could get tha rest of tha word out Maze was on his ass. Tha bouncers came over and broke it up.

"Maze what's going on?" one of them asked.

"This mafucka disrespected my girl and my sister."

By now Ahmad and tha rest of tha fellas were walking over.

"What tha fuck is going on?"

"This clown ass nigga grabbed Jade's arm and disrespected Bre."

Ahmad looked at me and asked if I was a'ight. I just shook my head.

"My man is there any particular reason you grabbed my wife's arm?"

"I was just asking her to dance, nothing more nothing less."

"Well, do me a favor don't ever put your hands on her again or you won't be alive to talk about it."

"I don't think you know who I am."

"Nah my friend, you don't know who I am."

King looked Ahmad in his face and said, "You be surprised who I know."

Killer said, "Man you tha police Nigga I know you. This tha nigga that told on Bop and all his peeps. They all got 20 while he got a nickel. If it's one thing I can't stand is a Fuckin' Rat!"

"I ain't no rat, I ain't in nobody's paperwork."

"You sure bout that?" Tiz asked.

"We gon' have to ask you to leave."

"He good, let 'em stay."

"You sure Swerve?"

"Yeah it's cool."

I took Jade back to our table.

"So, what you use to talk to that nigga?"

"Hell to tha no, he use to stalk me. Does he look like somebody I would even talk to?"

"I don't know."

"Now you being funny."

"You know he's on borrowed time."

"What do you mean by that?" I asked already knowing tha answer.

"Put it like this, he should have never grabbed your arm I don't give a fuck what he was asking you!"

"Awe you really do love me."

"Now you try'n to be funny."

Maze came over to tell me that King will be in tha boneyard by tha morning. All in all, tha night was a blast. It was around 2:30 in tha morning when I decided I was ready to go.

"Baby you ready to go?"

"Yeah, I was just waiting on you." We said our goodbyes to everybody then made our way to tha door.

"Honey let's take a couple pics before we leave so we will always remember this night."

On the way home, Jade let me know that she loved me wit all her heart and thanked me for giving her A.J. That night, we didn't even make love; we just held each other until we fell asleep.

CHAPTER 44

D.O.A.

"There he go right there."

We watched King get into his car and pull off. He made a few stops before going to his final destination.

"Come on before he gets in tha house."

"Chill he ain't even get out his car yet."

When we got down tha street he was just getting out his car.

"Oh shit, is that King?"

"Who dat?" he said half drunk.

"It's Lil' Man and Crack."

"Who?"

If he wasn't drunk he would have been able to see tha .45 Lil' Man had in his hand.

"Who you say you was?"

"Jade."

"Jade?"

"Yeah, she sends her regards."

Boom, Boom, Boom 3 shots to his face, he was dead before he hit tha pavement.

"Come on before tha police come."

When we got in tha car I lit tha blunt and turn the radio up.

CHAPTER 45

Happy Birthday

A.J.'s first birthday was coming up in 5 days. Even though I didn't celebrate birthdays or holidays, I didn't stop Jade from having A.J.'s first birthday at tha house. She also knows that this will be his first and last. There were balloons all over tha house. Tiz, Killer and Heem were bringing their kids over along wit tha other kids. My mom and Ms. Sady were in tha kitchen cooking. I told them just to order some pizza from Pizza Hut and wings from Waltz. But of course, our moms insisted on cooking party wings, meatballs, and seafood salad. When tha guests started arriving I made my way to tha den. Before long, there were kids running around everywhere. Jade made sure she put all that expensive things up outta their reach.

"Ahmad, Ahmad." I acted like I didn't hear my mom calling me.

"Boy, I know you heard me out there calling ya name."

"Why what's up mom?"

"Ya son is out there calling ya name that's what's up!"

"Is that chicken done I'm hungry as a hostage."

"Ahmad, that food been done a long time ago."

"Allāhu Akbar, Allāhu Akbar, Allāhu Akbar, Allāhu Akbar, Ash-Hadu an la Llaha Ill Allāh, Ash-Hadu an la Llaha Ill Allāh, Ash-Hadu Anna Muhamna Dan Rasul-Ullah, Ash-Hadu Anna Muhamna Dan Rasul-Ullah, Halya Alas-Salah, Halya Alas-Salah, Halya Alal-Falah, Halya Alal-Falah Allāhu-Akbar, Allāhu- Akbar la Llaha Ill Allāh."

"Mom, I'll be out when I'm done making Salat."

"Ahmad does that clock do that every time you have to pray?"

"Yes."

"Oh well, make sure you come out here when you're done."

"I will Mom."

"While I was making Salat A.J. came in and got on tha side of me and did what I was doing as he always did. For him to be one he was very, very intelligent. When we finished everybody was standing in tha doorway.

"Hum-Du Allāh," Heem said.

"Ahmad, he was doing everything you were doing," Mom Sady said.

"He does that all tha time," Jade said wit a big smile.

"Insha Allāh yall all gonna be deeming up in this house?"

"You need to get on top of ya Deen," Lexis said.

"I make my 5 and I go to Jumah every Friday!"

"I'm not say'n you don't but what I'm say'n is you don't study as much as you use to when you first came home."

"He's a'ight, we all fall off a little, believe me I can tell you firsthand."

"It's time to sing happy birthday and cut tha cake."

All tha kids and even tha adults sang happy birthday. When it was time to blow out tha candle A.J. got slobber all over tha candle and cake.

"Good thing you got two cakes," my mom said, laugh'n hard.

A.J. put his hands all in the cake.

"Mom, take a picture of him."

"I already did."

When it was time to open his presents, Jade was more excited than he was.

"This boy has more clothes than I do," Fresh said smiling.

Heem had gotton him this nice ass necklace and charm that said A.J. It was tha perfect size for a one-year-old.

It was about 9 o'clock when tha party ended and I was happy.

"Baby, you a'ight?

"Yeah, I'm just glad tha party is over. I love kids, but 4 hours of whooping and hollering will drive anybody crazy."

"So, what would you do if you had all of those kids?"

"Phh, yeah right, one more and you get ya tubes tied, burned clip or something!"

"How you know I don't want 3 or 4 kids?" I looked at her like she lost her mind.

"I don't, but what if I did?"

"Well, if you did then we would have to really discuss it."

"That's more like it."

I didn't even respond to that because it would have only led to an argument.

The next few months flew by fast.

"Jade."

"Yes Ahmad."

"I've been thinking about opening another biz-ness."

"What kind of biz-ness Ahmad?"

"I don't know, maybe a rim shop. Everybody buys rims for their cars. Maybe I'll call it Rimz for Rides."

"That's a catchy name; I like it. So, what made you want to open a rim shop?"

"Because tha first thing you do when you buy a car is put some shoes on it. I'll have tha latest rimz and customized ones too."

"Did Maze call your phone?"

"No why?"

"He called me earlier wanting to know about tha married life.

"I know he's not getting cold feet; tha wedding is in 2 months."

"No, he said that he hopes he can be the husband Bre wants him to be."

"I know exactly how he's feeling."

"Oh, you do?"

"Yeah, I went through tha same thing right before we tied tha knot. Not knowing if I would be able to make you happy or if I would be everything you wanted in a husband."

"Baby, you are all that I wished for in a man and more."

CHAPTER 46

Prom Night

My prom was in two weeks, correction one week away. I had decided to accept Das offer to accompany me to my prom.

"Hey Brother."

"What up Lil' Sis, you ready for your prom next week?"

"Yeah, I can't wait to show off my Vera Wang original dress."

"I've have decided to let yall pull up tha Rolls Royce."

"Oh My God! Are you serious?"

"Heads are already gonna turn wit that dress, so why not put tha icing on tha cake."

I have spent all day preparing and pampering myself for tha prom tonight.

"Iciss, don't you think you should be getting ready?"

"I'm bout to do that now Mom."

"A'ight because Jade and Ahmad are on their way over."

45 minutes later, Ahmad and Jade were pulling up at tha same time Das was.

"Damn Das, you killing 'em wit that Zac Posen."

He had on a cream Zac Posen suit wit a lilac shirt and a pair of lilac Giuseppe Zanoth shoes.

"Iciss better jump on him before somebody else does." I looked at J like she lost her mind.

"Ahmad, she's old enough to have a boyfriend."

"I know she is."

"So then fall back."

Iciss was coming downstairs when we came in. I wasted no time taking pictures.

"Daaamn Lil' Sis, you look beautiful."

Das said, "Iciss, you really do look beautiful."

She had on her lilac and cream Vera Wang dress wit matching Christen Louboutin shoes.

"A'ight, yall better get going, Mom Sady said."

Jade said, "Hold on, I know what you need to set it off."

"What's that?" Iciss asked. Jade went into her bag and came out wit a box.

"Don't just look at it open it up."

"AAAGH!" Iciss screamed when she opened it and seen tha diamond necklace that said ICISS in diamonds.

"I remembered you said you wanted one of these."

"That was almost 4 years ago."

"I told you when you got older; I would get you one." Iciss handed it to Das so he could put it on for her.

"Yall have a good time tonight."

"We will," they both said, walking out tha door.

"Hey, aren't you forgetting something?" Ahmad asked, holding out his keys.

"Unh, Unh, we got to get a couple pictures in front of this. I even had it clean for yall."

"Thank you Brother," she said giving him a kiss on tha cheek.

When we pulled up at tha prom, all eyes were on us. We had tha hottest car by far. And when we stepped out, our gear was undeniable.

"Iciss, Iciss over here!"

"Hey Laura, love tha dress."

"Thanks, you look stunning."

"I know."

"Hey Das."

"Hey Laura."

"Love that suit."

"Thanks where's Bo?"

"He had to use tha men's room."

There were people that I've never seen before at tha prom. All in all, tha night was wonderful. There were a few dudes that I wouldn't give tha time of day staring and grilling Das. There were also females rolling their eyes at me, but I didn't care; I loved it. When tha prom was over, everybody went out to eat breakfast. Laura and Bo had a room at tha Hilton. I thought Das was going to ask me to get a room, but to my surprise, he didn't. We pulled up in front of my house.

"Here's ya brother's keys. Iciss, I just want to say thank you."

"What are you thanking me for Das?"

"For allowing me tha chance to take you to tha prom. I really had a wonderful time tonight despite tha ice grills from your fan club."

"Boy pleeeeease you had a fan club wanting to kill me."

(Ha! Ha! Ha!) We both laughed.

"Well, I guess I better let you go; I know you got somebody waiting on you."

"Nah, I'm bout to go to tha crib and get some sleep."

"Boy what ever!"

"Iciss, I don't do too much lying. You got my number I hope you use it even if you just call to say hi."

"Das, you have my number also."

"I know I didn't hear you right."

"Boy, stop playing, you heard what I said."

"Don't be surprised if ya phone rings tonight."

He gave me a kiss on tha cheek and then got into his car. My mom was in tha kitchen fixing ice cream when I walked in.

"What's that?" Iciss asked.

"I wasn't expecting you to come home tonight."

"Mom, Das was a perfect gentleman all night. I thought that he would try to get me to go to a hotel wit him, but he didn't."

"You sound disappointed."

"Not really, 'cause even if he did, I would've went, but there wouldn't have been any sex jumping off."

"You want some ice cream?"

"Yes, I'm going to put my nightgown on. I'll be right back."

I was telling my mom all about tha prom when my phone rang.

"Hello."

"Hey Beautiful, were you sleep?"

"No, I was talking to my mom."

"Do you want me to call you tomorrow?"

"No, you good, my mom was on her way to bed anyway."

"No, I wasn't, but I'll go upstairs so yall can talk."

"Mom!"

"Don't you hate when ya mom does that?"

"Yup."

"I know, my mom does that too."

"Yeah, I bet she does."

"For real, a lot of times, I give females my house number instead of my cell phone. So, if I'm home and one happens to call, I'll tell my mom to say I'm not home and she'll say into tha phone, no, I'm not telling her you're not home if you don't want to talk don't give tha number out."

"Are you serious? Your mom says that?"

"Yes, she really does do that."

"My mom isn't that bad."

I couldn't believe that it was that easy to communicate wit Das. We actually had a lot of tha same likes and dislikes.

"See, Iciss you should have been giving me a chance."

Before we realized it was 6 o'clock in tha morning.

"Even though I'm not tired Imma let you get some sleep."

As bad as I wanted to say I wasn't tired, I just said, "OK, make sure you call me later."

"A'ight, if you don't have any plans, maybe we can go out to dinner."

"That shouldn't be a problem; I get off at 8 tonight."

"Well, I'll see you before 8, then."

"Iciss, you OK you been a little distant today."

"Huh, what did you say Ms. Thelma?"

I ask if you were a'ight because you haven't been yourself today."

All I could do was smile when I thought of tha reason why I wasn't myself.

"OOOOH, I know that, look that boy you went to tha prom wit must have put it on you something serious."

"Ms. Thelma."

"What Chile, I was young once upon a time too."

"Well, nothing happened last night."

"Well, if that's how you act when nothing happens, I'd hate to see when it does happen."

Ms. Thelma what's 61 years old but didn't look a day over 40. I could just imagine her in her prime. It was only 6 o'clock and I couldn't wait til 8. As I was think'n about my upcoming dinner date, Das walked into tha store.

"What's up Iciss?"

"Hey Das."

"Let me get two Dutches and a pack of Big Red."

"What you smiling for?" I asked him.

"Just can't stop thinking about our dinner date tonight."

"That's another thing we have in common."

"Iciss, you only have an hour left; go ahead I got tha store."

"I couldn't impose that on you Ms. Thelma."

"Chile, if you don't get ya butt out of here."

"We can always go to dinner and a movie."

"If you think I'm going anywhere looking like this."

"What's wrong wit tha way you look?"

She was looking fine to me wit a pair of black capris, a white T-shirt that said, *'Don't you wish ya girlfriend was hot like me'* and a pair of white sandals.

"Chile it ain't nothing wrong wit what you wearing."

"Besides tha fact that I've been working and sweating tha past seven hours."

"Well, go home, take a shower, and I'll be by to scoop you in about a hour in a half."

"Is tha restaurant casual?"

"Yeah, they don't care what you wear at Wendy's."

(Ha! Ha! Ha!) He and Ms. Thelma laughed.

"So, you got jokes, huh?"

"I was only messing wit you."

"Well, I don't want to go to dinner now."

"You gon' to really act like that." I watched as tha smile he once had disappeared from his face.

"I was just messing wit you."

(Ha! Ha! Ha!) I had to laugh at that myself.

"You sure going to be a'ight Ms. Thelma?"

"If you don't get ya butt out of here Chile. I might be tempted to take him out," Ms. Thelma said, winking at Das.

"If she doesn't want me, I might take you up on that."

"Well, Iciss, I'd suggest you hold onto him."

I was in and out of the shower in 30 minutes. Since th restaurant is casual, I decided to throw on my Citizens of Humanity jeans wit my red spaghetti strap Donna Karen shirt and my red sandals.

"Where you headed to?"

"Das is taking me to dinner and tha movies."

"Wait a minute, is this tha same Das that gets on your nerves and has too many women for you?"

"I miss judged him Mom."

"That's why they say never judge a book by its cover."

I heard Das pulling up and told my mom I would talk to her later.

"I know that look," my mom said as I was leaving.

I didn't respond; I just took a mental note to ask her later what she meant. I got into tha car and Das let me know that we would be going to Dave & Buster's.

"I hope you don't mind going there instead of tha movies."

"No, not at all."

"Do you know how much to roll?" he said, handing me a Dutch and some weed. I didn't answer; I just took tha weed and tha Dutch.

"If you don't know how to roll, I'll roll it."

"I know how to roll."

"I'm just say'n I don't want it all tight."

"Look, do you want me to roll it?"

"Nah."

"Well, be quiet then." (Ha! Ha! Ha!)

"What's so funny?"

"You can't take nothing."

"And can't!"

After I have finished pearling tha Dutch, I lit it and then passed it to Das.

"You ain't smoking?"

"Yeah, but go head."

After he took a few pulls, he looked over at me and said, "Girl got skills." I just smiled.

"Damn, look at all these people try'n to get in."

We paid tha parking attendant and then found tha closest parking spot we could. Once inside, we let tha hostess know we wanted a table for two. To my surprise, we didn't have to wait long before we were seated.

"Das, I am so hungry I haven't ate all day."

"Me either, I already know what I want."

By tha time tha waiter came back, we were more than ready to order.

"Are you ready to order?"

"Yes, I'll have the steak and shrimp meal."

"How would you like your steak?"

"Well done."

"And your side?"

"Mash potatoes and corn."

"I'll have tha shrimp scampi wit fried chicken."

"Would it be all?"

"Umm, let me have an order of tha boneless hot wings."

"Is that all?" she asked, looking at me.

"Yes it is." She started to walk off.

"Oh, I'm sorry. Can I have a bottle of spring water please?"

"Make that two," Das added.

"OK, no problem," she said, looking at Das.

"I see somebody has a admirer."

"So, I'm here wit you and by tha way, did I tell you how nice you look?"

"No, but thank you."

"That's a nice necklace you got."

"Thanks, my mom got this for me for a graduation present."

"Must be nice."

"I can't believe I'll actually be walking tha aisle in two weeks.

"I'll just be glad when it's officially over."

"Das, do you plan on going to college?"

"I've been thinking about it a lot lately. Maybe I'll take up law; you know, help my peeps out."

"That's what I'm taking for tha same reason."

Tha waitress came wit our food.

"If you need anything, please let me know," she said, smiling at Das as she walked off. (Ha! Ha! Ha!)

"What's so funny Iciss?"

"If you need anything, pleeeeease let me know." (Ha! Ha! Ha!)

"Make sure you tell her to give you her number."

"Nah, I'm good Ma."

"Boy please, you know if I wasn't here, you would be all over her."

"You really got me fucked up. I don't jump on every broad that throws herself on me. If I did, that would be a lot of broads. You act like niggaz don't be all over you too."

We finished our food and then headed to tha game room to play some games.

"I thought you don't play games."

"I don't," I said, looking him in tha face so he could see tha seriousness in my face.

I was really having a good time. "Are you ready to leave?"

"If you are."

"I was thinking since we already up here, we might as well go to Plush or one of these clubs."

"I'm not dressed to go to no club."

"Ain't nothing wrong wit what you got on."

"I don't know." By tha time we got to tha car, my mind was already made up.

"So, am I going left or right?"

"You driving not me."

"Say no more."

We pulled up at Plush; as soon as I seen the line, I said, "I'm not going in there; let's go to Samba."

"Where's that at?"

"7th & Girard."

I forgot on Fridays, they have 18 and up night.

"Now, this is more like it," I said as we pulled up.

"You have to park on this street."

Tha line was pretty long, so they opened tha side door and charged extra to get in that way.

"Damn, it's packed in here."

"Boy, it's always packed in here."

"Do you want a drink?"

"I'm not a drinker; I only drink Apple Martini."

"That's like drink'n Kool-Aid."

"It's enough to have me feeling it."

"I heard that, come on."

Once we got our drinks, we went upstairs to see what was poppin'. Two hours and 4 Apple Martinis later, I was half ass drunk and ready to bounce. Das must have been feeling tha same way because he asked me if I was ready.

"Yeah, let's get outta here."

When we got outside, it was as if they took tha party outside. "Excuse you," I heard Iciss say.

I turned to see who she was talking to.

"Damn Ma, you been play'n hardball all night."

"Aye, My Man, she wit me," I said wit out waiting for Iciss to respond to him.

"So what tha Fuck that mean!"

I could tell this nigga had too many drinks tonight. When his boys heard him get loud, they headed over.

Seeing this Iciss said, "Come on Das."

I wasn't scared because, thanks to my mom, I had been boxing since I was 8. My pride wouldn't let me be chumped, so I hoped he didn't talk stupid.

"Let's go, they might have a gun," she said.

I didn't think about that.

"You right, let's go," I said, grabbing her hand and walking toward my car.

All I had to do was make it to my car, where I had my .40 cal.

"That's what I thought Bitch Ass Nigga!"

I hit my alarm and told Iciss to get in while I did tha same, grabbing my .40 from under my seat. As I was pulling off, there was a loud bang on tha side of my car. I immediately put my car in park and got out. When I looked at my car, it had a big dent from tha brick that dude threw at my shit. Now I was on fire and Iciss saw it. She quickly got out and looked at tha dent.

"You Dumb Mafucka!" she said, now pissed herself.

"Fuck You Bitch," he said, walking toward us.

"Iciss get in tha car."

"No."

"Iciss get in tha car."

"Now!" I said, raising my voice.

This time she jumped in tha driver's seat and took tha car out of park. As soon as dude got wit in arm reach, he threw a wild hang maker, which I ducked and counted wit a straight jab that knocked his ass out cold. When his boys saw what happened, they started towards me. I pulled out my .40 Cal and they stopped immediately.

"If you Mafucka's wanna die, then try me." I walked around to tha passenger side, got in and Iciss pulled off.

"A pretty boy that can't fight or was that a lucky punch?"

"I been boxing for 10 years. Let's stop at tha Wawa."

"Nah, we can get something once we get home, just in case somebody gave up your tag number."

"I guess you're right."

After we got something to eat, we went back to my house, where we talked until we fell asleep on tha couch.

CHAPTER 47

A New Car

"Maze and Bre's wedding was real nice."

"I know, Maze told me Bre is also 4 weeks pregnant.

"Yeah, he's excited; he also told me he was also getting out of tha game at tha end of tha year."

"Yeah Insha Allāh, they'll all get out of tha game before it's too late."

Me and Ahmad have been married for a little over a year and I finally took my Shahada. Turk and Bre are my girls and I love them to death, but since I came into tha Deen, we don't hang out as much. We talk on tha phone often, but that's pretty much it.

"Jade, I never knew ya brother was Muslim."

"Yeah but he hasn't been on it in years."

"I know, he explained it all to me; I told him that all he has to do is repent and all past sins will be forgiven."

"What did he say?"

"Same thing I said when I was in the Dunya."

"Well, that explains why Bre has been asking me so much about tha Deen."

"Well, I hope you tibleeked her every chance you got."

"You know I did. I even told her a few good books to get, so Insha Allāh she picked them up."

"We better get a move on it."

"I'm ready, I was waiting on you."

When we arrived, there were a few people there being helped by salesclerks.

"Amulama-Laka may I help you?"

"It's As Salamu-Alaikum and yes, you may."

"Oh, I'm sorry."

"It's Ok, but we want to purchase a car."

"What kind of car are you try'n to buy?"

"We want a Maybach."

"Oh, that's top-of-the-line."

"We know, it's a present for my sister."

"Wow, she must be really special for this type of present."

"Yeah, she just graduated."

"Well, let me show you tha ones we have."

When he was done, we went to do tha paperwork. I let him know that we wanted tha car in Iciss's name. We ended up wit tha charcoal/charcoal. After tha paperwork was done, I drove it off tha lot and over to my rim shop to get it fitted for a pair of customized 22-inch Isani's. When that was done, we drove to Mom Sady's, where we knew Iciss would be. Iciss was sitting on tha couch wit Das when we walked in.

"You two have been spending a lot of time together since tha prom."

"Please don't start."

"Mommy, Daddy!" A.J. yelled, coming downstairs.

"As Salamu Alaikum."

"Walaikum Salam," he said in return.

"Brother, can I use ya car later?" I just tossed her tha keys.

"Thanks; what would I do wit out you."

"Well, good thing you don't have to find out."

"Iciss, won't you run to tha market and get me some more shrimp."

"A'ight, come on Das."

When she opened tha door, tha whole neighborhood heard her scream. Mom Sady ran to tha door to see what was going on.

"Shit!"

"Is this my car?" she asked in tears.

"You don't want it?"

"Ahmad stop playing; you know this is my dream car."

"We all chipped in to get you this car."

"Who's we?"

"Me, Jade, Maze, Killer, Tiz, Fresh, Heem, Bre, Turk and Lexis."

"Don't look at me like that."

"I know I could have, but why should I?"

"I didn't say anything."

"You didn't have to; I know what you were thinking."

"Now you know you're wrong for that Brother."

"I love you and enjoy your new car."

"Oh, I will."

"Mom, I'll be right back."

"Iciss, get my shrimp before you go showing that pretty car off."

"I am Mom."

I shot to Pathmark, got tha shrimp and dropped them off to my mom.

"Iciss, this is top of the line right here. I have never been in a Maybach."

"Oh, so you think I have?"

"Not only do you have a Maybach, but you got a fresh pair of duece on it as well. I better step my game up."

We drove thru tha city; all eyes were on us. When I drove thru tha hill, my best friend Laura was sitting on her steps wit a few other people. When I rode past tha first time, she didn't know it was me. I circled tha block and stopped in front of her house.

"Bitch I didn't know that was you. Damn Das, that's how we doing it now!"

"Bitch, this is my graduation present."

"OOOOH, stop playing."

"She ain't lying; this is her whip."

"Bitch I'm jealous."

By now, cars were honking for us to pull over or pull off.

"Fuck 'em," I thought as I talked for a few more minutes.

"I'll call you a little later a'ight."

"Ok."

By tha time I got back home, my mom had finished her curry shrimp.

"Das are you hungry?"

"Yeah."

Jade and Ahmad were upstairs doing their Salat when we first came in. I respected tha fact that they were Muslin my nephew was even Muslin.

"I see yall made it back."

"Everybody thought it was Das's car and I was driving it. I kindly told them this is my car and my sister and brothers got it for me for graduating.

CHAPTER 48

New Year's Eve

It was New Year's Eve and Maze was leaving tha game; instead of having a party, he decided to have a big dinner and invited everybody over.

Everybody was sitting around talking, smoking and drinking except Jade and Ahmad.

"Hey, I can't speak for yall, but I'm in this thing until I'm dead and gone," Killer said.

"Not me, I plan to be out at tha end of next year," Fresh said.

"Bre, that was delicious."

"Thank you, but I can't take all tha credit," she said, pointing to Turk, Jade and Lexis.

We continued to talk until it was time for tha ball to drop.

"10, 9, 8, 7, 6, 5, 4, 3, 2, 1 Happy New Years!" everybody yelled.

Jade and Ahmad was upstairs bringing their New Years in making Salat. When it was all said and done, Jade and Ahmad were happily married wit their son A.J. Bre and Maze had a baby girl who they named Brazia. Turk and Fresh were now engaged to be married. Killer and Lexis were still a couple. Fresh, Killer, Heem and Tiz still had tha city in a chokehold because...

"It Is Wht It Is!"

COMING SOON THA SEQUEL!

It Still Is Wht It Is

"Aye Heem."

"What up Tiz?"

"You need to check ya boy Gill."

"Why, what's up?"

"He talking to tha bitches about biz-ness."

"Word."

"Yeah, one of my young jawns told me her friend holla at him and all he talks about is us and how we got tha city on smash and how you be hittin' him wit 10 to 20 birds."

"I don't even give that nigga more than 4 ½."

"Just imagine if you did."

"I know, he's gon' fuck around and get us locked up or robbed wit his big ass mouth."

"I feel you on that; you know what they say, loose lips sink ships."

"So."

"Don't worry, I'll handle it."

"You know Jade and Ahmad are having a dinner Sunday."

"He called me."

"I'm bout to holla at Fresh, so make sure you handle that."

"No more said," we dapped each other and went our way.

"Hello."

"Hey, Hey, what up Baby? I been waiting for you to call; I'm ready."

"That's what's up, meet me in back of Scooters; I'll be there in 30 minutes."

"Make it 20."

"20 it is then."

I shot to my stash house to pick up what I needed.

"Damn nigga you tell me 20 minutes, but you take 40; I could have busted Tina's ass for another 10 minutes."

"Look, I ain't trying to know or hear all that."

"You still be messing wit her peoples?"

"Yeah, I need to talk to you about that too."

"About what?"

"All that mafuckin' pillow talkin' you doing wit Tina."

"What you talkin' bout?"

"Gill, don't play dumb; you know exactly what tha fuck I'm talkin' bout!"

"Nah, I don't."

"Well, let me jog ya memory."

"Hooold up, Heem we ain't got to take it there. I was just trying to score some points wit Tina that's all."

"Score some points, you dumb mafucka you already knocked her off."

"I know, but I wanted to make sure she wasn't going nowhere."

"By lying and putting our biz-ness out there?"

"It's only Tina Heem."

"Do you see how she ran back to Janeen?"

"That's her girl."

"Nah, because she dumb and young."

"Yo she won't say nothing, I promise."

"I know she won't because I'm gonna help her keep her mouth close."

"How are you going to do that?"

"Like this… PTT, PTT, PTT, PTT."

His head slammed back against tha headrest, then hit tha steering wheel. I got out made sure nobody was looking, got in my car then pulled off as if nothing ever even happened. When I got back to tha stash house, I unscrewed tha silencer, cleaned it as well as tha pistol, then headed back out.

"Did you talk to Heem about that big-mouth young boy?"

"Yeah, I just left him; he said he would handle it."

"We need to all sit-down and talk about a potential problem we might have brewing."

"What kind of problem?"

"Those Dominican cats. Call Heem and Killer, tell them to come thru."

We played Madden while we waited on Heem and Killer. When they arrived, we got straight to biz-ness.

ABOUT THE AUTHOR

My name is Jerz Toston, and I reside in Wilmington, Delaware. First, thanks to my fans for your continued support. This is my 9th book titled It Is What It Is. My other eight books are titled Bound By DNA, Wht U Don't Kno Can Hurt U, Trust is Ery Thing, Compromised, Street Dreamz: Ery Thing Ain't What It Seems, Da Game Ain't Fair, Betrayal & Deceit, Who Can U Trust?, and It Is Wht It Is are available now on all on-line-bookstores. Also, you can call my publisher directly at 877.782.5550 and have them shipped to ya door.

Writing books is my passion and I'll continue to give you page-turners. Just call me Ya Fav Author.

YA FAV AUTHOR